FRICTIONS II

STORIES BY WOMEN

Edited by

RHEA TREGEBOV

CANADIAN CATALOGUING IN PUBLICATION DATA

Main entry under title:
Frictions II : stories by women

ISBN 0-929005-47-3

1. Short stories, Canadian (English) - Women authors.*
2. Canadian fiction (English) - Women authors.*
3. Canadian fiction (English) - 20th century.*
I. Tregebov, Rhea, 1953-   .

PS8321 .F67 1993   C813' .01089287   C93-094754-1
PR9197 .3 .F67 1993

Cover Illustration by Chum McLeod

Printed and bound in Canada

*Second Story Press gratefully acknowledges the assistance of the
Ontario Arts Council and the Canada Council*

Published by

SECOND STORY PRESS
*760 Bathurst Street
Toronto, Ontario*
M5S 2R6

CONTENTS

PREFACE

SINCE THE PUBLICATION of *Frictions*, Second Story's first collection of fiction, the boom in women's writing has continued with unabated energy. Selection of the work to be included in this anthology was, perhaps, even more difficult than it was four years ago. *Frictions II* — the result of this difficult editorial process — presents, I believe, an intriguing and illuminating picture of what women are writing, and writing about.

What they are writing about — with energy, verve and intelligence — is identity; the social, political and emotional context in which identity is formed. For Canadians, this inevitably brings into question the allied issues of class, race, ethnic and geographic origin. Canada at this moment is unquestionably fertile ground for such exploration. We are a country in, yet again, an identity crisis; a country formed by its contradictions. I would speculate that the strength with which these writers are able to approach this national, and personal, conundrum is a product of the marginal position women continue to occupy.

Woven inextricably into this discourse, central to it in many stories, is the embodied presence of women, the placement of the female body within history, within culture, within the literary text. This grounding in the physical is a current running through the book, and I believe readers will continue to find in it affirmation of the sense that, in women's literature at least, our bodies are finally our own. We don't have to fall into essentialism, with its implication that biology is indeed destiny, to need to feel that we are at last appropriating our own physical space.

What was, perhaps, most exhilarating for me in reading the stories that came to comprise this anthology was the growing sense that, within the context of the women's writing community — a community of publishers, booksellers and reviewers as well as readers — and with the encouragement of a now very broad and sophisticated feminist literary theory, women are finding a new freedom to write. I find in these stories a fearlessness and joy, a spirit that we welcome as readers.

I would like to take this opportunity to express my gratitude to the women at Second Story Press who once again managed to coax me into another anthology project. My thanks to Liz Martin, Margie Wolfe and Lois Pike for their encouragement and advice, and to Terri Goveia for her able editorial assistance.

Rhea Tregebov
September, 1993

THE GIRL WITH THE BELL NECKLACE

Gail Anderson-Dargatz

WHEN I CAME IN from chores, flocks of birds chirped on our roof. I knew we had guests. Bertha Moses and her daughters and her daughters' daughters were in the kitchen drinking coffee left from breakfast. One of the daughters was dipping hot water from the reservoir on the stove into the coffee pot. I'd polished the stove with butter the day before — those were the days when you couldn't give butter away — and the woodstove shone black as the daughter's hair. I went back out the screen door and yelled across the yard at my mother, "Mrs. Moses and her family are here," and went about the business of being hostess. Bertha Moses and her family were walking from the reservation into town. I knew this because they always stopped at our house on their way to and from town. My mother entered the kitchen wiping her hands on her skirt. She wore milking clothes identical to my own: a brown skirt, white blouse, gumboots and blue kerchief.

"Bertha," she said. "Good to see you."

Bertha Moses wore a red dress, black stockings and moccasins decorated with porcupine quills and embroidery. She wore several strings of brightly coloured beads. She had no husband and no sons. She would not have a drunk man in her house, so it was a house of women. One of the daughter's daughters was pregnant. Another had webbed fingers. Some of the younger girls had blue or green eyes. Each of the girl's hair was black and oiled with bear grease so it shone, and tied back in all manner of barrettes and ribbons. Someone wore violet scented talc. One of the daughter's daughters wore boys' jeans and a western shirt that stretched a little at the buttons across her breasts. She was my age. My father never let me wear trousers. The girl wore a necklace of bells strung together. I coveted it. She saw me looking at the bell necklace and jingled it. The room filled with tinkling notes that lit everyone's faces. I watched the girl with the bell necklace. She smiled. The room grew womanly.

My mother told how my father tried to fool the hired men. My father hired older Indian boys, like Dennis and Filthy Billy, who ran away from the residential school in Kamloops. My father said he was doing them a favour because these were the days of Depression when no-one else would hire them. They worked for cheap and didn't talk back unless they got drunk. If they got drunk, my father fired them.

"John brought home a porcupine yesterday," Mum said. "He skinned it, cleaned it and said, 'It's chicken.' I said, 'That's not chicken.'

"He said, 'I said it's chicken, so it's chicken.'

"I said, 'Fine it's chicken.' I cooked it like chicken. Dennis and Filthy Billy come in for dinner and John says, 'Maudie cooked chicken for dinner.'

"Everyone helps themselves and then Dennis whispers, 'Porcie,' and Filthy Billy whispers, 'Porcie.' "

Everyone laughed because they knew my father. The laughter became huge and shook the house. The screen door slammed shut.

"What's this about?" said my father. "What are you laughing at?"

There was a pause, then one of Bertha's daughters said, "Men."

My father pushed me out of his way and stood over Bertha Moses. Bertha became an old woman in my father's shadow; he sucked the air from her cheeks and made her eyes dull.

"You told Dennis not to work," he said.

Bertha stood and her daughters stood behind her. Their combined shadows pushed my father's shadow against the wall.

"I said he deserves more for the work he does."

"You don't know nothing," said my father.

"You hire our boys because they don't know how to ask for what they're worth," she said. "You treat them like slaves. They're not slaves."

"Get out of my house!" said my father.

Bertha Moses' shadow gripped my father's shadow around the throat, forcing blood into his face. He stepped back and pushed open the screen door.

"Get out!" he said, and fled from the house.

"We should be going," said Bertha Moses.

"Yes," said one of the daughters.

The women made the motions of leaving.

"It was good to have you," said my mother.

The daughters and daughters' daughters filed out the door. The girl with the bells jingled her necklace as she went by. She had eyes of two different colours, one blue and one green. She was a half-breed then. Bertha stayed behind and patted my mother's hand.

"Stop in on your way back," said my mother. "Please. He won't remember. He gets angry and it washes away."

I followed the women a little way down the road. Their glittering jewelry attracted birds; purple swallows zoomed around them, crows hovered above them, and songbirds sang from trees as they approached. Bertha Moses and her daughters and her daughters' daughters sang hymns of praise to a white man's god all the way into town.

I spent the morning roaming. I followed the creek up to the benchland overlooking my father's property. Filthy Billy worked down below, stooking alone. My father said Filthy Billy was little more than an idiot. Bertha Moses said Filthy Billy was possessed. It occurred to me that if I ran down that hill, I could fly. I spread my arms and the air carried me.

Filthy Billy was hot and tired and agitated. He was skinny and his hair was greasy. He did not own his voice and this made him agitated. His voice made him say words no-one liked, and the best Filthy Billy could do was make the renegade words come out in a whisper. He saw me coming and looked more agitated.

"Hello (fuck)," he said. "Excuse me, hello (fuck)."

"Hello," I said.

"(Shit) your daddy doesn't (fuck) (shit) sorry want me talking to you (shit). Excuse me. Sorry (fuck)."

"Why do you talk like that?" I said.

"I don't know (fucking shit). Sorry. I can't help it (shit). Excuse me."

"What does fuck mean?"

"(Shit) you should go," he said.

"Why?" I said.

Then I saw the spirit around Filthy Billy's neck. It was a skinny, nervous spirit with hands like chicken's feet. The chicken spirit jumped on Filthy Billy, as if his lungs were bellows. Each time the spirit jumped, Filthy Billy spewed a nasty word as if it were a fart.

"(Fuck) sorry," he said. "You should go. (Shit) excuse me. Please. Go."

I ran to the farm. Something followed me in the grass.

There was a second path beside mine. I reached the fence, jumped over it and the sound of swooshing grass behind me stopped. I leaned against the back of the barn out of breath. Two parallel paths stretched out across the field; mine continued through the grass past the fence. The second did not. I saw a pair of hands clutching the boards of the fence, as if someone were leaning on it, but nobody was there.

I kept my back to the barn, my eyes on the fence, backed around the corner and ran smack into someone. I jumped and squeaked. The girl with the bell necklace was standing right there. Bertha and her daughters must have stopped in then, on their way back from town, even after what my father said.

"Hi!" she said.

"Hi!" I said.

She bent forwards and looked at the fenceline. "What you running from?"

"Nothing," I said.

My eyes were drawn to her necklace. She jingled it.

"Like it?" she said. I nodded. "I like your hair," she said, and she did an odd thing. She ran her fingers through my hair for some minutes without speaking. It felt good and calming, like my mother brushing my hair before bed. After a minute I closed my eyes and enjoyed it.

"You're beautiful like an angel," she said, and just then, I felt that way.

I opened my eyes. I became aware of the noisy chattering of birds.

"Where is everyone?" I said.

"In the house," she said. She stopped stroking my hair and sunk both hands into her jeans pockets. I tried to think of something smart to say. I felt silly asking her name because I already sort of knew her, though I'd never talked to her before. She'd been at the house with the rest of Bertha's family so many times, drinking coffee, looking at the walls.

"How was town?" I said.

"Dry," she said. "The streets are all dust, and everybody's kicking it up; all the horses were kicking it up. Town was full of people today, with school starting tomorrow. The dust filled your mouth. I had a soda."

She put her hands behind her and stared up at the red roof against the blue sky.

"I guess you start tomorrow," she said.

"Yeh," I said. I knew she wouldn't, so I didn't ask. She took my hand and held it loosely and we stared at the roof and sky together.

I heard my father yell, from some distance away, in the field. I couldn't hear what he said, but I could see he was angry. We let our hands fall. Finally he came close enough we could hear him.

"You!" he said. "You deaf? Get off my property. Get away from here. Lousy Indian! Get off my property."

He marched at us. I looked at the girl with the bell necklace. Her face had gone stony. She turned and fled, jingling, into the house, followed by my father. The birds on the roof lifted and hovered over the house. Presently the women of Bertha Moses' family filed out the door. They jingled, sang and fluttered, and the birds accompanied them. The girl with the bell necklace looked back at me several times, but neither of us waved.

The next morning my mother woke me with a butterfly kiss. She grazed her eyelashes across my cheek, fluttering them. She entered my dream as a moth carrying my mother's blue eyes on stalks. I shook my head awake and my mother stood straight and produced a butterfly from behind her back. The butterfly was made from petals of scarlet flax and my mother's fingers breathed life into it. This was a childish game and I was angry at her for it. I threw back the covers and dressed for school, had breakfast and did my chores. My mother went about the business of her day separately, with sorrow draped around her.

Guilt caught up to me on my way to school. The low clouds oppressed my spirit. At the crossroads something moved in the bush, and I got scared for no reason and ran the rest of the way.

School was a one-room building with a wood heater in the middle and a cloakroom at the back. All the grades were jumbled together; I knew their faces, but I'd never befriended them, my father had seen to that.

During hygiene inspection Mrs. MacKay found a yellow streak of manure on my forearm, from chores. That singled me out for the noon-hour initiations that always took place the first day of school. I'd been their victim before; I'd been forced to steal rhubarb from the Watson property next to the school. The house was haunted and I was terrified. One of the boys jumped at me from the derelict window and I ran home, screaming, sure that Rudy Watson had risen from the dead.

At noon a group of older kids surrounded me as I read on the steps of the school. One of the boys clapped his hand over my mouth, picked me up and carried me over to the Watson property. The other kids giggled and followed him into the house. They had kidnapped Gerald Kennedy as well and were holding him down and undressing him. They stripped me of my underwear and pulled my dress over my head. They pulled off my brassiere and laughed at my nakedness. They held down my legs and arms. Two boys pushed Gerald Kennedy down on top of me.

"Screw her," somebody said.

"Do it, or we'll tell MacKay we found you and Beth together naked."

Gerald humped feebly against my crotch and thighs, pulling against my skin. When the crowd finally had enough of this miserable performance they let Gerald up and I hurriedly put on my clothes. Gerald dressed and ran off. Somebody started a chant.

"Slut! Slut! Slut!"

They stood around me, not letting me get up. Finally I struggled away, and the chorus chased after me, yelling "Slut!"

I didn't stop at the school. I left my coat and lunch tin, and ran down the road, leaving the chorus behind. The clouds finally broke and the downpour began. At the crossroads I saw myself standing in the rain, wet through and sickly, my hands outstretched. I was pleading with myself to stop. I ran past myself and the invisible thing hopped onto the road. I saw its footsteps. I ran harder until I saw Filthy Billy sitting against a stook with his collar up against the rain. He smiled and waved, swore at me and apologized.

"Billy," I said, "something's following me."

"There always is," he said.

The chicken spirit hopped and Filthy Billy swore and apologized profusely. I found no comfort in his company. The thing that followed me took steps closer. I stumbled down our roadway and into the house; the footsteps ended outside, on the front steps. I ran to my room and threw myself on the bed and clutched my pillow. Immediately stones fell from the ceiling. The chair by the window began a slow march towards the bed and my dolls jumped off my vanity and began walking at me. I screamed and screamed and then it seemed if I were to stay very still, then everything would stop. I held myself rigid on the bed. The rocks stopped showering and the furniture in my room went back to its usual place. I felt my mother's footsteps and then her face was over me. She called my name and shook me but I focussed on the ceiling behind her head. She called my name louder and slapped my face. She said, "Oh God," and left my room. A little while later she came back with my father. His footsteps shook the bed so I knew he was angry; he looked distorted and huge.

"She saw me, she's awake," he said.

"Whatever could have happened?" said my mother.

"She should be at school."

"She wouldn't have come home unless something happened," said my mother.

She looked into my face.

"Beth dear, what happened?" she said.

Her voice was so tender, so forgiving, I almost answered. But there was a new peace here, in not reacting. Everything seemed in my control. As long as I didn't move, no-one could hurt me, nothing could penetrate. She tried for a long time, talking sweetly to me. My father huffed and stomped from the house. My mother cried. Then she left my room and fussed in the kitchen, and I must have slept. When I woke there was no-one in the house. I heard the rain on the roof, and my stomach grumbled. I struggled against apathy and shuffled into the kitchen. I drank a cup of milk and ate a piece of unbuttered bread. Then I shuffled back to my room and lay rigid.

I became aware I was being watched. Before I could think I turned my head towards the window. The hands, from the thing that followed, were on the outside window ledge. I threw a blanket over myself and looked again. The hands were gone. I heard footsteps and hurriedly arranged myself as I had been. The window slid open and someone climbed into the room. I heard bells. The girl watched me and jingled the necklace. I sat up.

"You were asleep," she whispered.

"No," I said.

"Your parents aren't here?"

"No," I said.

She sat on the bed beside me with the necklace coiled loosely in her hand. The thing that followed me followed her. It stood behind her with one hand resting kindly on her shoulder.

"Your hair is so golden," she said.

She reached out and gently combed my hair with her fingers. I took the necklace and jingled the bells.

"How was school?" she said.

I shook my head. She nodded as if I'd told her everything.

"Roll on your stomach," she said. I rolled over and lay full length, resting my chin on my hands. The bells smelled tinny. She arranged my hair to one side, and smoothed the material of my blouse as if cleaning a blackboard. She began to draw on my back. It felt smooth and tickly and I relaxed under her hands. After a while I said, "What are you drawing?"

"I'm writing," she said.

"What are you writing?"

"You have to guess," she said.

I followed the circles of her hands on my back.

"I don't know," I said.

"Guess!"

Slowly she formed big looped letters of three words, and repeated them over and over. I understood quickly, but didn't know what to do. I turned over and she continued to write, spelling the words over the sides of my breasts.

"You," she said, mouthing the last word, and forming a 'u' that cupped my breast. Blood tingled into my cheeks. I sat there for some time, breathless, sitting up on my elbows. She continued to draw a 'u' that followed the contours of my breasts, first one and then the other. She grazed her lips over my cheeks and forehead, so lightly it was barely a breath. She lay beside me on the bed and I did my best to imitate her. She ran her fingers up my arm and I ran mine down hers. She pulled me close so our breasts touched. She kissed me. I'd never heard of two people doing anything like this. I began to realize that if I'd never heard anyone talk about this, it must be wrong.

The kitchen door slammed and we jolted apart. The girl grabbed the bell necklace and ran. My father marched into my room, just as the girl was climbing out the window.

"Get out of my house," my father yelled, but of course she was already gone. "I'll skin you," he yelled. "Stupid little squaw."

Then he turned on me. He flipped me over on my stomach and turned up my skirt and slapped my bare bottom with his bare hand. It was an indecent act; I was far too old to be handled in this way by my father. After a few slaps he turned me over again and began yelling.

"You will not have that girl here," he said. "Do you understand? She's a breed. They're filth. They carry lice. Do you understand? It's for your own good. I'm only trying to protect you. Do you understand?"

I nodded. He said this about anyone who ventured to be my friend. I stood up, backed away from my father and fled from the house into the field. My father didn't bother to follow me. The storm had taken on a new fury. Wind blistered the rain and it boiled in all directions. Birds struggled for cover and were carried in the wind like sheets of newspaper. A whirlwind zipped by the hung laundry flinging my father's underwear and socks up to heaven. I ran back into the house as my father ran to the pasture, with his coat over his head.

I watched from my bedroom window as my father struggled to get the animals into the barn. The cows were excited by the storm and my father's attempts at chasing them looked clumsy and foolish. Seeing my father pitted against the storm in this way, I wondered how I could be frightened of him.

The anger of the storm ended abruptly. An awful calmness smothered the house. I pressed my face against the window, and saw a rain begin to fall, so gently the raindrops seemed to float. Then I saw they were not raindrops, they were flowers, violets, fluttering to the ground. In no time at all the rain covered the earth in flowers. I opened my window and crawled out onto the purple carpet. I took my shoes off and paddled around in pools of violets. Their fragrance was intoxicating. The clouds moved on, and still the violets drifted down, from a blue sky.

"The Girl with the Bell Necklace" is excerpted from a current novel-in-progress.

SUMMER OF LOVE

Jennifer Rudder

THERE IS A STADIUM on the corner. Walking west along Bloor Street you can easily pass it unaware. The academic fortress of a museum and ivy-covered music conservatory give way to a high brick wall which grows out of the sidewalk. Beyond the wall, the banked seats of the stadium reach out over the sidewalk and form an arcade under which the sports fans walk. I only know it as a place for outdoor rock concerts.

I don't find myself in this part of the city very often. At one time this section of Bloor was the main drag for me, linking Rochdale to Yorkville and Yonge Street. Now, twenty years later, I reach that corner and glance furtively at the site; cross the street quickly, my stomach a tight knot.

He waited for the child there in his car, parked a discreet distance from Bloor Street. Perhaps he used the phone in the lone blue and white booth to call her the last time. Today a newspaper is trapped in the booth, its pages blowing away in the wet November wind, one sheet at a time.

It's only a short ride from Summerhill station to St. George. Just two stops south and two stops west. Her favourite part of the trip is from Summerhill to Yonge, when the train travels above ground. Pink and

23

white blooms at the side of the tracks, green wedges of grass and bushes whiz past and the train pulls into the Rosedale station. Sunlight on pale green tiles that hot July day. Three older, teenaged girls get on the train. Giggling and pushing, they rush to find three seats all together and slide into place. The girl with red hair has that same pink Roots bag that Karen bought last week. She tried phoning Karen and Vanessa, but both their lines were busy. Probably talking to each other. She can't wait to see them and the rest of the team at the stadium.

Waiting at Yonge Street for the westbound train. The photographer phoned and said he wanted to take her picture for the track and field magazine! Clutching her gym bag, she files onto the westbound train with the crowd and squeezes into the seat closest to the door. Bay Street: one more stop. Next week they are all going on a bus to New Jersey to compete in the Eastern semi-finals. The coach is certain that their team will win, but has scheduled practice every day until they leave anyway. Jumping up, the skin of her bare legs pulls away from the vinyl seat of the subway car.

There is a small crowd waiting their turn at the foot of the escalator, but Alison takes the stairs two at a time, and leaves them all behind. Sprinting across the upper platform, she takes the next set of stairs three at a time, her long legs warming. Running past the newspaper stand, she sees her reflection looking back at her from the dark glass. She smiles, imagining her face on the cover of Junior Track and Field. *Bounding up the last eight stairs she emerges and heads toward Bloor Street, squinting into the sunlight. She checks her Swatch: 11:25. Five minutes early.*

With two weeks of school left, Jo and I go to our first week-end-long rock festival at Varsity Stadium. I meet Jo's friend Susie for the first time on that corner. She goes to the all-girl convent Jo left for my school. Beautiful and wild like Jo, she has abandoned her uniform and is decked out in nickel-and-dime finds from the Salvation Army Thrift Shop. In her wide-brimmed straw hat and maroon Forties housedress, Susie searches the crowd eagerly, disappears and returns triumphant. She pulls her hand from the pocket of her dress and unfurls her fingers, revealing a small wad of tin foil for our inspection. Jo reaches into the purple velvet pouch dangling from her belt and produces a beautiful blue enamel pipe. Our backs against the warm concrete wall, we sit out under the arcade on the sidewalk and smoke hash.

Strands of coloured glass beads stick to the warm flesh of my throat. My silver bracelets slide up my arm and clink together as I lift my damp, waist-length hair up off my neck. When I throw my head back to laugh the tiny bells on my Indian earrings tinkle. We join the throng filing in through the turn-stiles, and spill out into the sun-drenched arena. The bass guitar being tuned on stage reverberates in my stomach. Drifts of burning grass tickle my nose. A bare-chested guy with wide sideburns and round, blue glasses blows me a kiss. For one moment I lose Jo and Susie. Each face I stop at seems familiar: every young woman with long black hair and bright Indian skirt is Jo; every smiley, baby-faced blonde lying across a boy's lap is Susie. "Come," Jo whispers in her husky voice. She takes my elbow and directs me back to where our blanket is spread out on the grass, where Susie sits cross-legged, fishing in her basket for a corkscrew. It's June, the beginning of the Summer of Love.

Later that night Jo and I stroll along Bloor Street arm-in-arm, the pavement under our bare feet still warm from the heat of the day. A hot Saturday night, the line of cars filled with fun-seekers inches slowly forward, headlights blazing, headed for the coffee houses of Yorkville or the crowds of Yonge Street. We wear long skirts and no bras, and we have nothing but time. But at 1:00 am we panic and scramble into the clammy subterranean cool of the subway station, racing down the three flights of stairs, desperate to catch the last train which speeds us eastward, out of the city, home.

Soon after school ends, Jo phones me. She's crying and it's hard to make out what she's saying. Her mom tried to kill herself. An ambulance came and took her to the hospital and Jo has to go see her. Could I come with her? I hang up the phone on the kitchen wall and I'm out of the house like a shot, running up the street past the sprinklers, one on each lawn spinning, twirling, rotating silently. *It's O.K. Jo, I'm coming, I'll rescue you.*

I run the whole way up the long hill to meet her, taking the dirt path after the sidewalk ends, ducking under the low branches of pine, on the only original trees, in front of the only old house left in this suburb. I'm thinking about the word *suicide*, Jo said *suicide*. All those nights I lay in my bed wishing I were dead, crying myself to sleep. But her mom, so nervous and thin.

I run faster, remembering Jo's voice on the phone. I could barely hear her; she couldn't say the words. I'm glad that she phoned me, glad that she needs me. Her life is so much harder than mine, harder than anybody else I know at school. She has so many other friends from St. Joe's, but she called me and I'm happy.

I reach Sheppard Avenue and see 'the hills' as we call them. Hills that were there before they dug them up and built a plaza; they separate her subdivision from mine. I spot Jo, far away at the top of one hill, wearing the red blouse I bought her at the Salvation Army last year. She is running up and over and when we meet I clasp her to me and feel her wet face on my neck, her thin shoulders convulsing against my chest as she sobs.

Jo never waits for the bus, she hitchhikes everywhere. But she's so upset and the bus that never comes when I need it is pulling up beside us before we have a chance to argue. We climb on and I stuff two tickets in the box. It's a long, slow bus-ride across the north of the city to the spanking new hospital where her mother is. I can't stop talking. I tell her a funny story from when I was a kid, which usually cheers her up. She just pulls a dirty, blue and white polka-dot handkerchief from her shoulder bag and blows hard. The other passengers turn and stare. For some reason this embarrasses me, but Jo stares defiantly back at them, her red eyes burning. I look out the window, grey industrial complexes scud by.

North York General is set back from the road, in vast, ploughed-up fields. I leave Jo at the doorway to her mother's darkened room and wait in the lounge at the end of the hallway. It's so clean and silent, nothing like the crowded, bustling old hospital downtown where my relatives go when they get sick. It feels like Mrs. Stanton and Jo and I are the only people here.

Afterwards we sit on the steep grassy slopes of the road, waiting for the bus. I lie back, my hands clasped under my head, and watch Jo's back. She sits there stunned, hugging her knees to her chest, smoking cigarettes, the sky tomato red behind her.

"Want to spend the night at my house?"

She shakes her head. "I've got to stay with Billy and Fats tonight." Her little brothers. "They're with the neighbours."

I can't remember a time before when we had nothing to say to each other.

Five months after her abduction and murder, the trail was ice cold. Then the police seized the corner bank's video surveillance cameras. When the tapes of that particular day were scrutinized, the camera, in its slow, dumb sweep of the bank, had recorded not his, but her, small blurry image. Desperate for a lead, the detective scans the videotape again. The camera makes its silent, black-and-white swing of the room. Impatient clients cough and shift their weight in the line-up, glad for the air-conditioned cool of the bank on that hot July day. The teller discreetly closes a bank book as she hands it back across the wicket, a vague smile on her lips. They say "Have a nice day." The camera tracks over the shoulder of the teller, through the window. The bottom of the child's white shorts and long bare legs stride by, dark gym bag banging against her side. A clock on the bank counter shows 11:28. No killer. No make of car or license plate number. No clue. In the few seconds that it takes the camera to cross the room a second time, she is gone. The tall banks of floodlights perch high on their poles in the sunny stadium.

The week Jo's mom comes home from the hospital, Jo moves to Rochdale College. Susie has already rented a room there. I have a summer job filling orders in a book warehouse and visit them once. We sit in their open window ten stories above Bloor Street, drinking wine and calling out to people passing down below. Once in August I see Susie sitting slumped on the steps of one of the skinny, brightly-coloured houses in Yorkville. I go up to her and say Hi but she doesn't recognize me. I want to stay and talk to her, but she just stares dully in front of her as if she doesn't really see me.

On the first day of my last year of high school, I walk to school across the fields under the hydro towers, crying. I can't face another year of football heroes and cheerleaders and teachers who don't understand me. When I enter the front doors the excitement of the other students depresses me further, and I head for the girls' washroom, lock myself into a cubicle, sit down on the toilet seat and cry. Girls come and go. The bell rings. The bathroom is quiet, but someone is still outside the cubicle. She hears me sniffing and snorts, "I know how you feel, man." It's Jo. I jump up, open the door and let her in. She's back home and back at school. When she hugs me I'm so happy I start sobbing again. She says, "We can make it

Jenny; we just have to stick together."

Jo lasts about three weeks at school before she disappears from my life again. I stop calling her house; her mother just sighs and hangs up whenever I ask for her. One day late in November, she calls me from downtown. I skip school and wait for her in the Zumburger on Bloor near St. George. An hour after we've arranged to meet, and after I've made three trips across the street to Rochdale to see if I can find her or anyone who knows her, Jo walks in.

"I know I look like shit, Jenny," she laughs. "No sleep and no food."

And too much acid.

I use all of my babysitting money to buy her a burger and fries, coffees and a pack of cigarettes from the machine. I'm yacking away, telling her how awful school is, filling her in on her most hated teachers. I tell her about the new guy in my class, who rides a motorcycle to school and skips classes to read Dylan Thomas.

"He's so cool. Hey, remember *La Morte D'Arthur*? I'm working on this really big painting of Guinevere and Gawain."

"Susie just got outta the hospital."

I stub out my cigarette. "What's wrong? What happened?"

"Hep man. What a drag."

"Hep?"

"Yeah, hepatitis. I went to visit her and I found her sitting on her bed, alone in a room in the dark, right? I said 'Susie?' and when she turned to look at me, her eyes were glowing. Bright green, man. Fucking weird. I was so freaked out. It's her liver. Too much speed. The whites of her eyes were green."

I shake my head. I know she disapproves of Susie using speed but she doesn't want *me* to judge Susie.

"So now she's moved into some kind of weird house up on Bedford. Bad news man. I've gotta get her out of there."

"I'll go with you," I say.

"Really?"

"Sure."

We walk along Bloor past the stadium and turn up Bedford, past all the once-grand homes now rooming houses. It starts raining, and Jo keeps talking. She seems glad to have company.

"There's this rich guy," she says. "He travels all around the world and lives with some tribe in South America. He's letting them use his house. Kind of like a hostel."

We ring the doorbell several times and wait in the rain by the huge wooden doors. After a few minutes we try the door: it opens. Inside a skinny ginger cat stretches and rubs his patchy fur up against Jo's blue jeans. I follow her down the hallway, Jo calling out Susie's name in her husky voice, knocking at each door. Mattresses. Filthy, bare. Garbage everywhere, cat shit. At the back of the house there's a kitchen. It seems never used, though gluey pots and plates fill the sink.

As we climb up to the second floor, a guy with long, dirty hair leans over the banister. When Jo asks him if Susie is there, he hugs his sunken chest and nods down the hall. The house is cold, silent. The upstairs hallway has no light. Pushing open the door at the end of the hallway, we spot someone curled in a ball on the mattress, underneath an old fur coat. It's Susie. She sits up and rubs her eyes. Jo rushes to her side, kneels down and hugs her, then lights us all cigarettes. Susie sits on the bed smoking in a dirty T-shirt and panties and considers us sleepily. Her cheeks are marked with large, sore-looking pimples and her eyes are glazed. Jo rubs Susie's skinny arms gently. They're stained with dainty purple bruises like blossoms, and tiny points of dried blood run up and down.

I stand at the window and watch the bus speed up Bedford, its wires zipping along together like ski poles. I'm cold even with my coat on. Jo tries to convince Susie to move back into Rochdale with her, I press my forehead on the glass.

The rain has changed to snow. I'm sorry I spent all my money on Jo: it looks like it's been a lot longer since Susie ate anything. I hear the word 'morphine' and think of trenches in France, the First World War, see my history teacher jabbing his wooden pointer at the pink, yellow and blue map of Europe. I wonder if Susie studied the First World War too. How did we get from hash to speed to morphine so fast? Why does she look worse now that the drug sounds more legitimate, more pharmaceutical? I think about the owner of the house in South America — does he know how his house is being used, does he care. I think he doesn't. Care.

It will take me twenty years to remember this part. The summer after we got her out of that shooting gallery on Bedford, Susie and a friend were picked up by the cops for vagrancy in Yorkville. They were taken to the police station and held in the basement overnight. Two cops took turns raping them. No. In 1969 we wouldn't have used the word rape. What did Jo say when she told me? Ball? Fuck?

Susie and her friend were released in the morning; the cops threatened to tell their parents that they were dealing drugs. I remember I just shook my head when Jo told me this, as if she had said that she had been thrown out by her mother again, or that Susie was back in the hospital with hep. My sense of outrage still undeveloped, still mute, I was unable to comprehend. Police protect us, cops don't fuck young girls in holding cells. I didn't understand. It never sank in.

I sit in the Mr. Submarine on the corner, facing the stadium and the renovated bank and think about Alison. I remember I was in the back seat of our parked car, my newborn son asleep in my lap when I first saw her pretty face looking out from the newspaper box. A recent family photo: her head tilted slightly to one side, chin resting in her upturned palm. Calmly confident for an eleven-year-old, her large green eyes look up at the photographer dreamily. The black headline one grim word: MISSING.

4'10", 75 lbs. Blonde hair, green eyes. Good teeth and refined speech.

Later the Deputy Chief of Police would say, "It's a particularly savage murder of a fine young girl who is an example of what a young girl should be."

I met Jo in front of Varsity Stadium again, at the end of the summer of 1969. We tried to get into the John and Yoko concert but it was sold out, so we lay out under the trees behind the stadium and smoked a crumb of hash flecked with stray tobacco bits from the bottom of Jo's bag. She always carried a shawl in her basket, a grubby baby blanket really, and we huddled together underneath it that August evening, shivering in our thin jean jackets.

We never talked much about Jo's home life; she didn't like to get too heavy. The way she saw it we were two innocent milk-maids from a Thomas Hardy novel, thrown together in this harsh world. She felt responsible for me, wanted to protect me and sometimes regretted dragging me into her world. Like the beautiful stray dog you bring in out of the rain late at night to feed and pet, Jo would bask in the comfort and uncomplicated stability of my life: two parents who loved each other and loved me. They even loved her, and recharged by my dad's soup and corny jokes and my mom's concern, she would be off again.

I lay on my back, looking up at the dark shapes of the trees looming above us. Jo curled beside me, her arm across my waist, head turned toward me. Her nose almost touched my ear as she recounted in that deep, thrilling voice the details of our trip to Hardy's landscape in Dorset England. Jo always talked about these plans when things weren't going well. I loved to listen to her describe the salt sea smell blowing the curtains of our room at night, in our bed-and-breakfast in Lyme Regis. After a long day walking along the sea wall we would eat fish and chips in the pub and we could even order a beer there, even though we were only seventeen. Maybe we could rent a little cottage and stay a while. Beyond Jo's whisper, Yoko's spooky staccato wailing echoed over the city night, mingling with distant sirens.

THE TALE

Claire Harris

I STEPPED OUT of the air-conditioned airport at Piarco into the island energized by love. Now I know that's a strange thing to say ... but I hadn't been home for twenty years. I tell you the earth moved. Then I felt the tropical humidity, the dazzling energy of its crowded places slam into my face, wrap itself around my body, and I almost retreated. Back to the Air Canada desk, to the cool blue Rockies. Then I saw Great Aunt. Scrawny neck rising out of her grey linen shirtwaist, battered black leather bag, the smallest possible size in men's black Oxfords, she gleamed against the navy Vanguard sedan, circa 1970. Sun and age had burnt the flesh from her bones. She seemed shorter, frail, even as I noted how strong her hug was for a woman in the mid-eighties. And that if she was fragile, it didn't extend to her voice.

I see her hesitate a little, Marielle, as she stand there with one small small suitcase, and she beauty case in she hand. I have to confess the heart twist a little. She look so much like she mother. She sit quiet in the back of the car, holding my hands, looking at me like she making a memory. And I realize she change, but she ain't change that much. She exchange a little chat with Dokin; she even remember the names of he family. And though

it have a little Canadian twist to everything she say, it ain't
bad enough to give offense. Then we sit quiet while she watch
the road, and all the big houses, and the little shopping malls
it have everywhere now. A lot change in fifteen years, and is
fifteen years since she was last here. That time she come to the
mother funeral, and all told she was just here five days. Not
even time enough to realize what that kind of dead mean.
When we get to Arouca, she sit up well animated.

She ask Dokin to give she a little run through the town.
We turn off the main road, drive round by the church and the
convent, over by the cricket field, as far as the old airstrip
from the Second War when they had Americans here.
Suddenly, she laugh like she remember something. So I play
my part and ask, she tell me she want to see if the warden
house still have all those boulders paint white, and if they still
painting the trunks of coconut trees black with white stripe in
the warden garden. Is not very far, so though my mind didn't
give me to go out there, we drive all the way to the prison at
Orange Grove. Then she say she want to go inside the house
to see if the prisoners still have to polish the warden floor till
it shine like glass. Someting in she voice come like a warning
an' I think is lucky I don't know this warden. So we couldn't
visit.

"Of course we can, Aunt! Let's see. I could say I'm a rep-
resentative of the Organization for World Prisoners' rights,
and as I'm visiting the island, I thought I'd look him up."

I thought was a joke. Then I see Dokin looking at me in
the mirror, and I turn to face her. You know she busy digging
in she bag for notebook and tape recorder!

"Which do you think he'd be more comfortable with,
Aunt? I don't want to spook him."

Spook him? She serious! She don't want to spook the
man! She is a person I help bring up by hand and I ain't know
she. She grow up on my lap, and she ain't have any respect for

people privacy. She forget is a island! You make a enemy it
ain't have nowhere to hide.

Look, I love the islands! They're in my blood. I know them.
I'm not stupid. I would have sailed in there perfectly politely,
asked the prisoner/ butler to take my name in, asked the
Director for an interview. No reason at all for panic. It's
unlikely that he reads *This Magazine*. On the other hand it
might be read in Ottawa. The Island Embassy. We're good at
many things, we islanders, but we haven't really examined the
British premise. The colonial premise: he who is outside the
law is a slave. QED. (*Quod erat demonstrandum* as in Grenada,
as in Las Malvinas, as in Panama, as in Iraq.) You challenge
their 'law,' you lose all humanity. I tried to explain all this to
the Great Aunt, but she could only think that I would be
"exploiting the man"; that I would be "invading his privacy";
that it was "longtime custom." It isn't any surprise that the
island hasn't got it yet! Canada hasn't either. Of course, Native
American and Inuit have, but that's another story! Not even
mine. I have to admit, though, the island has less excuse. After
all, here the colonizer spoke a different language, ate a different food. Those who survived the hungry Atlantic, the savage
three hundred years, *should know* in the bone. Yet, in the island
some prisoners are used like house slaves, like 'boys.' It
seemed to me that I could, that I should do something! After
all, I had the tape recorder. I had access to the media. Publicity
can cause change. We all know that.

Besides, the sky was as brilliant as I remembered; the pas-
tel houses with their filigree of wrought-iron bars, their verandahs and patios still rain-stained. Hibiscus was still as red, as
white, the few dilapidated shacks visible still upright in spite of
weather; the birds still brilliant, jewelled, raucous; the country
roads as ragged, verges as star-spattered. My aunt beside me
still as vital as in my dreams. There was nothing to fear. There

had never been anything to fear. So I said, "Come on Great Aunt, you always know everybody! Besides, it's not your responsibility. I'm the adult with the tape recorder. I'm the write ... ." But even as I spoke, Dokin was reversing into the circular driveway, and we were going back the way we had come. I opened my mouth to protest ... and felt my aunt's hands hard on mine, felt, rather than saw the slightest inclination of her head towards Dokin's back ... 'not in front of the servants.'

'Not in front of the ... !' Nothing was ever going to change in those islands. This was the inheritance of slavery. This was why I had left. It was ... it was intolerable!

We get back to the main road in silence. When she start up, I squeeze she hands, and shut she up. I know is an argument she want, but I never invite people to disrespect me. Is a thing I not good at at all. But I see the horrified way she look at me. And I feel the contempt. So I sit in the darkness as we drive through the town, and turn up the Lopinot road, wondering what trouble it is I have on my hands. I listen to her start to sweet-talk Dokin in what have to be she Canadian voice.

"This road holds so many memories for me!"

What that have to do with Dokin? Where she memories an' his cross, he is boy in torn pants bringing water from the ravine, and she is missy in stiff starched cotton paying he ten cents per gallon tin while she father looking on. What in that Dokin go want to remember?

"I'd forgotten how quickly darkness falls in the tropics. Like a guillotine!"

'Tropics'! 'Guillotine'! She embarrassing the poor man. What she trying to tell him? That he barefoot in he father tomato patch while she going to Convent school in town? That she gone to University while he drive bus? That all the Barrett blood gone to she head and she is a fool like all that side of the family? She forget the way you get privilege in the islands is when slave master rape your mother. Meanwhile Dokin only giving me quick little glances in the mirror. I have no intention of saying anything. She is a grown woman. Everybody got to go to hell they own way.

Impossible to ignore the silence in the car growing heavier, Dokin's answers coming slower and more reluctantly. But I would not be beaten. I kept up a lively line of chatter asking about politics, and all the village characters whose names I could remember. Every time Dokin grinned into the mirror, I counted it a victory. It sounds like we'd been driving for hours, but in fact everything recounted here must have taken place within fifty minutes. Pretty soon we had turned into the lane, steel gate wide open so that everyone could have access to the river road. The car's lights punched a tunnel through the absolute country darkness. The trees still arched over the drive as I remembered, and the sweet heavy smell of night flowers and rotting mangoes mingled with the tangy river smell and the cocoa. The lane was shorter than I remembered it and very soon we saw the lights of the old house. Low and wide with wrought-iron windows and doors opening on to a wide verandah, it blazed with welcoming lights and music.

Dokin get out an' open the car door for that child and she look at me smiling, and in the verandah light I see she face all light up like a Christmas tree. The family start out on the verandah to greet she, and she hugging everybody and exclaiming. I stand up there watching she, thinking how normal she appear when one of the cousins come out and start fussing over me. I let him fuss. Then Dokin wife, Pretty, come out to tell me everything ready, she ask if I want to serve dinner or wait. I think is better if we wait till eight o'clock or so, then everybody really hungry. The party was already going full swing before we reach, and everybody settle back to serious fun.

It's really hard when you first get back, that very first night, not to get all teary-eyed. After I had broken away from the greetings, I went to my room to change. It was even smaller than I remembered. This is a really old house built like a railway carriage with back-to-back compartments, at a time when families stayed together. At various times, eight truly narrow bedrooms were added to the original two large rooms. Then about sixty years ago the two great verandahs, one in front and one at the back, were built on. Since I'd been in Canada, one of the tiny rooms on each side had been turned into a bathroom, and a modern kitchen had replaced the old Carib kitchen and showers. It's possible to trace family upheavals in each pair of bedrooms, and the additions chart the price of cocoa. My room was lined with heavy old mahogany furniture, dark with age, and touched at the corners with desultory carvings. The bed was as narrow as I remembered, and as hard. The old coconut straw mattress on woven leather supports was still there. But Pretty had put white ixoras on the dressing table, and my wrought-iron gate opened onto the back gallery, so I knew that there was a wonderful view of orange, cocoa and banana trees almost at my door, and a great stand of anthuriums. I could hear the river. In the morning I would see it. I was home.

I have to admit I notice the relax look on she face when she come out to join the party. She had change into an African gown and it well suit her. She sit down in the midst, and people gather round to talk. All the cousins educate in Canada or in England, and was a really good thing to see them together talking. It cross my mind that I happy she come here rather than go to the mother family in town. Especially now it look like she settle down, she listening and behaving normal. I sit back watching them, and they children, hoping the old house have another generation to shelter. Someone that love cocoa. Everything going so good I forget is the island. Suddenly without any warning lights gone off. One of the children scream in the darkness and I hear the parent correct him. By that time I was up trying to find the torches in the bureau drawer. Pretty come in with a candle, and start lighting the lamps. Soon the excitement over. Everybody settle down with lamp light well soft on everything and leaving shadows. Pretty and I decide to wait and see if the electricity coming back on before we serve supper. She had turn around to go back to Dokin in the kitchen when I hear Marielle.

"Pretty, why you and Dokin hiding out in the kitchen? Why don't you take a chair?"

For a moment, no-one said anything and I saw the look of surprise on Pretty's face. It isn't that I don't know that people have to cast off their own chains, I do. But I know that a push helps. I saw that she was going to make an excuse, and refuse. No-one had seconded the invitation. I stared hard at her and we teetered together on the brink. Just as she took courage to turn me down, one of the kids, it may have been Jonathan, piped up, "Yes, Pretty, you come and tell us stories."

"Get Dokin to tell us about the time the succoyant came to his house!"

"Yeah!"

"Ghost stories!"

The children were shouting, pleading as the wonderful idea took hold. It is possible to refuse a 'stranger who has come from away,' it is not possible to refuse 'young master.' In a few minutes, Pretty and Dokin appeared in the drawing-room, ready for their star turn.

Look at my crosses nuh! This is Marielle! This is my great niece. She inherit all what this family suffer in the gut to accumulate, generation by generation, and she ready to throw it away. And is not money I talking about. Is how, black, you work to make yourself different, to make yourself separate from the most. So they don't treat you like the most. So when they pick an' choose who to put in good school, they choose yours because they *think* you not like the rest. So they don't ignore you; you got a problem they fix; you go to hospital, somebody come immediately to attend to you; so you don't have to wait nowhere in the hot sun. So you walk in the front door. So everybody, no matter who, call you Mrs. Duceaux. Nobody overly familiar, out of place with you. And is only then you get to really talk for your people. Everybody take you serious, you can ease the boot a little, make a change. This family what grow cocoa or grow teachers and lawyers. But she in a hurry. The plane just land and she want to score big, she want to fix. For three hundred years we trying to fix. They say what you don't want in your kitchen, you does get in your drawing-room!

All the while turning down the lamps, blowing out the candles for Dokin story is so I thinking what happen in this child head; how she mixing up Canada-there and here. I thought was enough, all what happen in the short time she here. But it had more to come.

Dokin came into the room reluctantly, looked down at the kids and said, "Who wan' to hear story come wid meh on de verandah."

The kids follow him as if he were the pied piper, and we adults left alone, find ourselves leaning forward to hear Dokin's voice. Though in the clear country night it came to us easily.

It was night of de big storm, yuh cud say hurricane. Rain had stop falling, an' it ent have no real wind. Still de sky was full of clouds, an' every now an' again one of dem would cover de moon face. Was a trouble night. We was living dat time in de house dong below yuh uncle. In de hollow. All day Ma catchin' water in bucket an' basin. Now de rain stop is jus' drip drip all night.

Now yuh haf to know dat de week before, Saime tell we Succoyant take he taxi. We ent know weder to laugh or cry. Dey say every ting everyting possible. So my fader did buy de blue foh de crosses on de window boards, but we didn't have time to paint, or bring de Hindu priest. Dat night de groun' so damp, we sling plenty hammock, and everybody tumble in an' gorn to sleep. In de middle of the night, someting wake me. Some ting, someting what smell horrible, snuffling round de house. Ah tumble out de hammock an' crawl over to mi fader an' wake him. Yuh could hear it tryin', scratchin', at de two window, an' de door. Den it start roun' again, de two window and de door. Ah ent know how long ah listen to dis ting circling de house. Den ah hear it at de door and dis time is like shoving and ah cud see de door bucklin'. An de smell ... like somebody dead and leave for days, like rotten eggs ... an' it coming at yuh in waves. By dis time de whole family wake up. Mi fader move like cat, quiet quiet, an' pick up a board from de corner, he sneak over an' put it to prop de door. Ma praying quiet like. It start circling again, everybody turnin' in de dark to follow how it snufflin' round de house. De smell so bad yuh could hardly breathe. Den we hear de voice. At first it soft an' far.

"Samjeet, (dat was mi fader name) Samjeet, de Duceaux put me out! Give me a corner!"

Ma look at mi fader an' whisper, "Is a bad one! It know we name!"

Mi fader say "Shhhhh!" and it call again.

"Samjeet, Samjeet give me a corner."

Each time it call it getting nearer. An' nearer. An' de smell far worse. Den it stop suddenly. We wait an' wait, an' the smell go away. Ma say to keep praying. Mi brothers an' sisters an' me stiff like board. We frighten to move a muscle. Den we smell something sweet, like roses, coming though de door. Then a voice like a young girl leaning up against de door giggling an' putting she lips against de door an' whispering. "Samjeet is me! Is only me! Why yuh en let me in Samjeet? Why? It so cold out here!"

Is den my fader shout, "No gat room! No gat room! Samjeet send yuh back! No room!"

Outside de door we hear something sigh. Ah cyan explain to you what carry in dat sigh. An' move away.

Is then it happen. Dokin start to walk off the verandah, when Marielle call him. "Dokin, did that happen one Easter? There was a hurricane!"

"Yes, Ma'm. And it did use yuh fader name! Ah always remember dat."

As soon as she laugh that laugh, like she some bell, I knew was trouble. You don't have to have high intelligence to know this is Dokin story. This is he courage and he strength. He and his father, and his mother and his sisters, the whole family battle the supernatural and they survive. Was no ordinary trouble. Was the powers of darkness. Canada make her too smart to see that. She feel she have to educate.

"Come on, Dokin! That was no succoyant! All that smell, and scent, all that snuffling!" She laughed again. "That was my aunt, Winnie! You remember her. A real tease! She was teasing you. She told us she asked your father ... ."

Dokin stand one foot on the top step one on the edge of the verandah and he look at she. He stand there so still it seem like he hush the night. Even the cicadas freeze in he still and the children gone quiet in the rockers while he look. The room inhale an' hold. And Dokin what ain't even five foot seven grow tall. For a second she face fold into itself and it was like he break straight through she, look straight through the cracks to them streets in Calgary. I have to say ... a something like pity pass ... a something. When he turn he back and walk off, the room exhale. We sit there in silence listening to he foot-steps round the house while the world come back.

They talk, the cousins, they talk all night all through the heaviness of Dokin leaving the family. Mostly they talk about how they miss Trinidad or they miss London. Comparing what can't compare. They talk while Pretty clean everything every-thing in the kitchen. Wiping away before she follow Dokin. Is thirty years she had was to clear. She leave the place shining. Just before five she finish and we get to bed.

Everybody exhaust. But you old, you can't always do things when you want and how you want. Sleep ain't no differ-ent. Besides, since oil-glut nobody working. What Pretty going to do? Last week she tell me school books add up to $867 for the three children, and the girl need new uniforms for September. Is thinking about that, is worrying about every-thing, is thinking about why the children believe we so heart-less, we so backward in the islands as if it have a place where everybody everybody get to be doctor, I come to hear Marielle call out.

"Who is it?" My voice a little sharp and high.

"Girl, why you so nervous? Is only me, Jerome. Listen nuh, that night Aunt Win went begging for a board, was Terry's birthday, no? We were all staying over to celebrate, you remember?" He sat down at the foot of my bed and made himself comfortable.

I sat bolt upright, and kicked out at him, "You mean to tell me you come crawling in here in the middle of the night to ask if I remember? Of course I remember. I remember everything about Trinidad. It was his seventh birthday and she was teas-ing him ... ."

"And he kicked her out ... Marielle that was the night *before the hurricane!* You remember it was as hot as hell and they sent us out on the balcony to sleep? *It was the night before!* The night

they sent the helicopter! You remember the helicopter lights?
And your Dad ... . Mar? Mar?"

Poor child! Poor, poor child, Marielle.

THE BRAVEST GIRL IN THE WORLD

Holley Rubinsky

LIFE HAS A WAY of setting you up when all you're trying to do is get the laundry done. It's a Saturday in the week I've lost my job, bastard fired me, and I'm in the laundromat, the place full of immigrants babbling, washers chuggling. I spot two empty machines side by side. "Thank God," I say, so stressed out I'm talking to myself, my stuff banging against my bare legs as I make a beeline.

I get my first look at the stranger who is fated to enter my life and wreck it worse than usual. He's moving toward the empty machines, too. Actually, he's already standing at them; but what I do, I dart in front of him. I'm in a dog-eat-dog mood. I have days like that, when I charge through life, elbows out. Old folks and kids with any brains step aside when they see me coming.

This jock — I thought of him as just your normal jock and not destiny heading in my direction — he doesn't step aside when I push by. What he does is say something dirty. "Beg pardon?" I reply, proper as can be, all the while sizing up the place. The gals in saris aren't protection but their brats playing war create a reassuring, domestic scene. There's a muttering bag-lady type who looks like she could handle herself. Negotiating in the corner are some pit-faced Vietnamese guys. Okay. With this good Canadian crowd behind me, I start grabbing items from the pillowcases — including the three pairs of skimpy candy-striped shorts my ex-boss says I have to give back — and shove them willy-nilly into both machines with a kind of over-your-dead-body attitude. It's just bluff. I have a gin-and-292 hangover the size of Sudbury.

"Thems my machines," says the jock, who is now also, I hear, illiterate. He's bigger than I first noticed and beefy-faced, hard in the belly as though he works out. His type hangs around in the lounges I work at, but they're not drinkers; they sit at the bar nursing a Scotch till the cows come home, giving me the once-over when I place orders. They're harmless. When they let their hair down, not that this one has much, they're soft as babies.

In this instance I wasn't so smart as I usually give myself credit for.

"First come, first serve," I chirp. "It's the rule I live by."

"I bet you served plenty," he says, insinuatingly eyeing my legs. I'm wearing the first thing I found when I crawled out of bed this morning, a pair of black shorts.

I use the old elbow and pour Cheer into the machines. His hot breath in the vicinity of my neck gives me prickles. I'm living on the edge here.

When I go to find my stash of quarters, patting my genuine imitation leather jacket all over like I'm feeling myself up, they're not there. My fifteen-year-old has robbed me again. Since his father kicked off a year ago, the kid's turned into a petty thief. He thinks it's funny.

Suddenly the hot air I was so full of leaks out like a bad fart. I am about to tell this Godzilla to shove off or I'll yell bloody murder, when it hits me that I do not own in my possession a single damn quarter. All my new-found single-girl aggression is wasted. I burst into tears. Blubber a blue streak. Break down in the laundromat in front of a big dumb jock and half the third world.

He stoops to get a better look at me, his face soft as margarine left on the table. He lifts my chin with his hammy finger. "Why, you cry just like a little girl. You shouldn't be wearing them shorts and high heels. Give a fellow the wrong idea."

In my experience, fellows get any ideas they want, independent of me. I wipe my eyes with my knuckles and tell him I don't give a ham-on-rye what he thinks.

"I bet I got something you want," he says.

"Mister, you got eight quarters, then you got something I want." I am that desperate, to beg off a stranger.

Leisurely out of his pants pocket he takes a fresh $10-roll, Donald Trump fashion. He unwraps the package. "Want a ice cream, little girl?" He's snickering like he's told a joke.

Next door in the mall was a Baskin-Robbins. At first I didn't think he was serious — it was an odd-ball come-on — but it turned out he was very serious. He held the shiny row of slumped-over quarters in the palm of his hand. When I reached for them, he withdrew his hand with a cutesy "uh uh" like you do with a toddler you're blackmailing into good behaviour.

It worked. What the hey, I figured. I shrugged, took the quarters off him, slid them in the machines. I rationalized that my company over ice cream was the least I could do. Then I decided to go for broke. "You buying, right? I'm real tight this month."

"Deal," he said.

I'm in for it.

By now everybody and their brother knows about broads being battered. There was that movie, the one with something-enemy in the title, proving you weren't any better off being rich. Gals shoot fellows they live with, husbands even, and get away with it, driven crazy by years of beatings. I thought shooting the bastards was okay, because in my book girls are always given the wrong end of the popsicle. They still want you to buy into the Prince Charming bit, but what happens after the sunset scene they're a little vague on.

At the time I met George in the laundromat — his name turned out to be George — Buddy'd been killed in a car crash, leaving me with Donny, our only kid. (Donny was an only because I was the type to get pregnant at the drop of a hat — first Donny, then a miscarriage barely half a year afterwards — so Buddy went and had a vasectomy. He didn't mind. We weren't the maternal types. The pill made me allergic and gave me headaches.) Donny was nearly grown but recently grown stupid. He was imitating his movie heroes who took what they wanted when they wanted and got away with it, but not Donny. I was spending too much time answering the door and lying through my teeth on his behalf.

My girlfriend Sherryle, who moved to Brandon, was always telling me I had a one-track mind. Her point being that sometimes I don't pick up on things. Okay. I admit I missed essential qualities about George. What I'm getting to now is it takes two to tango. These movies and magazines about gals being hurt act like it's only the guy who's psycho. The innocent chick battered like chicken before you fry it. The loyal mom holding the family together while the deranged slob she's married to routinely breaks her jaw. What I'm saying is different.

There's layers of being a victim. From Buddy I already knew about the wife as punching bag when a guy's frustrated. To my thinking at the time, it was no big deal; it was a life a lot of girls expected and you learned to get around it.

Who George found in the laundromat was no Bambi. I was not young (thirty-two and should have known better), I did not have a pack of kids to raise (my one was a pill, but I was lazy in general and spoiled), and I was not dumb (even though I was pregnant at sixteen and got married, I did finish my high school diploma, whether I used it or not).

But mostly who I was, I was a broad living a secret life from herself. I had an impulsive nature but the causes behind it were hidden from me. I did rash acts that I didn't even know I was going to do until they'd taken on a life of their own. Example: Buddy took Donny and me on vacation to a pal of his's place in the woods near a lake. By the time we set out, the three of us cozily crammed into the ancient Corvette (at that time Buddy's latest buck-guzzling hobby), the bruise on my cheek from him straightening me around was almost invisible, thanks to pancake make-up, sometimes a girl's best friend.

We barely arrive and I go and blow the whole vacation by taking an unpremeditated swim in the lake just because Buddy says not to. He can't swim and I remember that I can and so I wade in, shorts and halter the same as a suit, and leave him and Donny both whining on the shore. Taking my time I swim to a lopsided old raft with a diving platform, and all the while Buddy's shouting, "You get your ass back here."

Something stubborn deep inside me refuses. Gloating that he can't even float, I am suddenly the bravest girl in the world. Water drips off my trim little desirable body, tanned perfect, toes painted "You're peachy," curly copper-coloured hair glistening in the sun. Then my mean streak takes over and I shake my head like a girl in a Pepsi commercial so he can benefit from the full effect.

I lie down and for a minute bask on the raft that's warm as a heating pad. I am in heaven.

Somewhere inside I sense I better get back or he will kill

me and the kid both. I roll over and look into the water and my eyes bug out, unbelieving of what I see. Long dark shapes drift in the murk around the ramshackle raft. Big-lipped sucker fish, just waiting for a piece of some dumb smarty-pants broad.

Glimpsing those ugly-snouted bottom-feeders makes my stomach churn. I'm stuck between the sky and the deep blue because I didn't do what Buddy told me. It seems like a lesson. But first I have to get to shore where Donny's wailing his heart out. He was ten at the time and a regular blubber-face, bursting into tears like a girl every time Buddy so much as looked at him sideways.

Dinner perched on the rickety raft, I pump my nerves, close my eyes and jump, practically fainting into the water. The fish don't bite, but Buddy has, taking my thongs and sun shirt and driving off, which was what the kid was blubbering about. Eventually, sunburned and feet bleeding, I locate the cabin and manage to swallow a few 292s, preparing myself for Buddy's being fed up. Some things you just know you're asking for.

Taking pills over the years helped me to see what happened to a chick's face once you started slapping it around. I understood how Buddy couldn't keep himself from it sometimes. Take a couple of 292s and wait fifteen minutes, then go stare in the mirror. Your face slowly comes undone, its sharp edges smooth down and drain away. Straightening a girl out causes that same look, I know from experience. At some point in being attacked, you abandon yourself, you give up.

I used to picture how it was for Buddy, a not-great mechanic trying to make a living for a wife he wouldn't let work and a bratty kid he didn't much like. He'd be frustrated on the job and pissed off and start thinking of his little woman. Thinking of her would make his mouth water, and he wouldn't understand why he wanted so bad to get home to her and would think sex was it. He'd come through the door and there

I'd be, watching a soap on TV, the apartment maybe a little messy (not expecting him home so early) and Donny whining or doing some other number. I had a habit of leaping up and checking Buddy's mood, and if the nervy agitation was there, my mouth went dry.

For preamble, he tossed a few things onto the floor or picked a fight, stalked me from room to room or circled me like a boxer, waiting for the fear signs I couldn't prevent, for my eyes to glisten, my lips to part, for whimpering sounds to rise from my throat, for my cheeks to redden from adrenaline kicking in, all this before he'd even touched me. It had to be a turn-on, how fear of him made me even prettier than normal. When he was ready, he caught hold of me with one hand and flung the other into the air, but not striking right away. He watched me not being able to help my automatic response. I hunched my shoulders and ducked my head, and then as I tried half-heartedly to make a break for it, his hand snagged me on the half-turn. He slapped my face sideways and yanked me into his line of vision, so as not to miss the change when it came.

He took his time. That was part of it, the waiting. The waiting allowed me to recover a little, always a mistake leading to worse on his part. His intent watching, his frantic searching of my face let me glimpse the excitement in his eyes that was better for him than sex. Then he batted my head again and waited. And so on. When I gave in and my face came undone and melted in a puddle of ice cream in the bottom of the bowl, he quit.

I took money from his wallet on a routine basis, dime by dime, dollar by dollar, partly to afford the perms for my hair that he liked bragging about but was too cheap to pay for and partly I didn't know why. I'd be in the bedroom, robbing him, going, "Yeah, great, baby," or "Way to go, hon," him talking from the living-room over the sound of the TV about his work day, some success maybe he had fixing something, and my fingers would be busy as fiends, nipping quarters, fivers if he was loaded, you name it. My stash was in the quilted bag I kept my nylons in and occasionally he'd come in just as I was managing to ease the drawer closed and he'd need me to find something for him or iron something; or if he'd been drinking and was in a lovey mood, he'd smooch the back of my neck and push me down on the bed and do his thing. Later I understood the taking made up for the way I'd turned out being, the longer I was Buddy's wife.

Mangos have a hide-like feel in the palm of your hand and they're heavy, too, heavier than you expect from just looking. They're pretty, yellow and green and red, but their shapes are ugly, like something an exotic dead bird might lay or what a bald lion would spit up: a fur ball without the fur. The point about a mango is, it makes a mess all over the cutting-board, this I learned, a runny orange mess that doesn't make you sick to look at: it isn't baby shit or barf. It's perfumed and sweet. The toughness turns out to be inside, in the texture of the pulpy, juicy part, that rips when you try to tear it from its seed.

Living at George's house, I slobbered over mangos and sometimes went so far as to lick the board. I read in a cookbook his wife left behind (he told me she disappeared one night with his two little girls) about how you can get hoity-toity with a mango. Make neat slices one way, then across the other, like the criss-cross lines on tic-tac-toe. The idea is to cut tidy squares that are supposed to make the mango neater to eat, but no matter how careful I was in working the knife, my mangos came out looking stabbed. They oozed most of their juices before the cuts were finished and I ended up digging in, face first, strings in my teeth and wet, fragrant slop dripping off my chin.

Learning about mangos was a major entertainment while I

was trapped at George's. His house was a fancy split-level in a new tract in the 'burbs. There was one snooty breeder across the street with a slew of brats, but otherwise the houses were unoccupied and unfinished. Donny was gone. George took care of him early on, put him on the bus to the coast for the whole summer, to his cousin who runs a deep-sea fishing rig. I thought it would do the kid good, getting away.

George didn't let me drive — he liked to drive his little sweetie himself — and so on Saturdays when we went to the supermarket I used to load up. (There was only so much TV a girl could watch, even if it was big-screen with remote control.) He let me buy anything I wanted, stuff I never could afford before, including shrimp and avocados and cheeses whose name you couldn't pronounce.

In the beginning, George was patient and sweet-tempered. Opened doors, helped me into the car, paid my way like a real gentleman. Once he went along to the police station to pick up Donny (simple loitering, big deal, you'd think they'd have other fish to fry) and the cops treated me different, a man of George's caliber in tow. George said what he wanted in life was a family to love and to love him back and he wanted me to move in, Donny too.

I couldn't believe my luck. I wrote Sherryle about this sweet goof who was in love with me. (It's hard to imagine it now, being so blind as to think what George had going with me was love. He didn't know me, nobody knew me, myself included. I never acted any other way than what a guy expected, and if George wanted hoops different from what Buddy wanted, what the hey, I could jump through them, too.)

About ten weeks into this set-up, George is in the driveway, pissed off and hosing down the Astrovan. The van is packed with camping gear — sleeping bags, a camp stove, lanterns — things I could care less about, not being the outdoorsy type. George has got it into his head that for his holiday, the two of us are going to hit the open road. He's wearing his new, rugged, heavy-duty, green khakis and a plaid shirt, the exact same that he bought for me that I am supposed to be putting on but am not. Still in my nightie, I am spying on him through the narrow window above the breakfast nook.

He puts down the hose and rubs the chamois on the van so hard the whole thing shakes. His being mad makes me queasy. I don't know what's happened to me. Until making a scene last night, I was working so hard to be his perfect little dollbaby. I'd shaved all over and was calling him daddy in bed like he wanted and I was putting up with his constant, rabbity sex, not being much into sex myself, and I was putting up with him treating me like his little girl. And all the while, not realizing it, I had moved into the second layer of being a victim, the mental layer where you go against your own instincts, your own mind. But you can only go so far, and sometimes a dumb thing can be your Waterloo and for me, camping was it.

Last night after supper I said I wasn't going, I wasn't the camping type. I said, "You arranged it all behind my back. You never once asked me."

He gave a mean chortle. "Who says I got to ask you? You do what I say and like it." Then he punched my shoulder, just a little bump, but I got the message. George'd never laid a finger on me and I was grateful. That by itself had been a holiday.

Now, when he stomps into the kitchen after ship-shaping the van, he finds me still in the breakfast nook, sitting there and smearing the sweat from a glass.

"I guess I got to spill the beans, you're so dumb. You ain't wised up yet," he says, washing his hands at the sink.

"You never asked me," I repeat, my best line from last night.

He reaches for a paper towel. "That isn't what I mean, sweetie. You have not clued in yet to your *condition*." He begins to chuckle in that wheezy way he has.

I ask "What?" despite myself and he delivers the insults he's into lately — that I dye my hair like a slut, that I'm a boozer — which I mostly ignore. He says, "I told you I wanted a family, didn't I? A man's got a right to a family. You think I don't get nothing out of this deal? Hell no. I want me a little girlie baby like the ones I used to have. And I knew you was perfect, with your sweet nature. I love you, dollbaby."

Pennies start dropping by the carloads. Stomach swirling, I move to slide out of the booth, but he clamps my wrist. "You don't understand the least little thing about love, do you, sweetie? After all I done for you."

I struggle to free myself.

"Pardon? You say something?" When I don't answer, he says in a high-pitched voice, "Pretty please, daddy, pretty please with peanut-butter on it?"

I whine, "You're hurting me, George. I have to go puke."

He gives his laugh and twists my arm harder. "Yeah, sweetie! Puking! How much you want me to let you go? Huh? Huh? How much you want to get to the can and check that diaphragm, huh? How much?" He takes to humming the tune 'Summertime,' his favourite. "I can wait," he says.

My fingers are turning purple. Seeing them there on the end of my squeezed wrist makes me snivel, I am in such a panic that he's right about my condition. My head has been stuck in the sand. "Come on, daddy, please. Pretty please with peanut-butter on it."

Next thing I'm in the can, door locked, running hot and cold water over my hand until it prickles back to life. Then I swallow a couple of 292s before opening the vanity and holding the diaphragm to the overhead light. It's pinpricked, all right, and I'm screwed, royally. I barf, not bothering to lift the seat.

George taps on the door. "Should I make some coffee for my little dollbaby? Should I? Well, I will. I would be happy to, you're welcome. You get yourself cleaned up, now, get dressed in those new clothes daddy got you and then you just march right on out there and get your goddamn butt in the car."

One morning in a Pancake House what I did was, I excused myself to go to the can. Halfway there, through an open kitchen door I caught sight of some faded grass in the watery glare of morning sunlight. I stared. Next I found myself making a quick tour of the kitchen, swiping a paring knife and dropping it into the pocket of my windbreaker — I wasn't Donny's mother for nothing — and then impulsively I dove out the door. I didn't have a clue what my intentions were.

Nobody said anything, nobody followed. I had finally become invisible, to everybody as well as myself. Maybe it was in my mind that I was running away, but I got only as far as a nearby alley. Just getting that far was like moving underwater with weights strapped to my ankles; I was worn down, gasping and puffing for air. I didn't even bother hiding behind the trash cans, I just slid down the side of a building and waited for him to find me. It seemed like fate he would.

Sherryle always said, Act like a kicked dog soon enough and the chances are better of not having your bones broke. I thought about that, how I was always acting out my life in a defensive manner. I thought about Donny on the coast, on a fishing boat, learning things. Feeling wind and waves and watching red sunsets, his arms growing strong from doing what he was told. Maybe seeing whales passing by.

I gave George a smile. I knew he wouldn't kill me pregnant, but I also knew he would hit me, he would get around to it, he would have to for the sake of his pride. Knowing what he didn't made me feel powerful. He said something and I didn't answer and his face grew redder. He was working up the nerve to change himself into a wife beater from a child diddler.

For I suspected he was, I had suspected it in secret all along, and I began right then thinking about what if it was a baby girl I was carrying, what about her, as I stepped toward him and from habit turn sideways to brace myself, in this case to keep my head from hitting bricks. Then I changed my mind and jerked my hand out of my pocket instead.

Talk about surprise. "Nadine," he said. My name.

(GIRLS' OWN)
HORSE STORIES

Elise Levine

THE MOST EMBARRASSING MOMENT in her life.

At the track. Exercising a wired two-year-old with legs-for-days in front of the horse's investors. Just past the quarter mile she realizes her sanitary napkin has bust loose and is booting it backward between her legs with each pounding beat. She's coming in to the home stretch now in front of the big shots and she's praying Dear lord in heaven don't let me don't let me lose it.

I'm going back to tampons, she announces to Louise during dinner that night. Let toxic shock take me.

Louise almost dies laughing. Almost.

❖

Black Beauty. Ginger. Coco. Buckskin. Midnight. Hoot-Owl. Palomino-Pal-O-Mine. Stalwarts bedding down for the night, having crossed the crooked stream, the mountain path by day. Benjy. Liebling-My-Love. Hey Dude.

Ariel, Sergeant, Big Bay: ten cents a ride at the Dominion

store. She's tall in the saddle, the plastic mount cantering back and forth, back and forth.

This is the finest moment of my life, she thinks, age ten, riding home in Mrs. Taylor's Mustang, clutching an orange Honeydew and a hotdog from the grocery store snackbar.

National Velvet. My Friend Flicka.

That girl's horse-crazy.

Mrs. Taylor is too old to knock before she enters through the kitchen door. The old woman snorts and tosses her frizzy dyed hair. Mrs. Taylor's got pep.

She'll grow out of it, her mom says hopefully.

Mrs. Taylor smells of powder and nail polish.

Mrs. Taylor's hair, fine as a feathered fetlock.

Chestnut.

Hanoverians. Trakehners. She has a crush on Christilot Boylen who wins the Bronze for dressage in the '76 Olympics. Oh beautiful, the commentator gushes. Look at that control!

She imagines cleaning tack together: lathering martingales, polishing spurs and stirrups. They take to the ring. Oh exquisite *passage!* Their habits chaste, alluring. Layers float then fall like apple blossoms. Lips meet once. Then it's round and round the ring again, flying lead changes everywhere. It's like slow-mo on CTV Sports. It's like love.

By the end of their first week as roommates in the apartment above the tack shed, she and Louise get along fine.

They watch John Wilsey turn out Bare Breeze — worth a lot of bananas, sperm $15,000 a pop — in Northwind's west pasture. John Wilsey has the metal chain of the lead shank across the stallion's upper gums for control. Looks like Mr. Ed's grumpy today. The horse shies at a puddle on the driveway: for two mil you get shit for brains. John Wilsey better rip his lips, she sure would, though only guys look after the studs. Bare Breeze side-slithers two steps then bunny-hops the remaining four yards to the pasture gate, bouncing John Wilsey up and down in the mud like a ball.

She and Louise muck out the yearlings.

She raises the pitchfork. Stops and looks up: two down, twenty-eight baby Mr. Eds to go. Louise pushes the wheelbarrow over. Louise is strong for her size. Twenty-seven, twenty-six stalls left. A horse is a horse — she walks across the aisle to Louise — of course, of course. Louise laughs. She knocks a wisp of straw from Louise's hair. Mr. Ed x 30 nickers softly. Louise puts the wheelbarrow down.

She believes this to be the strangest moment of her life.

The rape of brood mares. Three men holding the dam, two others assisting the stud, poor dumb fuck cock eighteen inches long four inches thick. He's so excited the whites of his eyes are tapioca and the men have to help him find the right hole. Yeah, they say. And more. She probably would too. She slams the apple juice into the grocery cart. Oh fucking right Louise. You're always fucking right. Her Firebird a junk-bucket but it goes, stereo cranked and sparkling. She knows how it's done.

Lying in bed late at night, *Flipper* re-runs on TV. Drunk enough (just enough), she imagines she's on that track again, a big dumb two-year-old beneath her. She's riding short, and it's like the first time because she's scared, bum barely grazing leather every fourth beat. She can feel the napkin bunching up, it must be halfway out of her jeans by now but she doesn't care, let the sucker fly. Black Beauty, Ginger, Coco. Benjy!

Cooling down, she drops the sweaty reins over the slackened neck. Leans back, pats the steaming flanks. When she was a teenager she shared part-board at a stable on a friend's quarter horse. She remembers another boarder at the same stable, Ann Richmond, how her horse went colicky one spring and died, Ann at age fifty-one walking that horse for days and nights to turn the twisted gut right-side-up again.

"They call him Flipper, Flipper, faster than lightning." She and Louise used to know the words off by heart. "No-one you see, is smarter than he."

The Jack Russell outside yips in his sleep.

"And we know Flipper, lives in a world full of wonder, lying there under ... ."

What kind of moment is this? she wonders, knowing it's mostly what she is now: alone, coarsened by time and love, regret brushing her face like a mane in the darkened paddock of night.

JESUS AND THE TOUCAN

Susan Perly

THE TOUCAN IS A FRIEND of Jesus. He comes often to see him in prison. He comes often to visit with him in his cell. They'll sit on the cot and smoke a cigar or three, they'll share some dreams, they'll get into some of the old stories. Which is what is happening right now — the toucan is listening to Jesus tell a story. This one is the cuento of the day the sky rains birds wearing pictures. Jesus tells the story:

The gringos were busy painting the picture of the Saviour, el Salvador, on blue paper. They wanted to bring the news of His return to a tribe of small creatures who lived in the jungle. They painted the message in the picture language of the tribe. But the gringos painted Jesus in their own image. A pale white body with a dot of red rouge on each cheek, a little turned-up nose, thin red cupid lips, orange hair, eyes of blue.

"I mean, give me a break," says Jesus to the toucan. "Do I look anything like *that*?" He puffs on his puro — it's a Romeo y Julieta, the kind he saves for special visits — and the cigar smoke drifts around his face. Jesus has a broad nose and thick lips. He has a skin of red lake. He has snakes of amber resin wrapped around his wrists; he has dainty turquoise beads encircling his ankles. He has a tiny jade spirit hanging from his silver necklace. He has wide black eyes. "But they give me these baby blues," continues Jesus to the toucan, "and then they paint me sitting in a chopper like Rambo or something, aviator specs on, green fatigues if you can believe it, the blessed cross still stuck to my back and I'm flying this helicóptero-looking *thing*, which — let's face it, these guys are not exactly Van Gogh — looks more like a turnip than a chopper."

The toucan is dreaming the passion. He is catching the sun. Jesus goes on:

> The message: *Convert to Christ / Your Ticket to Heaven* is coloured in pictures on blue sheets which are first flat, then folded into birds, then taken in bundles on board helicópteros.
>
> The helicópteros arrive at the most sacred region of Above, which lies over the jungle. They drop the bundles. The sky rains birds. Down to the earth region of Below flutter hundreds of pale crucified tickets to heaven.
>
> The helicópteros have loudspeakers. They shrill: *The Prince of Peace*! They shrill: *The End of War Is in His Hands*! Shrill their syllables like cicadas through the forest near-night, giant electric cicadas setting on edge the teeth of the small creatures under the canopy, quietly painting their stories.

The toucan keeps on dozing. The thing is, you see, is that he is just incredibly jet-lagged. He got in very late last night from a travel in which he had to go all the way to the river on the Other Side and back. His sparkling feathers look like hell. The rubies are all scratched up, not to mention the sapphires which have flaked off into almost sky. His head drops into dreams. His beak hits his chest. An emerald rivulet trickles out of him and rolls down over his amber belly.

"Go ahead and snore, it makes no never mind to me," says Jesus to the snoring toucan. "As long as you're getting into the story."

You see, the toucan is able to hear the story even as he puts himself into dreams, even as he snores away in a cloud of cigar smoke, because the toucan is a shaman. And not just any ordinary kind of shaman, either. The toucan is a psychopomp — a guide and a bodyguard for the souls of the dead — and as he goes on travels carrying away the dead ones' souls he listens to the stories Jesus tells him. The toucan is dreaming of palms at the beach. This is what he hears through his snores:

He whom they call *Jesus, Eternal King* is shown as a gringo soldier on the cross piloting a turnip. This is the picture on the birds' stomachs. On their backs the birds say: *Do Not Worship The Sun.* When the small creatures unfold the blue birds, looking at the warning in their own picture language taught by someone to the gringos, they laugh. It is an orange laughing which they laugh, pulsing orange through the green trees, a very giggly orange.

The helicópteros hover in Above. The Sun yawns. The Forest tickles her awake from behind. He whispers in her ear about the message on the birds not to worship her, and the Sun and the Forest get silly and they giggle and they giggle and the choppergringos go, *What the ... ?* and the Sun as she rises on her lover giggles with him with their smells inside each other, and they giggle That's A Good One till they doze.

Snoring deeply on the sand is the toucan in his travel.

Says Jesus, "You see, it's not just birdies they are dropping. That was the first part; that set the stage. That was the diversion. Now comes the good part, now comes the real part. We are talking bombing, we are talking bombs. It was not me who was coming, good old Jesucristo. I was busy having coffee and a puro in the jungle with the creatures, we were playing cards. I was not coming with the flapflap and the flapping; I was with the others, looking up." The toucan's head jerks back. His eyelids are closed. Jesus continues:

> The small creatures look up.
> Drops a bomb.
> (!boomh!) (!boomh!) sounds first. The echo.
> !BOOMH! !BOOMH! sounds then. The place is
> already on fire.

"Then," says Jesus, "then I see it in replay. Right before the fire: the bomb in slow: the bomb falls in slow: and in slow I see it graze a palm leaf falling and it falls in slow down through the yellow jungle steam and big wide bounces it up from a leaf and slow down it falls from the bounce and falls it down to the creatures who look up with mouths so opening I see wide in the slow !BOOMH! shreds their faces.

"I rewind to before the bomb falls in slow through the trees. I see the trees. I see the green trees and the small creatures under the green trees, painting their stories. !BOOMH! — giant trees on fire topple, old ones are fleeing, children are riding high on their shoulders."

The toucan is visiting diamonds. His snore snorts are purrs now. Jesus stories on:

> Children in flames. The crackle of the wood of the jungle. The milk leaks out of the rubber trees. Another bomb whistles down — ! — the dwelling place a place of black smoke. The small creatures die with their hollow sockets throbbing, *Eloi, Eloi, lama sabachthani?* in the vision of them and the lament of all ones who die feeling forsaken. The children die burnt in their arms.
>
> This is a story of those who are gone. This is a story of those who are no longer with us. This is a

story of a tribe which is a memory. This is the story of the day the sky rained birds wearing pictures.

The pictures said, *Smile, Jesus Loves You.*

"With one of those little happy-face smile-button smiles, I'm not kidding," Jesus says to the toucan, who is off collecting bags. "I mean, my lungs are so full of smoke the old asthma gets going and I can't breathe for wheezing out chirp-chirp, I'm sweating who knows what poison crud from the bombs like a dog, then an arm comes through the air, whizzing at me about a hundred miles an hour, I say to myself, 'Wait a minute, I *know* that arm, it belongs to the old ... ,' then she's at my feet, the old grandmother (one of the best professional mourners around, by the way), on fire like the blazes, then the flames on her dress catch onto my cross and we're both pretty much burning alive, and then — wouldn't you know it? — the stitches on my hide pick that very moment to split wide open and blood is dripping all over the poor little mourner of a grandmother and — hallelujah! — down from the sky, here it comes: *Smile, Jesus Loves You.* I mean, give me a *break*!"

The toucan makes a nothing yawn. He itches his eyes. He rubs rainbows into them. On fire, meanwhile, is Jesus in the story along with the rest of the gang:

> And wind pumping is what the sound of the fire burning whoosh-sounds sounds like, as rolling and falling and rolling and bumping into each other come rolling down the mountain the rocks which have been dislodged by the bombing and onto the jungle burning roll the rocks of the avalanche crushing the already charred bodies under their rolling which stops.

> The Forest wails and the children of the small creature tribe, the smallest of the small ones, they wail on their knees, begging for life from the Sun. The Sun tries to bring a soothing to her creatures as she watches

her lover the Forest burning to thin sticks from his greenness. Skeletons of trees have no shelter to give skeletons of small creatures.

The evil Jaguar dips his ladle into the purple volcano. He lifts up bubbling green lava, and pours it down over everything in Below gone to dead, and every other thing left living.

It is all buried there under the green molten blanket. The Sun bakes the bubbling blanket to hard lava rock. The rainy seasons beat the rock with torrents of rain. The Sun bakes it until it cracks, the earth quakes it until the cracks are wide and jagged. The wind off the ocean whips at it in a frenzy. It peels to rawness.

Tremors from Below vibrate the air of Above. Through the same trajectory of sky where a giant tree of the jungle once toppled flaming, a skyscraper falls. The concrete giant collapses on workers praying under their desks. Rocks bump and tumble down the mountainside. The Jaguar lifts up his ladle. Over the rubble of the rascacielo he pours green molten lava.

Under the layers and layers of lava blankets, many secrets are hidden: secrets told inside the stories of dead ones, pressed to their fossils in old carbon, marooned at the bottom of older oceans, buried deep inside the ancient legends, and now they are gone to us.

It is a flat dry place along which flows the rut of the river of the valley. Once, in this place, a tribe of small creatures lived under great green trees, painting their stories.

"Yup, the good old days in the jungle," says Jesus, sitting on the cot with the toucan. "Paradise, right? You and me and Rousseau and the boys, getting ready to show our work in Paris. 'Primitif,' they say. 'These paintings, how *wonderfully* primitif. How very much in the tradition of the naïf.' I'll give them na-*eef*: three and a half tons of volcano smack on top of your schnoz, how's that for naïf? The smell of your own skin seared like a pig on a spit, that's about as primitivo as it gets, boys and girls."

The mere thought of it makes the toucan itchy, and he scratches his skin with his beak. He scratches and scratches and itches and scratches until his feathers bleed. He flies up to the wall of the prison cell and rubs himself up and down against it like sandpaper with wings. In the cell next door waits the soul he will escort next, a young man whose eyes were put out and whose genitals were electroshocked and whose skull was crushed with a beisbol bat. The toucan rubs himself all around, making ruby smears and amethyst jags. He twists a curvy itch down the wall, making an ultramarine meander. He is incredibly worn. He rests the side of his head against the wall, his eyelids closed. His wings open up. A small stick appears under his left wing. The toucan picks it up with his beak. He flies to the top of Jesus' head. He swings the stick hard against the air. Dropping it, he flies to a corner of the cot, to a second, and a third and back in a swoop to the head of Jesus, safely home.

The young man was playing beisbol when the strangers came for him. Top of the ninth they arrived. They watched him from under the palms near third. His eyes were to the sky. The high fly ball he felt already in his glove. He ran backwards into the ocean, he fell back on his back, soaked wet and salty. He caught the ball, rolling over and over in the waves. Bottom of the ninth. The strangers come forward from under the palms. They take him away.

They remove him from his village. There, the people tell the story of the days when there was a tribe of small creatures who lived by a cool blue river on the Other Side, many many times ago. They tell the story of the beginning of things, the way the tribe painted it. Says the story, "'This is our First

Page,' said the small ones under the trees, and they showed each other their stories."

And this is the first page, the beginning of things, the way the small ones painted it:

From the void shines out the shape of the first diamond.

Rubs itself into appearance the first plate.

Silence sits upon the face of the void. In the silence many plates rub.

Then the passion fills the void. The cry of the passion is "Play ball!"

All take their positions. Jesus takes the outfield.

Crack of the first skin on the first wood is heard.

Comes it to bases loaded, two out, three and two.

The first rains begin to glisten the diamond.

Comes the first delay.

Appears the first rainbow.

The starting lineup climbs up on the rainbow to look down at the diamond which has no colour except transparence, only the ripple of the mirror on the toucan's foot.

Soon the entire home team is up on the curve. It cannot hold them all. It breaks. It falls down in bits and pieces on the great mirror below. The team sits in glorious nothing.

The toucan takes off and flies the mirror around and around like a wild thing and the prisms of the rainbow multiply out along the mirror. These are the first flowers. These are the very first colours seen upon the void.

The toucan meanwhile is off flying, spinning the mirror so the flowers go falling to all curves of the void. Orchids and lilies and sunflowers float. They are so beautiful the toucan rubs his eyes in disbelief. His eyes drop tears. The tears drop down hot upon the mirror. They flood over the mirror, which becomes the hot aqua ocean we know, and the colours dive down deep inside the ocean and they are the first fish.

The players are dipping their heads down with the fish. "Play ball!" squawks the ump macaw from the diamond. The players hear the call down there in slow aquamarine. Up they come in air. They swim to ocean shore. They crawl with legs on rock. They walk with two legs, upright. They take their place with lungs. Jesus takes right field.

Crack of wood against skin is heard once more again. The ball is hot when it hits the glove of Jesus. He holds on to it tight as it burns his hand. It hops out. It is above, on the curve, burning. It burns hot and orange. It is the Sun.

"You see," goes the story told in the village beside the ocean, "this is how the Sun came to us for the first time. This is shown on the first page of the book of stories painted by the tribe of small creatures from the jungle."

So spoke the beisbolero to his little baby daughter; so had his grandmother spoken it to him — the legends. But the thing is, you see, is that these legends, these stories told in paintings, are prohibida. In other words, it is forbidden to pass on the small-creature version of what happened. It is banned. The beginning of things, the end of things — uh-uh, outlawed. The prophecy of the death of their own race by strangers who will speak in sounds which will hurt the ear, and who will end the dwelling place by fire dropped from flying things — disallowed, careful. The Sun and how she first arrived — a verboten no-no.

That is why the strangers wait under the palms near third base, watching the beisbolero catch the fly. He is a master storyteller. He tells leyendas prohibidas. So when bottom of the ninth he hits a grand slam homer way out past the outfield out to somewhere there where the blue waves meet up with the blue curve, the strangers catch him running home and take him away. They throw him in prison.

They throw his wife in prison. They throw his baby daughter and his grandmother holding the baby to her in prison. And that is what brings me here — to airlift out the souls of their dead and tortured bodies. With the able assistance of Romeo y Julieta, my all-time favourite cigar, my pure clear eagle for entering into the travels.

I take the souls to a place beside a cool blue river, a place where big green trees grow overtop in a canopy and pale pink orchids grow in all profusion hidden and scarlet macaws mate by a salt lagoon. There sits the purple volcano. There on its rim sleeps the black heart of Jaguar. There, I record the end of things in my paintings. There, I am the chronicler of the conquest.

There, I revisit the places of extinction. I trip running, I smell my flesh burn, I carry the children, I am crushed by a boulder. Electroshock courses my body; I try to rub it away, rubbing my feathers raw against a tree. My sapphires go to bruises. My feathers rub away. My rubies start to open. My wings go arms outspread. My feet go legs with toes. My nose is broad and my beak is lips. My eyes are black and white. I wear a little toucan in jade around my neck. Me, Jesucristo, my hands held by amber nails, my legs held by amber too. I am skin upon wood. I am bleeding from my wounds. I relive the small ones. Memory is a mercy. I am in the mercy itch. I smear my liquid body. The smears are pictures. Look: there is the ancient river, the old old blue. There is the umbrella plant. There we are under it, cigars in our mouths, dealing the cards. There we are, back to work, mixing up green. There we are, looking up. There are the turnips dropping the birds. There we are unfolding the blue birds. And there is the orange, and the giggles, at this Me, the Prince of Peace in green fatigues, the Smile He Loves You Saviour, with my cupid lips and my orange hair and my cute little baby blues. There are the gringo screeches. There is the smoke making us sick in the yellow. There is the biggest green tree beside its own grey skeleton. There we are, a pile of ashes, with freebie glory ashes, all the same.

Each picture a story; each story painted on wood, the wood of my cross. The paintings which flow from my suffering are the echoes of the acts of them, the small creatures painting their pain in the jungle. When they painted it, I was with them and we soothed each other, and they hurt, reenacting with me my own death.

On the prison wall here, it is all on the cross, one large painting, which in our picture language feels something like, using the language of words, one single word which might sound like this: *the-picture-of-a-suffering-which-shows-at-the-same-time-all-the-sufferings-of-all-the-creatures-in-what-happened*. This is the outlawed image containing all the banned, painted stories.

So remember folks, you never heard a word.

Anyway, gotta run. Jet lag time again in the jungle.

The old skin of red lake grows back white feathers. The painting rewinds from the cross to my body. Presto! Story? What story? A mystery murder? Nah. My feathers are but innocent jewels: ambers and rubies, sapphires and emeralds. My head is emerald's sister, all aquamarine. My eyes are diamond glitters in old socket light. My tail is a dip in the purest melted gold. I fly to the cell two doors down. I cradle the soul of the dead beisbolero's wife. I carry her to the river on the Other Side. Me, the wonder of worlds. And I take her to the river of soothing, water of grace in the valley. And I lay her down. And she goes out to meet him. Going out to her husband, way out past the curve, on the long blue meander of us all.

HAIR

Pauline Peters

THIS STORY IS TOLD on a round head that is growing a forest of hair that has to be washed, oiled, combed, braided, unbraided and combed again. It grows dark, shiny, curled and close, so close you cannot always find the scalp. This hair requires work. It is thick hair, solid hair, beautiful hair, different from any other hair. It is the uncompromising and demanding hair that grows untamed on the beautiful island that is your head. It is a strange and powerful plant made of tightly curled fibres strong and firm when woven together but ever so delicate when left alone a single strand because the journey is long everywhere a turn at every junction a twist a corner a stopover — London, Jamaica, Germany, Brazil — this hair has travelled everywhere and may be fragile as a single strand but powerful when braided together into one long rope of never-ending hemp ...

I am the Storyteller. I have come very far with fragments of memory clenched in my fists, some unrecognizable, some sweet, some so bitter they will not say their names. I have taken all these memories and spread them out across the floor in no particular order, selecting those that contain the most concentrated oils to soothe my scalp in times of need when there is no-one to part, no-one to comb, no-one to untangle the knots from my head. I have stored my combs, my afro picks, my hot combs and chemical relaxers. I have stored my olive oil, my pomade, my natural moisturizers and my petroleum jelly. I have stored my Saturday afternoon visits to the barber and the feel of fine brush bristles running hard over my scalp. I have washed my implements, my tools and my hands and now I am ready to tell the story.

My parents were born in a place called Jamaica: Xamayca, land of fountains, where things grow overnight, where colour is a force to be reckoned with, where soil is so rich as to be edible, where the sun hangs so low you can touch it. Xamayca is in the centre of the world and the people there eat what the soil gives them so they look like her, rich black and fulsome. Their tongues are made of laughing water so that when they open their mouths they do not speak, they sing. Jamaica is a hot place where things unravel and where it is possible to have someone slit open your belly and pull out the intestines just to see how far they will go. But then, this could happen anywhere. For example, in Canada — the only difference being that you can stand for a long time in bloodless conversation with someone before you realize their hands are full of your guts.

I am the Storyteller. I know about ghosts because my father became one in a way I do not like to remember, wide-eyed and unbelieving death would come in the blaze and cut of fire and metal. He was a handsome man but this was no excuse or even reason for the metal edge to my mother's voice or the texture of her voice ground raw with shame. It was not the lies that sent reason running but the day my mother sought her own mother, long-dead, in the closets and beneath the cushions of the couch. I did not know her voice. I did not know her smell. The voices on the end of the line spoke only in curses and the house smelled of sulphur. And through all this you drifted smiling sometimes shaking off a woman like a crab stuck to the end of your finger. No. Beauty was no excuse, but I will give you a reason perhaps this: a strand of iron braided through a whip that bore your name, or perhaps a mother too gentle and a father too rough, or perhaps it was the promise that power could be stepped into like a pair of shoes readymade. But a heart is not a rock daddy to be burnished with sandpaper. A heart is not intended for experimental art. And although I wish that you had died better I can no longer line my throat with excuses for you are a ghost and I am not your mother I am today no-one's mother but my own. Three times I have seen you enough to know that your eyes are big and yellow and I tell you not to grieve but to take account. Go back. Go back and learn what the old ones can teach you. I have now at my disposal miles of rock and plenty of water and do you know how long it takes to turn rock to soil? I say it can be done in a lifetime with the careful sifting of dirt and water in a shallow pan and I am fully expecting to find a glimmer of gold.

I have seen women sifting with hands soft and quick so that all my life I have wanted to have a woman's hands. They say that if you are looking for a miracle, find a woman and gently hold her hands. Now it is true that my mother, on days when her blood was transfused with fire, when the ends of her nerves cried out individually each with a separate voice and a new name for pain, it is true that on those days she may have said many times and in a treble voice that her husband my father would receive the end that he deserved. But even she who with only her eyes could tighten a rope around my neck, even she who was so driven as to stay up all night beating the white back into her uniforms, even she who could so well lay out a string of curses that if reversed would have helped the blind to see, even she could not have expected her husband my father to return home in a closed coffin burnt to ash and bone.

I am Storyteller. I once had two grandmothers, one black and the other gold. In the photo my gold grandmother wears a pink and green dress. She is soft with cheeks like pillows and hair smooth as the fibre of milkweed. I remember now her voice tumbling into the neckline of her dress and her hands holding the pillowcases embroidered, one for me, one for my sister. We stand, me with one hand on her shoulder, proud of her, my new acquisition, a soft pink, pink, yellow, gold and green grandmother.

My Grandmother Gladys stands alone in her photo. She is blue-black and seems to me not just a woman but a force of nature who commands machete, cooking spoon, whip, calabash, hammer, knife, shovel and pot. I am told she was a market woman and that she raised eleven children and two husbands. In my memory she is leading the way through the bush at night and to my eyes then seven feet tall, leading the way through the black night no stars saying to my father in a voice like a millstone grinding, "Sam, do you believe in duppies?"

My people speak sometimes in a sign language that we do not remember. I have seen my aunt, steeped in religion and righteousness hold out her hands and make the sign of the dead. It was Thanksgiving dinner and for a moment the shouting stopped as she held out her hands and turned them over, one palm up and one palm down. This is the sign for death, for passing over, and for a moment the silence was taut as each spirit acknowledged the sign and then picked up a fork to resume the clatter as though nothing had happened.

History is a long rope and I keep pulling. Witches with screaming hair who can only breathe water. I keep pulling. "There is no-one else alive on the end of this rope." This from the latest witch with fraying eyes and clothing from the wrong era. You cannot believe what she says. I keep pulling.

I loved my mother once with a fierceness I am ashamed to admit. It was a love that shook the walls of our house and broke out into seeping wounds of hatred, tumbled into fist fights and taught me to bare my teeth and chew religiously on my own tongue. Hatred black and searing as burning tar has tunnelled through my bones. And I refused to be born. Kicking and tearing at the damp walls, kicking with calloused heels at aging bones, I refused to be born. (And when I dreamed of food you came bringing. And when I dreamed of shoes you brought those too.) It is a shame to carry for so long a child who will not be born. It is a shame to carry a raging demon inside so small a body. I have consented now to be born, my teeth filled with abscesses, my body sewn together with large uneven stitches. I have consented now to dispel my rage into the sky, into the story, into the earth. And I consent now to the presence of hands attempting to soothe the demons inside my heart. May these hands emerge unbitten.

I am the Storyteller. If you walk through my head at night you will sometimes find people who do not sleep even for a moment. They are old. Sometimes you will find them sitting in the dark leaning against the trunks of trees and talking to the sky. There was one night a woman came and sat down speaking low sometimes dropping words and letting them lie. She said "and blackness wraps you sometimes with the soft weight of tired voices, constant assurance that the voices will never stop seeps through your fingers so that hair, heart and hand make the sign. Say forever blackness is the berries and blue as in the serious navy blue of my sister whose features are so fine and regular you can measure nose to eye and come up with an even number. And I have seen it the balls of your feet hard and yellow dipping you into a curve that wasn't there before and in the lines of your palm talking about the flight yesterday, testifying to how many minds souls and sorrows rolled into one for you to treasure or dismiss. They say the Lord never gives you more than you can carry. I say the Lord needs help too. They say, "come, carry, it can hold you, let us take you further into this one square inch of blackness weighing more than the whole universe." I say, "who are you?" They say, "Now take the light and throw it back." Sometimes I think the only way is to remember that we are the blackness and then some.

My people are made of darkness and I like it. I like the smell of it and the feel of it between my fingers. I like the way it sighs and the way it holds a secret. I like the way darkness gives birth to colour, nursing and blending, giving judiciously a share to every eye. I have learned how to hold darkness on my tongue, letting it dissolve into tiny grains and to listen for the sound of hands shaping darkness into light. I have learned to weigh in both hands the swell and the promise and I am learning to wait.

I am the Storyteller. I asked for names and was given these: Tata, Henny, Austin, Elcanaan, Vincent and Miss P. Papa French, Mum-mum, Theophilus, Grandmother Gladys, Estry, Archilles and Lillian. Priscilla, Lydia, Olive, Ezekiel, Sonny B, Clarissa and Hermine. Tatty, Coolie, Winnie, Gladstone, Joyce and Miss U. Grandmother Irene. Papa David. And the rest? The rest are in fields of white stone under black earth warmed by green winds. The rest are seeking water under burning sun soothing bent backs with knotted hands. The rest are in a fast long sleep, bones curled on bones, bones piled on bones, bones crossed on bones. The rest are taking bones and sorting bones and pouring new spirit into old bones. The rest are waiting, they've been a long time waiting, they are still there waiting for somebody to remember their names.

I am the Storyteller. I learned how to braid when I was very young. It wasn't easy. You had to learn how to make the braids lie flat, how to knot your fingers in one smooth knitting motion, how to make tight braids that would stay put even when you slept on them. And I learned how then when I was very young and my mother braided my hair into tight plaits while I sat on the floor trying to hold my head still and intuit by her touch which way to turn, I learned then how to carefully store this memory of being sorted out, put to rights and set in order by strong hands and with rare attention.

The thing about this hair is not only that every single strand of it twists in a way that is different from all the others or that it can be braided, twisted, sculpted and shaved into patterns, rows, towers, tunnels, ropes and maps, it is not only that. It is that someone, someone with strong fine hands when you are very young must take the time to show you how to make the rows, the tunnels, the patterns, the towers, show you how to tend, how to care, how to oil and how to braid. Show you to find your way by the map on your head ...

... this hair makes a deep road. This hair makes a kinky road. This hair makes a silver, blue-black and winding road. This hair will identify and horrify. This hair is not easily swayed by wind. This hair can stand up, shout out, curse and justify. This hair remembers.

WEDDING IN SASKATOON

Elisabeth Harvor

October 10, 1959

IN ONE WAY Saskatoon is exactly like Düsseldorf: once again Norman and Maria have been assigned to bunk beds. But now that they're back in Canada again their room is one of the rooms in the back wing of Maria's parents' house, and although it's equipped with only four bunks, the remaining two beds are occupied by two of the visitors who flew into town earlier this week to attend the big wedding.

Their two roommates are Ruth and Frances. Norman calls them his harem. Maria thinks he gets a kick out of watching his three women get up in the mornings — the way they all try to pretend they aren't modest, the way they all yawn and haul on their dressing-gowns in ostentatious slow motion but then go into high gear to tie themselves up harshly with cords tied tight as a six-year-old's shoelace. Not that any of them will ever see six again, or have anything much to do with six-year-olds. In fact both Ruth and Frances are women in their late forties, both good sports (which is how they came to end up being billeted with a married couple), both bangle-wearers, both women who smile a little too quickly. And then their smiles die just a little too fast in their eyes. Like Maria, they press their bunched-up clothes tight to their breasts as they scurry down the dim back hallway in the early mornings to hoppingly haul on their skirts and stockings in awkward coldness in the back wing bathroom.

As for Maria and Norman's luggage, it hasn't arrived yet, it's still on its travels. Norman keeps calling the people at the airline office in Regina, and they keep telling him its arrival is imminent. "We'll believe it when we see it," he says to Maria with a husbandly sigh.

The bedroom that belonged to Maria all through her childhood has been reserved for Donna Northrup, Jens' bride-to-be. She's been acting wide-eyed and tense in Maria's presence ever since the night Maria and Norman got back from Europe, which makes Maria feel guilty because she keeps thinking it must show in her eyes that she wishes Donna would offer to give her old room back to her. The wedding is only three days away by now, though, so it's not that much longer to wait. In the meantime, Maria finds herself wanting to talk to Norman about things (about their not having any privacy, for starters) but for some reason she's not able to get his attention; the closest they come to being close is on their first morning when they lie on one of the bottom bunks for twenty minutes or so and kiss hotly while their two roommates are over at the church, practising for the wedding. (Ruth is to be the organist, Frances the soloist.) After the kissing, they end up lying on their backs, shoulder to shoulder. They breathe in stale air of mattress while they stare up at the poster Maria's mother years ago taped to the bottom bunk's ceiling. It's a photo of a white cruise ship honeycombed with black windows, and it's leaving a bridal wake of foam behind it as it makes its way across a Norwegian fjord the colour of ink. They talk about Ruth and Frances. No, they don't talk, they whisper, as if they're afraid their two bunk-mates will be able to hear them all the way from the Anglican cathedral, halfway across Saskatoon. They make little complaints but mostly it's innocent stuff, things Maria remembers about them from childhood, this and that. She tells Norman that by the time she'd graduated from high school she'd figured out that Frances was sort of a self-satisfied type — "very magnetic, though," a lot like the teacher who led her in Christmas choir practice the year she was in grade ten. Husky-voiced, glamorous, unmarried, a puzzle to everyone. And then she tells him that she can remember being a little kid and loving being hugged by Frances. Partly because of her perfume, which was so subtle it smelled like the silk lining of her fur coat. Norman whispers into her hair, "Well, probably it *was* the silk lining of her fur coat. You always make things so complicated, but mostly they are what they appear to be."

She wants to dispute this, but when she does he whispers, "Give me an example from real life then." And she can't think of a thing. But then she remembers something funny: a dream she had at some point during the night. She remembers it because she had to get up in the dark to go to the bathroom — a thing she hates to do when she's sharing a room with other people, her stomach always gets such a cringe in it. Her heart, too. And her feet are pure cringe, every creak she makes. She tells Norman she was peeing in her dream, squatting on a hillside somewhere in southern France peeing, and there was a man (a stranger in a dark business suit) standing peeing beside her. Peeing and singing. A strange song (half-French, half-English) sung to the tune of *La Marseillaise*. The words made perfect sense in her dream — they were *On boire a chanson!* and they meant "The earth needs us to rain on it." It wasn't till she was on her way back from the bathroom that she realized the French part of the song was total gibberish. And then she tells him that as she was doing her little tiptoe back into the room, Frances moaned a very deep sexy moan and just as she was crawling into the bunk across from Frances's bunk she heard her groan "Oh, *God*" in a voice so like an orgasmic man's voice that she looked up at Norman's bunk to see if the sound was coming from him. "It wasn't you, though, you were sleeping still as could be, like a stone knight on a tomb. But it was just so incredibly sexual."

The minute she has finished telling him all this she starts wishing she hadn't told him any of it. It just kills her, the way she's her own worst enemy every minute of the day. How can she act so dumb? How can she act like she hasn't noticed the way he keeps trying not to stare at Frances in the mornings when she bends down to her suitcase to gather up her slinky ivory slip, her shining nylons? And why tell him about how she was childishly peeing in her dream in the first place? Childishly peeing while Frances, in *her* dream, was grown-uply groaning? Anyone can see that Frances is still awfully attractive even if she is a woman in her forties. And that what men think of how she looks still really matters to her. You can tell by the kinds of nylons she wears (smoked taffy); you can tell by the sexy cut of her skimpy little dark rayon suits, and her rickety high-heeled sandals, you can tell by all the bangles.

But Norman can't have been thinking about Frances at all because what he asks next is "What about the bridesmaids? Do you know any of them?"

"No," she says, almost in a whimper. "No, I don't." She hates the way he always frowns and sounds so worried and fake-decent when he's trying to find out if unknown women are attractive.

On the way into the supermarket parking lot, Maria's mother tells her that the reason the wedding is to be held from the groom's house, not the bride's, is because Donna's mother is sick. "Out in Alberta, in Foothills Hospital. Maybe even dying. So don't even *mention* her mother to her, it's all very hush-hush."

It seems to Maria that her mother is expecting her to say something that'll be sympathetic to Donna. In all likelihood she wants her to say some extolling thing about mothers in general. But she can't bring herself to say anything. She briefly thinks of Donna's mother lying in a hospital bed and slowly dying, then tries to imagine her own mother dying, how she would feel. An illegal relief is what she imagines. She looks out the window. Sometimes she's taken over by a dread that she'll shout out something totally inappropriate. "Masturbation!", for instance. Or "Saliva!" Or she might be driven to make some unexpected confession: I think about sex all the time, but the way things have worked out — especially lately — Norman and I haven't even had all that many chances to *do* it. Living in youth hostels, living in Europe, sharing an apartment with someone else the whole time we were living in Denmark. And anyway I almost always end up with the feeling that what he really wants is to do it with every goddamn woman he's ever laid eyes on and then if he has any time and energy left over he might just condescend to do it with me. But how could she ever say this, or anything even remotely like this, to her own mother? There isn't really anyone in the whole world she could say something like this to, and this goes for at least ninety percent of the thoughts running around inside her brain. Besides, confessing her anxieties to her mother just never ever pays; it's the way to guarantee getting told to get prettier, get more charming, cater to him more.

At the supermarket she waits behind her mother at the check-out counter with a cart stocked with packaged jellos and bottles of pickled herring and olives. In the line next to theirs, there's a young mother with a toddler. A tall redhead, she's glancing irritably at a fashion magazine and bumping her grocery cart along with a hip while waiting for her turn at the cash register. She's quite the fashion plate herself — a bit gawky, true, but classically gawky — and she's wearing a pale-cream voile dress patterned with pencil-thin silver stripes.

Maria's mother has noticed her too. "Attractive," she says in a low voice to Maria. "And what a darling baby."

They both look over at him. He's been plunked into the cart with his plump little legs hanging down through the wire mesh of the basket-part and he's already sucked most of his bottle of apple juice dry. Maria feels sorry for him, his face has such a smudged, mucus-rubbed look, as if he's spent most of his short life having colds and crying. He's dressed in tiny yellow ankle-socks and pale-blue overalls with a bib that has darker blue smocking on it. He peddles his legs in the air and then arches his back in order to do feminine and desperate little reaching-out stretches with his feet, pointing them like a ballerina's feet (looks like he's getting ready to wail) and as his mother is lifting him up out of the cart, one of his arched feet gets caught in the cart's upper basket-part and when she's yanked him free of it she sits him too hard down on the floor beside the cart and he starts to howl. She decides to give him a banana at the same moment that it's her turn to start unloading her cart, and in a flustered fierce instant she grabs up his bottle from among the groceries, pokes its nipple into her own mouth to free her hands so that the bottle bobs like a lightweight plastic penis from the rubbery give of its nipple as she swiftly drops to one knee to peel the banana and then shove the top half of it into his mouth.

The banana works like a stopper. There's a surprised glug and then he sits much more quietly down on the floor, chewing, the tears still streaming down his rubbed-looking face.

She's not a good mother, thinks Maria, and for some reason she wants her own mother to witness this, but her own mother has already passed through the cashier's line and is on her way out of the store, although at the moment she's been waylaid by an animated woman in a shining copper-coloured raincoat. Maria wants to go up to her mother and take her by the elbow and say to her in a low controlled voice, Why are you always looking the other way when there's a chance for you to learn some new way not to blame me?

But what, exactly, does her mother blame her *for*?

Nothing she can put her finger on.

Everything.

For being who she is.

Now that the wedding is only two days away, the tension and bustle in the house have been stepped up. Neighbours and friends of the family have come over to give a hand with the cooking. A lot of tomato aspics with bay leaves and basil are being poured into giant aluminium jelly-moulds, and other moulds are being filled to the brim with lime jello bobbing with pineapple chunks, sliced bananas.

Maria wonders if Donna is worried about her mother. Or maybe she's only having her period. She seems quieter than usual and has a listening look in her eyes as if she's trying to gauge if people can smell anything. She's wearing a green rayon sheath with slits up its sides and there's a fine mist of perspiration on her upper lip. One thing Maria has noticed is that she and Donna have something in common — they both keep trying to help out in the kitchen. She can feel how carefully they are both poised on the sidelines of the big sunlit room, aching to join in with all the chopping, dicing, tasting, and basting women, and it's like standing ready to jump into the pattern of a square dance but you just can't find the right moment to enter: with heartlessly cheerful energy the elbows of the dancers keep closing you out.

They end up sitting in helpless formality out in the front room. All Maria can think is: Don't ask her anything about her mother! It makes it hard to come up with a more acceptable topic. Finally she asks her about where she used to work, and it turns out she's had jobs in libraries, too — in Red Deer and Lethbridge.

"Which city did you like the best?"

"Lethbridge. Probably because I had closer friends there."

After she's told Maria this, the conversation dies. A miserable silence, then they hear the sound of Jens' car turning into the gravel of the driveway, the quick deluxe gulps of car doors being slammed shut. They go to the windows, saved at last, see the bridesmaids start to clamber out. Maria realizes she's been feeling incredibly tense about their arrival. All she knows about them so far is that they're all unmarried women, all close to her own age. She's afraid that some of them will be stunning. Probably only one of them will be spectacular, though; this is the way it usually is. But even only one is too many, because if one of them is spectacular, Norman won't be able to keep his eyes off her.

Seeing them out on the lawn, she feels reassured. They look pudgy and brisk, like five fat little athletes. They all have short hair and short noses. They are all dressed in dark slacks, cabled sweaters.

When they come into the house to be introduced to everyone, she discovers they all have short names as well: the tall one, introduced by Donna as a college basketball star, is Mo; the others are Rae and Kay and Joy and Pat. But then Maria sees that one of them — Pat — is, after all, astonishingly pretty. She is the smallest and most pert of the five; her short fair hair is sun-streaked, partly a waxy yellow, partly dark as the dark meat on a roasted chicken, and her plump quick smile is flirty and dimpled.

They all sit awkwardly perched in the living-room, drinking

sherry at ten in the morning. Even Hansie and Luff have come in to give the bridesmaids a quick male once-over. But they end up more looked at than looking, as if the year Maria was away in Denmark has turned them into farm boys. They don't seem to know what to do with their hands, their eyes.

After fifteen minutes of hard-working conversation Jens, at some signal from their mother, says, "Listen, why don't I take you girls to your new homes, get you settled."

He turns to Donna. "Want to come with us, hon?"

She stands up at once and with sorrowful swiftness goes to the hall closet to lift out her jacket.

The house, noisy though it still is with all the company and activity out in the kitchen, feels totally empty to Maria after Donna and the bridesmaids have all gone off with Jens in his car. She decides to go upstairs to write a letter to a friend down on the East Coast because although she doesn't much enjoy feeling invisible, she also doesn't want her mother to notice she isn't doing anything useful and so give her some disgusting chore like scouring out toilets.

On the way to the bunk-room she passes the doorway to her old bedroom. She stops at the threshold but feels shy about stepping beyond it because Donna's hairbrushes and scarves and blouses have been arranged or draped on bureaus, on chairs. This high up, the house seems eerily quiet, though — quiet enough for her to go in and take a quick peek around. She steps in, holding her breath — a tourist, a thief. The crook come back to haunt the scene of the crime. But what is the crime? Childhood? It seems such a good little girl's room to her now, the room of a virgin. At the same time there's something ghostly about it. But then maybe girlish goodness *is* ghostly, especially if you no longer consider yourself to be a girl. Or maybe the illness of Donna's mother is making her uneasy. She goes over to her old closet, opens it to see Donna's wedding gown hanging in there along with a short row of dark jackets, retired plaid skirts with a lot of grey and tweedy beige-flecked black in them. Stilled and queenly in its zippered clear polythene box, the wedding gown looks beaded, spectral, more headless than a short wedding dress could ever be.

She goes over to her old window, her old view. The bird-bath is still the same giant stone soup bowl, half sunk into the lawn and filled almost to its tilted brim with lethal-looking, leafy cold water. In the winters, when it would freeze over, Hansie and Luff used to help her flop her dolls all over it. Looking down at last summer's leaves in the water, she can hear again the high amazed little cries Luff used to make for her Lapland doll. In November they could see the dome of the Ukrainian church down on the corner, but for now the leaves of the big maple in the bottom of the garden obscure it. She loves the colour of these leaves — somewhere between wine and bronze; turning, then falling, they always used to signal new beginnings to her: the fall, new clothes, school starting up again, all those old sweet young hopes for the future: populari-ty, a boyfriend, being invited to school dances. And however unanswered those prayers mainly were, she wishes she could still feel hope in exactly that young, hopeful way again. But she can't; hope has changed — hope is no longer tied up with something wonderful happening, hope is by now only tied up with praying things won't get any worse, praying she can somehow, by hook or by crook, hang onto what she has. This is what she learned living in Europe. Living in Europe and being married: how much life is not equal to hope.

She can't write the letter. Not unless she wants it to be nothing but lies. It's just too insane to pretend it's exciting and terrific to be home. She recalls the trip back from Denmark and her head starts to fill up with the sucked, metallic roar of the plane as it carried them homeward across the dark ocean, the mechanized sanitized dimness. But what she remembers best are the wobbly walks to the aircraft toilet past the polished bald heads of some of the older male passengers, skullcapped by reading lights, and her romantic sense of Canada as a dimly populated iceberg, looming lonely and pale beyond the black ocean. The place they had so desperately wanted to make their escape from. At one point she recalls whispering to Norman, "We must be close to where the Titanic went down," and he whispered back "Maybe," and then she fell asleep and dreamed she was drowning — a drugged feeling in her legs like a bad case of the flu. Then Gander, an hour ahead of them, down in the bottomless dark. A thrilling name for a place, or so she'd thought then. She'd pictured it as an historic little village situated on a long neck-like inlet of inky water and flanked by green grass and long beaches of white sand. But the real Gander, in the dead hour before dawn, turned out to be a bleak and makeshift place, at least the part of it that was flocked around the airport, all shacks and the explosions of planes arriving, taking off. They'd tried to sleep there, their whole nine-hour stopover, in a cheap motel close to the runway, the hot late September sun beating down on the tin roof above them.

Norman comes to find her. "I'm phoning the airline again. I don't think they're telling us the truth about our stuff. First they said it went on to Calgary and they'd be sending it back to us, but when I talked to them twenty minutes ago they were vague about it again. I have a feeling it might still be in Montreal. Maybe Montreal, maybe Regina. Or maybe somebody just walked off with it, maybe they smelled the liquor in it."

"Maybe it's still in Newfoundland," says Maria, and she

pictures the little bud vase they bought for Norman's mother in Stockholm — a thick clear glass vase with a rainfall of teardrops and glassy bubbles inside it. She remembers not being able to decide at the time if it was hideous or adorable. But it makes her think of her own mother: her mother's going to lend her one of her cocktail dresses for the party tonight. She says, "God, I wish I had my own clothes."

Norman wishes he had his good suit. "Maybe I'll have to borrow something from Jens. He seems to have gained a good bit of weight, though."

"And he looks so worried all the time! As if he's not all that sure he wants to get married yet."

"Oh, I don't know about that. Just nerves maybe."

"I wish we had the presents we bought for them."

Norman wishes it too.

Tonight there's a big buffet supper over at Ralph Hickson's place. He's going to show everyone the movie he made of Norman and Maria's wedding — close to this time two years ago. He's been out of the country a lot himself since then, which is why nobody's had the chance to see it yet. Maria's stomach becomes untethered when she tries to imagine seeing herself up on the screen. She had the flu the day she got married (stomach cramps, diarrhea) and now she experiences the bizarre fear that when people see the movie they'll somehow be able to tell that she's not wearing any panties under her wedding gown.

For the rehearsal, the bridesmaids are already dressed in the party dresses they'll wear for the wedding supper tonight. And high-heeled silver sandals. Exactly like Maria's own silver sandals, still lost in limbo in some unidentified airport.

Frances stands beside the pulpit to sing a song from Mahler. She looks very dignified in a navy-blue crepe dress with a branch of seaweedy sequins glittering on her left shoulder.

After the central players have been put through their paces, they all move out into the vestry of the cathedral and then make their way down the stone steps to the cars. The bridesmaids are all wearing male-looking dark coats caped over their shoulders so that they resemble girls standing out on a floodlit lawn after a private dinner and dance.

Cars pull up. Bridesmaids dip into them. Only Pat and Gary, one of the ushers, hold back. Possibly Pat is waiting to see which car Norman is going to decide to climb into. Jens and Donna are the ones who end up taking them — Pat and Norman and Gary and Maria, along with Frances, who at the last minute runs up to the car, raps on the window, then hauls herself awkwardly but fragrantly in.

At the intersection just before the turn-off to Ralph Hickson's street, they have to stop for the light. As they're sitting waiting for it to change, a wedding party comes out of the United Church on the corner. It's clear and cold twilight by this time — the church's square windows are golden behind their thick thumbprint glass and the bride's dress is a short white sheath made out of the sort of fabric that sparkles like the sugar that's used to simulate snow on Christmas cards. She looks very happy. So does her puffy groom.

"Look at that, honey," Frances says to Maria. "The whole world's getting married."

Maria doesn't know why she always refers to Ralph Hickson's place as Ralph Hickson's place. Maybe because he designed it himself. He does have a wife, after all; she comes from somewhere in the American southwest. Amanda Lynn. She has the pot-bellied vivid warmth Maria associates with true glamour, but then she's had a soft spot for her ever since the Saturday night when she was in grade five or six and was sent over to the Hicksons with a basket of plums and Amanda Lynn opened the door to her and said, "Hello, beautiful one." Other times when she'd go over there, especially if she arrived on a Sunday afternoon, she would sense — particularly if Amanda Lynn and Ralph would come to the door together, one just behind the other and both of them darting their shirts into their jeans — that they'd just had sex. The embarrassment she would feel at that moment for what she imagined to be their embarrassment when they understood how embarrassed she must be because she knew what she knew about them would be almost unendurable to her.

Amanda Lynn, tonight dressed in a peasant blouse and a dull-red wraparound skirt, leads the wedding guests across the large polished living-room, then down into the sunken fireplace-room and over to the glassed-in back of the house where the buffet tables have been set up. Harry Belafonte is on the record player, singing the part of "Mathilda" where his voice tilts elastically back and forth on little cat feet. The tables are set with glazed hams and salads and huge bunches of daisies. Maria recalls that Mathilda is Donna's middle name — on the wedding invitations it said "We request the honour of your presence at the marriage of Donna Mathilda," and because Donna is standing close by, she puts her arm around her new sister-in-law and says, "Hey Donna, this song is for you!"

Donna turns to her swiftly, her eyes frightened and grateful, very bright. She says, "I love this song." They end up shyly swinging hands together. "Maria, I just want to thank you and your wonderful family for all of your kindness to me."

Now what? But then Jens comes over to Donna and gives her a peck on the cheek. "Sweetheart, come and say hello to Ralph Hickson."

Where's Pat? Where's Norman? Where's Gary? There are so many people in this room. Maria noticed Gary looking at her when they were back at the cathedral. She was staring at Norman staring at Pat and then was aware of someone's eyes fixed on herself and when she looked up, she saw that the eyes belonged to Gary. It made her feel strange, scared almost, as if in that moment he must have known her better than she'll ever know herself. She had a momentary wish to peel the expression she was wearing right off her face so that she could hide it away in her pocket. And then when they got here, he waited for her at the bottom of the path up to the cantilevered house. For a moment she was afraid he was waiting for her because he pitied her.

Norman has gone upstairs to try the airline again. A few moments after his departure, someone hits a dessert spoon against one of the wineglasses and then Ralph, looking flushed and slightly drunk, shouts, "Ladies and gentlemen, your attention please! Time for the grand feature!" He lifts a chalky landscape of driftwood and pebbled grey beach down from the wall above the fireplace while Amanda Lynn moves down the length of the buffet tables, blowing out candles.

The projector starts to whir and Maria takes a deep breath to prepare herself for the self-consciousness she knows she'll feel when she sees how self-conscious she looks when she's up on the screen. And right away there she is — the shy bride in her bower, smiling the uneasily bemused smile she remembers inventing for Ralph. There's something ghostly about this shot — a faded, ghostly light. Now she's starting to make her cautious way down the main stairway, the lacy tail of her veil draped over one arm, but at this point she hears Norman coming down from his phone call and gets distracted from her own image while she tries to figure out if Pat has saved a space for him next to her back there in the dark. She turns back to see Pat hitch herself into a corner of the sofa she's sitting in, then glances up at the screen again to see Norman's hunched and enlarged shadow trying to duck its way down to his new little lady friend as if he's afraid people will see his head up on the screen. She allows herself one final peek back and so turns in time to see him slump down beside Pat just as she hears pandemonium break out — hoots, cheers, foot-stomping, wolf-whistles — and for a split second it's like being in the middle of a bad dream and she's convinced everyone is howling because Pat and Norman are sitting together, but then there's another howl — from Ralph this time: "Oh, Christ, ladies and gents! I shot Norman and Maria's wedding over the movie of our Mardi Gras party!" and Maria looks up to the screen to see a shot of her mother dressed in a pair of faded red ski-slacks and one of her father's white shirts, smoking and squinting as she's hesitantly arranging a tall bouquet of faded red tulips. She's walking backwards, still squinting to examine her handiwork, and so almost collides with a man dressed in a clumsy black top hat and black frock-coat. Probably the Mad Hatter. Inger doesn't seem to see him, but then how could she, he isn't even in the same movie. Someone else comes into the picture at this point — an orange-haired girl in a tightly-laced black bustier and a hoop skirt that wobbles in an ungainly way as if it's powered by the wired supports of two unsynchronized lamp shades. Fuschia satin cow-patties cap its side-awnings, and as she moves, they too seem to waddle. The orange-haired girl and the Mad Hatter dance a lumbering little jig together, a sort of Sailor's Hornpipe, while Inger, still squinting and smoking, does her own little solo dance of one step forwards, two back. The audience roars at the comedy of Maria's mother's dance, then begins to applaud a short parade of tanned middle-aged women in silver sheath dresses and Lone Ranger silver eye-masks, then there are more men in top hats, this time eating hamburgers — some of them beer-bellied, some of them gaunt — and then there are crowds of tiny wedding guests wandering among Mardi Gras guests blown up big as billboards. Also

the reverse: wedding-guest faces looming huge as pale balloons
while Mardi Gras guests frolic among them like Lilliputians.
The next shot is of her father wandering past two giants in two
black stovepipe hats. It's as if her father has been transformed
into a hatless little Father of Confederation. She thinks: My
father! I've hardly even spoken to him since I got back home!
And she is all at once overwhelmed by the thought of his death;
it's as if he has died and she hasn't had the chance to say good-
bye to him. Her tears of laughter seem to alter their chemistry
right up in her eyes at this point, start to sting, as if from grief.

Maria has news, but feels she must whisper it. "Norm, I think
she burned it."

"Burned what?" He's dressed in his tan cotton pyjamas
bottoms, a damp blue towel hung boxer-style around his neck,
and he seems, in his response, to be peering at the mystery of
this burned thing above his Christmassy beard of lather as he
shaves himself in the bathroom mirror.

"The movie of our wedding."

"Your mother?"

"Yes."

"How do you know?" he whispers.

"I just had breakfast with her down in the kitchen and she
was just so evasive about the whereabouts of the thing. I told
her how terrific we both thought it was and how much we
want to take it to Calgary so we can show it to the people we
used to know when we were living up there and she said,
'Sweetie, why don't you just leave it here with us until you get
settled, then we can send it along to you.'"

"And then it gets lost in the mail, I betcha."

"Precisely, my dear Kaminski." And then she says that
there's also a really queer chemical smell down below. But then

there are lot of fabulous cooking smells too. Everybody's down there now, she tells him, eating as much as they can in case things get too crazy at lunch time and they have to go off to the church hungry. And she itemizes all the fantastic food smells: ham and bananas fried up together; sausages and pancakes; hot muffins and coffee. "Oh, and it's raining too — did you know that? Isn't that supposed to be good luck or something? To have it rain on the day of your wedding?"

"I think it's good luck in Greece."

"That's pretty cynical."

"Yeah, it is. But you know the Greeks, they're a pretty cynical people. Anyway, you're the one who keeps saying you think this marriage is going to be a total disaster."

"I don't know if I think that. I don't know what I think." She studies her reflection in the mirror, keeping it neutral. "Anyway, it smells very weird down there. Especially if you go into the den and stand up close to the fireplace."

"I wonder why she did it." He raises her left arm straight up the way a boxer's manager will raise up his fighter's arm after a fight, watches the two of them in the mirror for a bit, then brings her fist down to his mouth and kisses it, his eyes in the mirror watching the performance of himself doing it.

"Maybe she thought it was a bad omen."

He considers this. "That's so nutty, though. Like she's still living in the Middle Ages or something."

Maria sits down on the rim of the tub. She says, "I agree." But the bad-omen thing has occurred to her as well. And for a moment she almost dares to say, What *about* us, though? Do you think we're going to make it? Or are you going to keep looking at other women for the rest of our lives? Is this going to be the story with us forever? But then she doesn't think she has the right to say anything at all because she remembers a dream she had last night, about Gary. They were dancing to "Mathilda" but the words were being sung very low, very slow, and they were dancing slow and close.

"Have you talked to any of the bridesmaids much?"

"Not much," she says. And then she thinks: Have *you*? Should she say this? She studies his back — the pale freckles, the male pads of fat on it. "Have you talked to them much?"

"Not all that much," he says in a light careful voice. She's aware of the way he's watching her in the mirror even though she keeps looking down at her knees. She feels sad as a wet bird, her hands clamped beside her on the cold rim of the tub.

"Hey! Want to hear a riddle Luff told me?"

Fire away.

"What stringed instrument does Ralph Hickson play?"

She looks up at his back blankly. "I don't know, I'm no good at riddles."

"Do you give up?"

"I give up."

"Amanda Lynn."

She hits her fist on her knee and calls herself a prize idiot.

"We got hitched without a hitch," says Jens, pouring extra glasses of aquavit for everyone. Maria can't tell whether he looks desperate or relieved, they're all so tired by this time and there have been so many small and tall drinks to drink.

"Ah yes," says Gary, holding up his glass of aquavit to respectfully inspect it. "The infamous and lethal little caraway-seed drink."

One of the bridesmaids (Rae? Kay?) smiles over at him with tender approval. Maria noticed her looking at him before — her sweet eyes, protruding teeth. The fascinating thing about her smile is that she doesn't seem to be trying to hide anything when she smiles it. In fact, the reverse: it's as if her smile is in love with her teeth.

Hansie and Luff look flushed from all the drinking and seem shyer than ever as Frances moves from guest to guest to get a hug for her performance in church. Maria can see each brother brace himself for her kiss. Two solid boys with fair brush cuts, holding their breath. As for Frances, she's looking very gleaming and happy; she's braided her black hair and pinned it up at the back in a sort of elegant figure-eight arrangement and she's wearing a bronze taffeta suit without any blouse under it. Maria's positive that her mother disapproves of this suit. No, it's not the suit, it's the fact that Frances isn't wearing a blouse underneath it. Before they left for the church she overheard her mother say to her, "Sweetie, listen, I've got the most stunning silk scarf that would look really fabulous with your dear little taffeta suit." But Frances wouldn't hear of it. She said, "Oh Lord, Inger, no — I always get so damn hot when I sing in a church."

The rain had stopped and the sun had come bridally out at the very moment that Donna stepped out onto the damp porch in her beaded long gown. But then on their way to the church the sun hid itself again and it was as if all the dark in the world was being held in a giant sponge and a giant fist was squeezing it tight and then just before they turned onto the street where the Anglican cathedral stood, the whole day went dim with a kind of reverse-squeeze of shadow that spread out over Saskatoon in a subdued racing grey city blush of darkness that seemed to do some moody thing to the heart.

Donna and Jens slip away from the reception sometime before supper time but while the guests are still eating their salads and cold cuts they reappear together at the top of the stairway. They look dwarfed and royal up there behind the stair railing. Donna waves her bouquet, and the bridesmaids, all in yellow georgette dresses, surge towards her, holding up their arms like small girls chanting an imploring grace to God. The bouquet is tossed high, then plunges to be caught by the wedding's basketball star. So, thinks Maria: Pat didn't catch it. It's at this moment that she realizes that Norman isn't here and then she recalls that he mentioned at lunch time that he had a headache.

She wonders if he's lying upstairs somewhere, maybe she should go look for him. But then she decides not to move because people are starting to make toasts to Jens and Donna and so this just isn't the polite moment to be making an exit.

And by the time Hansie and Luff are circling the room, pouring fresh drinks for everyone, people are not only toasting Jens' and Donna's future, but the future in general.

"To the new decade!" cries Ruth.

"To 1960!" cries Frances.

There's the sound of a car door being slammed shut out in the driveway. Footsteps come up the porch stairs. They sound important and hollow, but possibly this is only because the wedding guests have decided, en masse, to listen. The door opens, they hear someone step inside, the front door being latched.

A moment later, Norman appears in the archway to the front room. He's carrying a heavy tan leather suitcase, belted with paler tan leather straps. For a bizarre instant Maria is convinced he's come to tell everyone he's leaving her, marriage over. But then she understands: it's their luggage, home at last.

Norman drops to one knee to undo the straps. It must be raining again — there's a spattering of dark spots on the shoulders of his raincoat. Maria glances out the window and sees that the day is bowed down and gloomy with it. Wet cars in the driveway, wet cars lining the lawn, somebody's black panel truck parked under the wet yellow maple at the north end of the garage.

"Jens." says Norman. "Donna. Your wedding presents. Direct from Copenhagen."

People stay quiet, ready to give the suitcase their undivided attention. But at first it's only clothes. Norman lifts out one of his Icelandic sweaters, then an old blouse of Maria's that looks dingy from having been washed in the tin sinks of too many youth hostels, then a gored red rayon skirt with a stain on it that could be anything — wine or coffee or blood. He holds each article up, impersonating a drunken auctioneer. People laugh, they're drunk enough by this time to laugh at anything. Maria's the only one who's not drunk; she might have been drunk two minutes ago, but now she's bathed in such a cold sweat that she feels crouched up inside herself, terrified. When Norman gets to one of her silver sandals and holds it spinning from one of its silver tails, she feels as if she could throw up from shame. She doesn't know where to look. No, not true: she looks towards Gary and sees that he's looking startled for her sake. His shock feels so much like love that she has to look away.

But something is wrong. Norman is feeling his way through their clothes with both hands, a man in a blind search for something precious he's lost in a fast-moving brook. He looks to Maria, then to Maria's mother. "We've been robbed," he says.

People cry out "Aw!" and Inger cries *"No!"* and Luff says that the liquor was probably swiped in Regina.

"No, no," says Gary. "Probably in Gander. Probably some guy in Customs in Gander saw the label on the Cherry Heering and said to his buddies, 'Herring, eh? This here little bottle must be some kind of newfangled Newfie drink.' "

People laugh, then everyone is all at once trying to outdo everyone else with robbery jokes. Only Ralph Hickson tries to cheer Norman up. "What the hell, Norm. It's the thought that counts."

Maria doesn't want to go and sit beside Norman but feels that she must. He shouldn't be left all alone over there, with no presents to give to anybody, all by himself on the sofa, it makes him seem too unlucky. But her legs feel drugged, heavy with sleep. Still, she does manage to stand, walk stiffly over to join him.

There's the depressed sigh of her weight as she sinks down beside him. He turns to her: "We were never robbed once, the whole time we were in Europe, were we, Maria?"

And she says no, never once.

People are still watching them, to see how all this will end. And Maria is convinced that they'll sit before their audience like this forever, the centre of attention at last, empty-handed.

FLAT MOUNTAIN TAXTAILS

Serena Lee Mis. Ta-Nash

MARY WOLFTAIL OPENED her eyes and noticed the upset in her stomach immediately. Didn't feel very good, but the house was too cold to worry about that now. She jammed her feet into icy moosehide slippers and padded out to the front room-cum-kitchen.

She lit a candle and carried it in that slow sure step that keeps a steady flame. She glanced at the big round thermometer on the inside cardboard-covered wall. It confirmed why she was shivering: minus twenty-two. And still pitch dark outside, although it was 8:30 in the morning. She moved quickly now, crumpled newspapers, stuffing them in the old barrel heater, following up with wood chips and rounds of spruce. As she held the match flame under the fuel she hoped Miss Piggy would cooperate and not smoke the place up.

The stove took off real good. Henry had cleaned the pipes yesterday. He had done it while Mary was freezing her butt off at the pay phone. She stood as close to the Pig as possible. "Too bad I couldn't get hold of that government lady yesterday. Seems even colder today. Wonder if Henry can get that truck going. Should have enough propane in that tiger torch," she thought.

Just thinking about the government lady made her stomach

tighten. Four letters had come and she'd gotten her daughter to help her answer them all. But the lady at Revenue Canada kept on sending back those forms from the computer with questions you only got to say 'yes' or 'no' to.

There was no room on the form for a proper answer. On the bottom there was a message about what you could go to jail for. And what would happen if you didn't phone this certain lady in Vancouver. Miss P. Cratchitte her name was. Something like that nurse in the movie they'd rented to take to their in-town friends' place. "One Flew Over the Cuckoo's Nest" it was called and if the Vancouver Cratchitte was anything like that, Mary was in trouble. Mary wasn't nearly as brave as that Indian man in the movie had been. He didn't let that nurse scare him.

Mary knew this was why her stomach hurt. Fear. I'll have to face it, she thought, only way to overcome the things you're afraid of is to go up against them. Use the fear wisely, know when to advance and when to retreat. Try to balance the fear, try to understand Miss Cratchitte. Tell her about how I don't understand all this tax stuff and I'm trying to pay.

Mary and Henry had no idea why the government thought they owed money. They had been getting papers and letters from the government for years now. Mary always read them word for word, never quite sure if she really knew what they said. She kept them carefully sorted in used file folders, leftovers from her daughter's office.

Whenever one of her four grown-up daughters came for a visit they would check out the newest pile of mail and try to make sense of it. All of her daughters had finished high school; they did better than their mother in the school part. Mary tried to remember all the things the girls told her to do with the papers. Sometimes, though, she just got fed up with the mail and shoved it, envelopes and all, in a drawer. Especially the contest forms and the other ones with boxes to fill in.

112

Now it seems that some of the papers with the boxes were pretty important. Miss Cratchitte sure must think so anyway. She wanted a phone call or she'd call the law.

Henry had been prodding Mary to phone Vancouver and so she had finally walked the ten miles to the pay phone yesterday, even though it was forty below, and worked up the nerve to call Miss Cratchitte.

It had turned out Miss Cratchitte couldn't talk to Mary, even after dead-tone hold for ten minutes. Being cold and scared was bad enough, but they didn't even play music while you waited. They did when you phoned the CYI or the Band Office, and it made the wait a lot nicer. She wondered if she should tell Miss Cratchitte about the five-hour walk if you couldn't get the truck started in the cold and couldn't hitchhike a ride.

Mary walked over to check the temperature. Up to five below; time to pour her second cup of coffee and call Henry. He liked the house warm when he got up and Mary sure enjoyed her time alone in the morning. She always stood at the window watching the day break over the mountains. Morning was a good time for her, most days, and she promised herself she wouldn't think about Miss Cratchitte anymore. At least not until she was at the pay phone. No sense aggravating over something that might not even happen.

Henry had put his foot down. Yesterday Mary had frozen her fingers, toes, nose and cheeks, so if he couldn't start the truck again today, she wouldn't be talking to Miss Cratchitte anyway. Or maybe she'd try to call and Miss Cratchitte wouldn't be there.

Henry came out of the bedroom, looking over his shoulder at the thermometer as he headed straight for Miss Piggy, "Up to zero now. You been up for a while, eh?"

"Ya, for a while. Looks like it might stay cold out today. Sky's clear and that sun seems pretty late coming up. Won't be much heat in it today," Mary replied.

"Well, I'll go out about eleven, once it's daylight, and try that truck for you. You got to try that Vancouver lady again, Mary; keep on trying until you can talk to her. I'm sure she'll understand why we can't send her all that money the government wants, once you tell her the whole story. Guess she didn't know what you were saying in those letters. It will be alright, don't you think," his voice trailed off.

Silence took over the room, Mary and Henry sipped their coffee, alternately standing beside Miss Piggy and the window, the view ever-changing, mountains fused in red, then pink, gold, yellow and finally blue white light.

As the house warmed they quietly slipped into their separate morning routines. Mary put the dishes to soak in the tin dish pan filled with soapy water warming on Miss Piggy's flattened-out back. She always left the supper dishes till morning in the winter; hard to get them clean by candlelight at night. They only used the kerosene lights for reading for a while each evening; candles were cheaper.

Henry pulled on his heavy outdoor clothes. Enough light outside now to chop wood and cart in the daily food supply for the Pig. She lived up to her name. Or was it the other way, she'd earned it? Either way, he had work to do.

Promptly at eleven, Henry rigged up the propane torch and stove pipes under the truck. He hated this chore, standing around outside trying to thaw out the truck yet not set it on fire with the flames from the tiger torch. "Sure hope Miss Cratchitte appreciates this," he muttered. He couldn't even go in to warm up, had to keep turning the motor over, moving the warmed up bottom oil to the top.

"Truck's running." Henry's voice cut into Mary's thoughts. "Better get ready and go soon. You got enough gas to stay there and try to call a few times."

All the way to the phone, Mary tried to think about something else. Good things. But her throat tightened as she got out of the truck and climbed the snowbank to the pay phone.

"Operator, I want to call the tax office collect," she said, then added the number. Damn — someone answered in Vancouver on the third ring.

"Will you accept a collect call from Mary Wolftail?" asked the operator.

"For whom is she calling?" asked a crisp male voice, clear in spite of the 1,800 mile distance.

"Is Miss Cratchitte there, please?" asked Mary. "I'm supposed to phone her." She tried to hide the fear in her voice.

"Your name and social insurance number please," demanded Mr. Crisp Talker.

Mary didn't know the number right off like that. "Just a minute, it's on that card in my pocket; I'll find it for you." She finally found the plastic card and read the numbers off slowly. Three seven nine, dash, six oh four, dash, three eight five.

"One moment please." Dead tone again. How long this time? Where did he have to go to find Miss Cratchitte? Mary had been to Vancouver once, knew how big some of those buildings were. Person could get lost inside them. She had.

Mary was startled by a new voice, this one nasal, with an accent that made the words sharp and hard. "Is this your social insurance number?" the voice snapped, rattling off the nine digits. "Are you Mary Wolftail? I'm so glad you finally responded to my repeated requests," it said in a tight, unfriendly tone. "I'm Miss Cratchitte, in charge of your overdue account, you're very hard to contact, I must say."

"I — uh — er, I wrote you a letter, more than one, and sent you that money, I thought you got them; nothing came back. You did get them, didn't you?" Mary felt better now.

"Yes, we received your correspondence, and your overdue payments," Cratchitte snapped, "but we need to discuss details of your account and a repayment schedule."

Mary gulped; she wasn't sure she understood all the words but the meaning was clear. "I explained all that in the letter. About being sick. And not working last summer and all that. I explained all that in the letters. Did you read them?"

"Of course I read them, but they don't provide enough specific financial information and these overdue accounts require special attention to get them collected. The deficit, you know."

"I didn't know we owed that much money. Do we? Do you think it will help the deficit! I've been trying to think up ways to tell that Michael Wilson finance guy about that might help but I let the one thing I could do slip right by me," Mary was at once very interested. She'd never thought that her money could help with the government debt. Sure seemed funny, though, that all those times the government owed her and Henry money they didn't seem to care about their debts.

She wisely decided not to mention this to Miss Cratchitte; she might not take kindly to it. "We want your money immediately; there certainly wasn't much in your bank account, was there? Where do you keep the rest?"

"What rest?" Mary asked, scared again, getting colder by the minute.

"Well you must have some money. People can't live way up there without money, can they? You must have an income, for pity's sake; what about your assets and savings? I need to know everything to fill out these forms."

Mary explained, as patiently as possible, her voice going soft, just above a whisper. "We don't have much money, only what Henry gets from UIC. And we need all that for food. Not much game left around here to eat. Too many people. Those rich big game hunters always want their trophies. Killed too many."

"We will decide how much you'll pay each month," Miss Cratchitte interrupted. "It will be based on the financial information you provide me. Now, how much rent do you pay?"

Mary took a deep breath, then stamped the cold out of her feet. She'd have to answer these questions and she already knew she and Miss Cratchitte were in for a good chin wag. She looked around her at the snow covered mountains and remembered what her Grandma had taught her about laughter and fun. How when you laughed with someone, you had formed a good bond with them.

The crow's-feet at the corners of Mary's eyes deepened with her smile. She'd see if she could have a little fun with Miss Cratchitte. Make her laugh. Would be good.

Miss Cratchitte was talking again, "I need to know your total monthly expenses so I can calculate a budget that will assist you in paying your debt in a timely manner. Rent was what I asked about. How much?"

"We don't exactly pay rent, we sort of own our place. Well Henry and me and the YTG, that's the government, we all think we own it. But I don't know if any of us do own it." She felt that was good funny stuff. "The government here thinks it owns all the land. Calls us squatters even though my family's been around here for a long, long time."

Mary thought of how silly people had gotten about land since that highway was built. Close to the towns they showed you maps with lines for where you lived and told you to fill out papers and apply to the government so you could keep on living there. Then after the Yukon Territorial Government said okay, they started to send you bills, wanted money for everything they thought they had done for you and for things they said they would do to let you keep your place.

Three years ago Henry had had to go to town and find a job, even though he was almost sixty. The government wanted money for making up all those papers. Then Mary had to pay a man for drawing lines on a map to show the YTG where they lived. And that government man was standing right there on their mountain when he said that.

Last summer they dug a trench alongside the road. All the way up the mountain. Said Henry and Mary could get a phone now. First they had to give the telephone company $650.00 to put in a pole. Henry had to clear all the trees out in a twenty-foot swath. He could get a pole easy; the bush behind the house was full of trees, good ones, but only a special pole would do, something about codes.

On top of that, the YTG wanted over $700.00 a year for putting the trench up the mountain and for the next fifteen years too. Maybe the YTG wanted them to have a phone, but Mary and Henry only made a few calls a week, usually from a phone in town when they went for their shower and filled the five-gallon water buckets for home.

Everybody wanted money and now they wanted you to have a phone, seemed more for them than for you. Maybe so they could phone you for more money.

The conversation with Miss Cratchitte continued. Mary's try at humour went on, but the only one having fun was Mary. Around and around they went, Cratchitte's voice stiff, the words hard and square, Mary now clapping her hands. She could hardly feel them.

She imagined the warm place where Miss Cratchitte sat behind a desk. Probably had a navy blue suit on, with a white blouse — plain. Short blonde hair likely. Glasses, long sharp nose. Must be, for her to talk that way.

Mary tried to help Miss Cratchitte understand and finally knew there was only one way this would ever happen.

"I'm not going to answer any more questions," she told Miss Cratchitte. "I'm nearly frozen and I have to go to the truck and warm up. I'm going to hang up now. But before I go, I'm inviting you to come to Flat Mountain and see our place. You can stay at the Cardboard Palace with us. That's what we call our place. Save money for the deficit," she laughed again. It was getting harder and harder to laugh.

Miss Cratchitte did not laugh. "I'm in total agreement and I'll be coming to Whitehorse in two weeks," she said. "I'll see you then to do an audit of your books and records. Please have everything ready and in good order when I arrive," Miss Cratchitte went on. "Now, how do I get to your place?"

Mary and Henry sat in their favourite chairs sipping cups of Hudson's Bay tea. Mary had picked it last fall and a few cups always relaxed them. Light from two short candles spilled over the table edge onto the hides they 'd been scraping with small, sharp knives.

Henry got up to check Miss Piggy. "You make out okay with that government lady?" he asked .

"Well, okay I guess. She's coming to see us. Didn't say exactly when. But soon. She wants to look at our books and records. She asked a lot of funny questions. I said she could stay here. Then we can explain things, easy," Mary answered.

Henry returned to his chair, picked up the hide and started scraping again. "If we got to give that lady a lot of money, sure hope we get lots more lynx. They're bringing good money now. Don't know where else we could get it."

"Still don't think we owe her any more money. She said she got all we sent. I never got a chance to tell her about that guy in town. The one who helped fill out them forms. Doesn't matter anyway. She'll come and she'll go. Hope she explains things real good. For the next time."

Henry sighed, put his hide down and went outside, flashlight in hand. "Still real cold out there," he told Mary as he came back in. "I'll fill Miss Piggy up real good. Time for bed. I need to go check those traps tomorrow. Going to warm up real good, south wind blowing those clouds over. Be a good time for lynx."

100 Times I Looked at the Window and Saw Your Reflection There

Beverley Daurio

YOU WALK A LONG WAY into the wind, your cheeks and fingers increasingly cold. It is after school. Twilight comes early in December; the sky is a rigid, military blue. Brown trees line the sidewalk; brown cars pass you, raising salty slush with their tires in the road.

You climb a snowdrift and cross a narrow parking lot that is furrowed with ice and badly in need of repair. You turn along a cement walkway studded with posts, then knock on her numbered door, one of twelve in a row. The varnish is worn off the wood; the door is corrugated, like cardboard.

Your grandmother's motel room never has enough air. Her room smells musty, as if she keeps cats, but cats are not allowed. Only a tiny square of her front window, framed in flaking metal and covered by stiff flowered curtains, opens at all. There is a little sideways handle sticking out over the cold stone sill to crank the window open, and that is the first thing you do when you arrive. On tiptoe, you lean your forehead against the glass and look out at the neon sign advertising HOUSEKEEPING ROOMS, at the wind-stunted pines edging the parking lot, and, if it's dark, at the yellow squares of windows in brick houses across the way.

For your visit tonight, your grandmother has lighted a score of tall red candles, in ashtrays, on saucers, in shallow tin cans, on every surface. It's pretty. Candle flames reflect and flicker in the window, in the white steel of the refrigerator door, in the chrome trim of the chairs. Distorted shadows stretch away across the rug and up the walls.

With your elbows on the wobbly Arborite table, you finger the tinsel that flutters from the miniature white Christmas tree. You sip at vaguely sour milk, poured into a thick pink glass from the same waxed carton as last week. The strips of silver waft and glitter in the hot wind rising from a heat register on the floor. The tree sparkles on the table in front of you, its base surrounded by a gold-flecked cotton batting skirt.

Your grandmother has trouble with her legs. As soon as you take off your coat and boots, she pours your milk, then lumbers over to the thin plaid couch and sits down. Slowly she lifts her feet up onto the coffee table, beside her used dishes from dinner. The fork is smeared with mustard. The fabric case containing her broken eyeglasses rests on the arm of the couch. Sometimes when you visit you play dominoes on the table where her feet are now. Sometimes you describe the pictures on television, or read to her; sometimes you do somersaults until she smiles. Your grandmother is fat and grey.

She lowers her feet to the floor with a sigh, and pads in her slippers to the cupboard in the kitchenette. She splashes liquid from a tall green bottle into her coffee mug. She pours with her back to you, the cupboard door open, half-hiding the bottle.

Last week on the news a Buddhist woman set herself on fire in a public square. Barefoot and wearing a simple white

robe, she knelt and doused herself with kerosene, then lit a
match and carefully folded her hands before her, disciplined
and still in the orange black flames.

Your grandmother is a drunk, your mother says.

The woman on television burned. Your grandmother shift-
ed her legs and listened to your voice. You did a headstand
then, your arms shaking; you brought two store-bought oat-
meal cookies from the tin canister and gave her one to eat,
thinking how later she would remove the cushions from the
couch and unfold the bed, smoothing out the linens and the
pillow with her hands.

Sitting on the floor, you bend against her. Grit from the rug
drives into your forearm. She reaches down and rubs your
hair. You sing a song about a shadow that you learned at
school. Your grandmother claps her hands, toasts you with her
mug, and grins.

Around seven o'clock, her eyes close and her head lolls forward on her neck. Her shoulders slump, her striped cardigan
bunches across her stomach. She breathes softly, smelling of violet perfume and onions and whiskey. You take the mug from her
curled hand and set it on the table beside the tree; you stack her
dishes in the sink. A famous actress's paper face is wrinkling on
the cover of a magazine under your boots. You rescue her, knock
the sand onto the floor where it doesn't matter, and replace the
magazine on the battered vinyl seat of the nearest chair.

You slip on your coat and go around the room snuffing red
candles. You hesitate over the last flame and then you blow
against it, hard, so it vanishes into the wick.

Outside it's dark and cold. Running, breathless, you throw
yourself down into the simple white robe of the snow, and let it
burn your lips and eyelids and burn against the skin of your face.

This story is excerpted from "100 Times I Looked at the Window and Saw
Your Reflection There," a current work-in-progress.

VIOLENCE OF A RACIST DIALOGUE

Fauzia Rafiq

"PUSH," THE WHITE WOMAN in white said, without making eye contact.

"A-mma."

"Don't scream." The woman poked icy fingers into the base of her womb. "Breathe." Her blue gaze flickered past Saleema's face.

"I am b-brea ... ."

"Take a deep breath."

She forced her lungs to take a deep breath. "Th-th-thank you." It felt as if she could not have taken this breath without being told to do so.

"The head is in place." The nurse probed parts of her body. "Everything seems okay."

"Th-thank you, Miss."

"This time when pain comes, push. Don't scream; it wastes your energy."

"O-oka-ah-ha-yaa—" The suddenness of the new surge of pain went to her head, blinding all spots that knew outside. Inside, she was afraid to go. Now when there was nothing but a storm of pain.

I need to be on the outside, my child is about to be born. I have to make sure ... . Yes, you have to Saleema. And stop being afraid. This is the world's most efficient medical system. Technologically advanced. Fully sanitized. Women are giving birth to children all the time. It's part of the normal function of your body. Your body knew how to grow a baby; it knows how to deliver the baby. You just relax. Look at your veins, Saleema, so taut. They are spread over your body like a net of barbed wire. Let go of them. Let them become veins again so your child can pass through.

She began relaxing her veins. Where to start? Hands, fingers, thumb. Arms, shoulders, back of the neck — neck ... . Awaaaa — wooah — haaye — yeyaah —

"Don't scream, push."

The pain raged through her head.

"Push," the woman spat in her face.

"H-ha-oow?" An incredible shame surfaced, taking over the space being emptied by the pain. Despite the growing hold of shame, another scream escaped. No, no. Don't scream, Saleema. The growing body of guilt was towering over her.

Okay, okay.

You are again not doing what you are expected to do, Saleema.

Why am I expected to do things that are so impossible?

You are again trying to put more into it than there actually is. Just to feel good about yourself. The enemy inside knows you are defenseless. No, I am not. How can I not scream when there is so much pain? Why can't I scream? I have to scream, it's too much. You are supposed to, expected to, use that energy into pushing the baby out.

I don't know — how-ahhoo-haaaaa-owwwww —

"Push!" The enemy outside screamed in her ear.

Push. Push.

"Push. Now."

P-push.

Push. Keep Britain Tidy.

She pushed using all her strength. What came out was a broken stream of water from her eyes.

"Push."

C-can't, can't push. Please, what to push, where? How to push?

"Push."

C-can't, please can't. The surge of pain gripped her guts.

"P-U-S-H."

"Ha-how? Don't don't want scream, it happen. Sorry." She reached for the hand of the woman.

Who snatched it away.

I need to hold your hand, oh please, I will push. I just need to hold your hand. I need to hold on to someone, anyone.

She wanted to be with her mother. Her tears came out with sobs. Shameless. Sobs were turning into cries of helplessness.

"Why are you crying?"

Saleema clutched the hem of the nurse's sleeve.

"Don't touch me."

Why not? Another onslaught of pain.

"PUSH."

"How, how t-to push?"

"Bloody 'ell, she doesn't even know how to push," the woman said in absolute disgust.

"Isabelle!"

"Yes, Mary."

"Can you come? She doesn't know how to push."

"Oh, dear." Spoken with the self-righteous horror of an eyewitness to an unspeakable crime.

Why is it so horrible to not know how to push? After all, it's my first experience in childbirth.

"First child," she informed Mary crossly.

"Yes, but luv, there are pre-natal classes. Did you attend them?"

"No."

"Why not?" Mary was primed to milk the cow.

"I — I don't know where they-ey had th-these classes." Oh please leave me alone, I might be a criminal but I am in labour. Prove me guilty later on, this pain is killing me. Please tell me how to push. I will learn fast and — haooow — ahhaaaa —

"Push."

Ha-oo-wo-l —

"Push, now."

Oow-hah-hooo —

"You have wasted this one too. You keep on doing that and it's never going to come out."

"I can push, but I won't." Saleema bluffed, simply to malign Mary.

"What?"

"I will push; one condition."

"Pardon me?" The nurse did not think Saleema was in a bargaining position at all.

"You let me smoke a cigarette."

The nurse looked at her with a blaze in her blue eyes and left the room.

Saleema alone in a deadly room, too white, too clean, too cold.

Yesterday she had been sitting in a deserted house in a poverty-stricken neighbourhood in Blackburn. There, she been patiently waiting for the last five months for the time to come. Alone, with rats, peeling wallpaper, damp broadloom and a black-and-white TV. Day in and day out.

Don't worry. Don't think.

She had entered Britain on a six-month visitor's visa when

she was four months into her pregnancy. Her motive: to have her child, alive and healthy. Away from everyone she knew, amidst total strangers, she felt safe. If I am safe, you are safe, she had told her baby.

She had not tried to find a doctor because of her fear that the authorities might find out and send her home before her baby was born. Nor did she feel it was mandatory for a pregnant woman to see a doctor. She had known many women who had gotten pregnant, borne it for nine months and then had given birth to healthy children at home. She could not recall any problem with any of the women she knew. Only rich women went to doctors all the time.

We are not rich, baby. And I am fine. Don't worry, you will be okay too. You haven't moved for a while. You sleeping in there? Saleema was gripped with fear at such times.

Keep moving in me that I know you are okay.

Her baby floated peacefully inside her.

Yes, you are fine. She caressed her huge tummy knowing her baby needed that touch.

Apart from talking to her baby, her only fulfilling activity was to prepare a suitcase for when the time came.

The time came at two in the morning.

She was pretending to herself she was asleep, as she did every night. Suddenly she felt very wet. She panicked, thinking that her self-control had become so weak that she was urinating in bed. She jumped out as quickly as a nine-month pregnant woman could, and raced towards the toilet. To her satisfaction, she soon realized that her self-control indeed was unscathed. She had 'broken water,' as it was called in an information booklet on pregnancy and childbirth.

If her self-control was intact then everything was fine. She took off her shalwar kameez and changed into her official maternity pants and top, picked up her suitcase full of diapers, toiletries, baby clothes and began descending the stairs.

She had been told by an old woman at the nearby grocery store how important it was to wear maternity pants and tops. Feeling it was an integral part of childbirth, she had spent the last of her savings, excepting a small portion for groceries, to buy those clothes. Cost her one month's living expenses but she went ahead with it. Because she did not want to appear 'ignorant.' Because she had not bought anything except food for months.

She also made it a point to spot the hospital nearest to where she lived. Only two miles. The taxi would not cost more than five pounds, she figured. But now when she checked her left-over change, it came to only three pounds. No problem.

She began walking.

Her new, expensive and uncomfortable maternity pants filled with water, she advanced with her suitcase on the deserted Blackburn street much like the British Indian army: massive, slow and deadly.

After a while, she began having pains. She had been expecting that, but the water was supposed to break after the pains, not before.

Don't worry, don't think, walk.

She had entered the lobby of the hospital just before three. A half-asleep male receptionist saw her protruding womb, the huge suitcase and looked past her. The door closed behind her. She kept walking towards him.

"You on your own, love?"

"Yes," she huffed.

He dived towards his left and pushed the emergency button with full force. Next thing she knew, she was being forced into a wheelchair.

"It okay, can walk, no worry." She did not want to put her entirely wet bottom on the clean British wheelchair.

The attendant pushed her into it and almost raced the chair into the deep of the huge and very clean building

"Push."

"H-ha-haoow, howww?" Saleema howled, the mounting slash of pain cutting through her body.

"I told you not to scream, PUSH."

"How ... ." Tears were making tiny waterways through the clusters of sweat beads on her face and neck.

"Push like you are moving your bowels."

"W-what is moving — moving your balls?"

"Not balls, bowels. Like you have constipation and you want to relieve yourself," she snapped out in disgust. "Fucking stupid Paki," she said between her lips.

Did she call me "fucking stupid Paki"? Why did she call me that? Fucking is okay, it is even used in a friendly way. What about the rest? I am not stupid. But she is right; I am from Pakistan. How did she know?

"How you know me from Pakistan?" She tried to obstruct the path of the flow of mutual hostility.

"For Christ's sake, can you fuckin' push?"

Oh, please, woman, my sister, I am alone here. This is my first baby. I stole it from the enemies. I am panicking for last nine months. Please help me. Accuse me later, prove me guilty later. Please, Amma! I am guilty, punish me some other time, Amma. Do you know this pain is tearing me apart?

You shameless whore, you maligned me, you disgraced our family.

Yes, I am guilty of having sex out of marriage, for wanting to give birth to a 'bastard child,' as you put it. But punish me later. Let me have my baby. I have no one. I need someone. Please Ammaaaaaagh — hoooo — ahaowwwww —

"I am alone." Let me hold your hand, please.

"Why are you alone?"

"I tell tomorrow."

"Why, what did you do, luv?"

Yes, what did you do? Will you face up to it? They banish women who bear children without getting married first. If you are poor, they might even rape you, mutilate you before killing.

"Are you married?" Check-mate.

Saleema's body cringed.

"Another coloured bastard, I bet." Mary murmured to the other woman, walking away from Saleema.

The vulture rose above her, knowing she was vulnerable. Saleema felt a surge of hatred engulfing her heart. Her body turned cold.

All was well.

She did not feel any pain any more.

Her vagina cringed back into place, small, dry, and cold. The baby froze in her womb. She felt a dreadful calm descending over her, creating a blanket of cool, silent and invisible threads. Saleema felt her womb was filled with a huge stone, heavy and unmoving.

Baby, don't turn to stone yet. Hold on, we will make it. Don't worry, just stay moving for a little while more.

From behind that weaving blanket of death, she caught sight of two women with contempt in their eyes. Her focus was Mary.

"Understand Punjabi?" She asked as if there was no child in her womb.

The contempt in the blue eyes faded, giving way to disgust again. The question was not worthy of an answer.

We have a history together, Mary my love. You and me. You enjoyed it a little, I suffered it a lot. You enjoyed it only a little because you did not take from me directly, the riches, the advantage, the privilege. Because you were not privileged enough to come over there. Women came, looked like you. But not you. I have come to you. In your territory. Now you want to take from me, directly. You don't know me except for a name, 'Paki.' I know you. I will not give you what I did not give to my own kind. My baby is not moving in my womb. But she will. Because I will not let you make my baby still.

"Get doctor."

"What?"

"Get doctor. Fucking bitch."

"You stupid ... ."

"Shut filthy mouth, and get doctor. No pains, not right."

Mary's blue eyes flared madness, her colonial instinct aroused.

"Hey, Bell or Isa, get doctor. Now."

Mary was about to swing her arm at Saleema when Isabelle contained her.

Sometime the same morning she heard a man talking to her.

"I am Dr. Dwight."

"Hello."

"What's your name?"

"Saleema."

"Sa-lama, we need you to sign this form. It is to give us permission to operate because you are having problems giving birth naturally."

"Know why?"

"Your pains were weak and then they stopped altogether ... ."

Yeah I would know that, wouldn't I? "Know why?"

"It could be anything. Tension, panic. Listen we don't have much time. The baby might ... ."

"What you want?"

"I suggest we operate."

"Will hurt?"

"Oh no, you won't feel a thing."

"W-will — push?"

"Push? Oh, you would not need that, we will bring the baby out without you pushing it."

"Baby okay?"

"Yes indeed; your baby is fine so far."

"*Acha? Shukar hey.*" Her eyes moistened.

"Pardon me?"

"S-sorry, nothing really?" She was overwhelmed with gratitude. "W-where the — paper?"

When she came to, it was peace all around.

"Congratulations Mrs. er — Miss Sam — Sa — " Someone came towards her.

"Saleema." Drugged, she giggled.

"Congratulations; you have a daughter."

"Where, my — my — ?" She is not crying. Why is she not crying?

A Mary brought a little bundle towards her.

"See, my baby is not stillborn."

"Oh, no, luv. She is healthy as a pup."

The baby was lucid with a head of thick black hair.

My first gift from life, my daughter, mine alone. Saleema brought her to her heart. Thank you for coming to me. She placed the baby on her chest. The baby was warm and did not make any attempt to jerk her body away. They snuggled into each other. Her tiny heart beat was comforting, reassuring. Saleema smiled to her.

What are you called, little one? What would you like to be called?

The little one pushed her knees into Saleema's stomach. It did not hurt at all.

And listen. If you feel people having problems with accepting you as an equal, here or over there, just remember they won't mean anything to me so then they won't have any power over us. So, what would you like to be called?

AN IMPORTANT PERSON

Anne Campbell

Chapter One

PADDOCKWOOD: SHE LOOKS STRAIGHT into the camera. She is not, as I had remembered, standing on a sidewalk facing a house to her right, her side to the camera. No, she stands on the ground behind the wooden sidewalk, her right hand resting on the right side of her stomach, the first finger of her left hand in her mouth touching her upper gum. She is looking straight into the camera.

I put the first finger of my left hand into my own mouth, now rub my upper gum as she does. I find the place where this finger might have rested. Her right hand, my right hand, is on my stomach where, even now, I have a tenderness.

Behind her, thin poplar trees hide an outhouse and further back, beyond the reach of the camera there are small but thick spruce and pine trees. She is eighteen months old and ready.

This photograph was taken in Paddockwood, in the northern part of Saskatchewan, in the middle of Canada. The pine scent is so strong there that one begins to smell it nearly one hundred miles south, and as you drive into the scent your brain cells begin to dance.

Chapter Two

Maria Masich is in a field, it is green; there are mountains on either side of her. The fields are full of stones. Maria is tiny, her features gently arranged; her eyes are deep brown. The field is warm and the grass smells sweet. Maria has a feeling that in someone else might have been a thought: there is such abundance. The smell of grass, warm sun, mountains guarding flat valley land, goat's milk, and cheese, and tomorrow beginning to embroider the engagement cloth; with wine red thread she will make the names Maria Masich and Paul Tomlenovich come together on thick woven cloth.

When we knew her later, when she was our grandmother, she spoke little; she was still tiny and her face was still gentle. Before she died, not even seventy, when she sat with one of her daughters who brushed her long silver hair with granddaughters watching, she often wept.

Maria is in the south of central Europe; her home is fifty miles inland over mountains from the Adriatic sea. She is seventeen years old, the year is 1902. Tomorrow Paul Tomlenovich, who Maria does not know well, will leave for the place they call America. Paul is tall, and strong looking; he will leave with two friends who are also cousins.

Chapter Three

Mary Ellen Kerfoot is quite the young lady. While her manners are well taught she has about her a kindness that is not taught, that is natural to her. Mary Ellen's world is well ordered; her father has, and his father before him had, what is called in north England, a plum job: bank manager of a section of the Leeds and Liverpool Canal. Mary Ellen is somewhat taken aback by young Robert King and his ideas of emigrating to Canada; what, she wonders, is wrong with little Chorley here in England, or the much larger Preston nearby for that matter.

Robert, like his father, works at brick laying and at plastering, but this is not what Robert has in mind for himself. He sees more. He believes that in Canada he will have the opportunity to show the thought that will make him respected in the community. He reads about North America. If Mary Ellen Kerfoot will marry him he will leave for Canada; he will do it. It is the spring of 1909; he hopes by the fall he will be married. He is nineteen, Mary Ellen is twenty-four and steady.

Chapter Four

The memory of a dream or an early silent knowledge: I won't walk. Even though everyone else does, I won't. Laugh they might, but I won't walk. I'll keep safe crawling on all fours. Did this dream really take place or did I make the decision myself, young, conscious and awake. How then, if this decision was made, did the walking start. A drive silent and deeper than the urge to safety.

Walking in London to get my bearings, lost twice in the night. Bearings lost I retrace my path, map in one hand refusing a cab, retracing my path until I find my error and am on track again, back in my temporary London home. I am in London to look for my bearings. I will dream later of a baby speaking and small, unable to walk.

Today in the British Museum wanting a pass to the Reading Room; wanting to get in there. And I do. I have my pass now, I can go there. That knowledge: I want to get into all the places, to be able to get into them. That thought followed fast with: no you don't, not all the places and the memory of my last trip to London, stalled in the underground full of people whose homes I did not want to get into, or even near. I know these homes too well, the ones I left (reading Peter Hall, the British theatre director, grown away, unfortunately, he said, from his bearings); in Torre Annunziata in Italy last year: I took a wrong turn on my way to Sorrento; instead of the scenic coast, it was miles and miles through streets looking like my memories of the houses I lived in as a child. Houses whose only function is to make some kind of refuge until their crowded grey can be left.

The English in me though, is a home, unspeakable: the pleasure of my grandmother not since equalled in person or place. (When did I turn away from that.)

Here in London this room, painted the palest shell peach, almost white, suits me. As soon as the electric heat meter is repaired, or emptied of its load of coins (whichever is causing it to refuse coins) I shall be fine.

Leaving my room today to find the repertory film theatre, I am transfixed by my good fortune. Gerard Depardieu will play in *Trop Belle Pour Toi.* This French man, this plain actor, produces in me a quickening. To say it straight: de-light inside I feel the word moving. De is a beginning, a prefix from Latin meaning undo. Light is being undone inside me; it is moving and I can feel it. Is this feeling in and around me some kind of love, the physicality of goodness. One senses in these people, this actor, my grandmother, that even in their failings they are good. Like

Martin Luther, one thinks, they would "sin boldly" with all their energy and spirit moving. Do they capture love for a moment as it flows in the air, then release it as others experience that love in them. Are they the ones who move love about stirring the world, stirring the earth.

Chapter Five

In the picture that I do not have in front of me, she is dressed in white. Her dark hair not pulled away from her face as usual but brushed into loose round curls. She wears a carefully made white dress; around the neck and wrists of this dress is carefully but generously sewn lace. She wears a veil and carries a prayer book. The wreath that holds the veil in place is white with tiny pale blue flowers wound into it. On her feet are white shoes, she has her first pair of white long stockings. This picture has been taken just before or just after her first communion.

First communion: when was that, for sure not that day, though she did with her body conjure such feelings. Focussing all her attention on the mystery of the host she did, as the altar bell rang, feel something.

Thinking of communion, first or otherwise, remembering a time with her first lover when her body of its own volition, without conscious direction from her, moved forwards or with another one. Such surprise: ah, that's how it works. It's different when the body moves on its own from a place within. Different than when you move under direction.

In another picture taken at the same time her sisters are with her. They are too young for communion but wear special Sunday dresses with matching bonnets their mother has made.

The wooden house in the background is banked with soil; it is her father's way of keeping the family warm through the cold prairie winter in Saskatoon which is just south of the pine scent.

Next door live Mr. and Mrs. Fisher with their dog, Tippy. They have a piano and the idea is that she and the oldest of the two sisters will learn to play it.

Chapter Six

Maria's brothers are as handsome as she is lovely; they have thick dark hair which will turn white before they are thirty. They will leave for America later than Paul Tomlenovich; they will wait for word on the settlement there.

Maria believes in Paul Tomlenovich; she does not know fear. Everything is taken care of, ordered in the farm yard by the family and beyond that in the fields and mountains by God. Maria is a bud, a worker bee, a flower closed. She is in her place in the world, and everything has a place. She does not doubt. There are no questions.

Chapter Seven

Mary Ellen Kerfoot's father is a Bank Inspector on a section of the Leeds and Liverpool Canal; his father before him was as well the keeper of the canal. Her home is plain but substantial, well constructed.

Mary Ellen is even tempered, her body and moods self regulating, and now she finds she has young Robert King on her mind. She knows he thinks of bettering himself; she believes this is unnecessary, that the order of things is fine. But she believes also that this will do no harm and may be a good sign. She understands that he wants to rise above his place in Chorley, rise right out of Chorley to be transported to Canada. Robert King wants to be an important person.

CARTOONS

Clare Braux

IN MONTREAL are many hilly streets, leafy trees. A greystone house on a shady dead end, artist's studio on the top floor: a famous artist in his white-walled studio fashioned with many-fingered hands out of acrylic gobs the Garbo of his dreams. Fervent, anguished work. You, his wife, shared his greystone if not his dreams. The life to which you were accustomed. What happened to him at the university where he taught & monkeyed around? His paintings clouded, darkened. He stormed. He threw you out.

You hive to the bus station with your luggage. You're thirty-seven, no spring chicken. You swallow hard, compose yourself, scrutinize the faces in the bar. Life is amassing evidence: what place is assigned to you in the universe?

Next to you, a middle-aged couple laughing. He's balding, a pigtail nevertheless. She a brushcut. You ask if they think the right brain is different from the left. They shrug in irritation. Their four dark eyes continue to peer at the screen. Most patrons peer at the top right-hand corner of the bar, watching cartoons of proto-humans chasing each other with hammers at a frenetic pace. Cruel little brown creatures & little green creatures fleeing to oblivion beyond the screen. Letters explode: rat-a-tat-tat! TV sound turned off & rock music blaring from hidden radio. You feel numb.

Crowds in the station through transparent curtains: people's feet walking, their minds on Exit signs. He was hit over the head, his right brain damaged.

You feel nothing. Fighting back tears.

You were called hysterical.

Your bus is leaving.

Sitting by a window, scraps of memory on the edge of your mind: your parents were old-fashioned shock-troops; fixed in self-denial, they kept faith with a psychopathic God.

Maximum 50 km

Polk Realty Co. — The Friendly Folk — Votre Ami

Surveillance Aerienne

You took up research in your teens. To figure out the circumstances in which you were placed: artless filing clerk dating a student at the university. He wanted to be a dentist to make a lot of money for his future family. You didn't think you could fit yourself into this future family, but he was a great french-kisser. Almost as good as the German DP you met at an artists' orgy. Artists are pretty good at sex. They try harder.

Chez Denise Beauty Salon

Auberge Qui Vive

1500 tons — Dumptruck. You are dumbstruck.

You love the steady hiss of the fat rubber wheels on the wet highway. Who are you anyway, a woman alone? They also serve who only stand & wait. Who said that? What does it mean? Lies, all lies. Your woman friend in Vancouver, an activist, says we wait no more. A pale man from Cobourg, Ontario, is sitting beside you. He tries, driving through this lovely countryside, to convert you to the Jehovah's Witnesses. Don't you see, he says, Jesus is sad to see all our young people drug-rock freaks. He's dead, you tell him. Do you think the right brain is different from the left brain, because I have been a victim?

Maximum 100 km

Chez Kim's — Yogourt Glacée

Ouest —

Your research foundered for a while. Your young woman's circumstances led you into many dark doorways, hidden copses beside highways, the back seats of moving cars. A physical awakening. Some kind of electric charge went down your legs, up into your thorax, centered around your 'Down-There' as your mum called it. The opposite sex, your daddy belatedly said, will be researching your female contours. Never yield an inch. Or else!

Welcome to Hawkesbury — Your Home Away from Home!

Bar Nun Beds — All Original Materials

On a gas station attendant's T-shirt: Loose Girls Tightened Here.

The Ottawa bus station is airier, boxier. TV cartoons alive with ruthless clay parliamentarians hurling mud at each other. Whack! Bump! Travellers mesmerized, gaping. You sit like patience on a monument, smiling at grief. Who said that?

A greystone house on a shaded cul-de-sac in Montreal, a leafy crescent. Famous artist, a hesitant man, & his colleague, his best friend, hurled insults at each other. Who is the greatest of us all?

You were under his roof, under his orbit, a hesitant man can be ferocious. You loved him still. Ah, love, that precious, so rare a thing, pressed at your heart still, when you looked at him. A life to which you were accustomed. You were called hysterical whenever you opened your mouth.

Nova Scotia bus driver enters the station. Anybody for the far east? he yells, grinning. You are going west.

90 km maximum

Falling Rocks

You sit towards the back of the bus to get the feel of the moving coach. Vaulted, shiny ceiling, flashing windows that superimpose on the landscape a mirror image of the opposite lane. Crossing the country in a tranquil mood. Keep calm, this may change you forever. You were told you'd be an artist when you grew up. You didn't really want to grow up. You just wanted to get away from home where a stranger at the door caused panic in the house.

You left home to be free of oppression. But you got scared walking alone at night, & walking alone in afternoon parks gave you standing hairs on the nape of your neck. Cleaning his brushes in his basement you felt safe if not ecstatic.

Well's Chicken Wings — Well Come Inn

Speed Limit 60

Angry cartoon creatures on TV at the Happy Hour in Toronto. Mindless spacemen warring for territory on the small screen. Military formations with coarse gestures. Vicious. Savage. Splat! Pow! Bang!

In the crowded bar, this middle-aged man with muzzy dark eyes offers you a seat at his table. You're not bad looking even at this advanced age. You don't like men judging your appeal from nothing but the nice hollows in your cheeks in dim light anymore. You hold subversive opinions which you treasure. They would peter out his peterkin.

The advantage of having brains is that you can entertain yourself over a beer. Today, your brain is a mindless refrain: he was hit on the head, an accident to his right brain, his ambitious left brain ticking, paintings became sensational: violent sex, swashbuckling colours. He developed impotence. You were not hysterical, you were feeling feelings not connected to anything. In distress, you look around you. Life is amassing evidence. People's eyes dart about, slide away. What defect of spirit divides us? Concentrate, you tell yourself.

You were an artist in your youth. You painted in oils, then in acrylic when it became the rage. You took courses at the university yourself, with young men accredited art teachers who had studied the New York School reproductions. They were a jolly bunch with leapfrog eyes. Explained hard-edge to you. Gave you earnest looks. Lowered their voices, their eyes from your face to your bosom. Hard-ons on their minds. Your earnest questions dismissed.

The better to see you with, my dear, said the famous painter, unzipping. Women artists make the best models, he said, they understand what is required. The female body is divine. Yours is exceptionally fine. Marry me. A famous artist's wife a desirable estate; a wife is cheaper than a model. He dressed you in a black velvet bikini. Stand like a statue, good girl! Don't move! That's perfect, hush.

He out-talks his envious friends. Depersonalized language. Where does that leave you? Must you always be trying to fathom his needs?

Here's the bus
Deer crossing 6 kilometers
Jesus is coming!

Famous artists at first can give you sizzling orgasms; they have long blue fingers, their left brain, right brain working together. Your mind fizzes, throat secretes aphrodisiac, ears go deaf, tuned to your inner power dive. Down-There erupts in tremors that shudder your thighs & numb your extremities.

Later when you danced — dancing is a very ancient religious experience — with him you'd get a charley horse.

Crossing 48th Parallel
Sault Ste. Marie.
Thunder Bay. Crossing space-time.

In bus stations men & young boys sit hypnotized before video screens. You stand behind them & watch brutal hobo figures exterminate miniature robots in empty arenas. Their violent trek to nowhere. Crash! Blast! You look out the windows at the scattered aluminium-sided houses.

Your Vancouver friend, an ecologist, says eco is Greek for house & logy means science. The science of houses. What houses you. Your habitation & abiding place, your native home, this earth of majesty, this little Eden built by Nature for herself, this precious stone set in the universe. Who said that?

Maximum (missed it)
Soft Shoulders
Singing Creek

You do not fly. A passive peregrine you progress across the country according to bus schedules. A feeling of comfort, a sense of safety in the swerving, rocking motion of a speeding cross-continent bus. For days you sit & watch stretch after stretch of pointillist forest, forest fullness, lakes & rivers glimmering through spruce, birch, pine & alder, maple, tamarack & aspen. The prairie spaces bald & naked scream down the sky. Where is your place in all of this?
    Rumpelstiltskin Restaurant
    Well Drilling — 10 kilometers
    Watch for Grimm's —

Bus depots along your westward route: a home away from home. Your friend says ecology studies the relation of living organisms to their environment, their communities, their households. Famous artist wasn't often home. At the university, a hesitant but popular teacher. Other models posed for him. At least once in your bed. In his dead-end house. The awful power of his desire, he said. Where does that leave you? Is it pity you should be feeling?

Your money is running out. You work as a waitress in Winnipeg. For a month you put up with the boss' pinching your hips. He smiles & winks at you. A hip man. Has trouble with the awful power, too. When you object, he gives you the rabid eye. You recognize this man. His name is violence.

Life is amassing evidence. Wittgenstein once said: The zeitgeist of these times operates to produce a cartoon bluntness in social behavior.

Your artist got hit on the head with a mallet wielded by his best friend, his best rival in ambition. In great pain at first, his deformity didn't show. Began storming & gnashing his teeth. His gestures became coarse & he couldn't satisfy his wife. She noticed a swelling on his left brain, his mustache drooping. His right hand saluted with an orgastic military snap. His wife began to duck. People said she was hysterical. He threw her out.

On your prairie schooner, on your whirlwind grand tour of Canada, you are trying to connect. You are trying to feel yourself alive.

Well Drilling — 6 km
See O. Weill's Animal Farm
Grimm's — Coming Up —

You haunt the bars in Regina & Saskatoon. Asking questions. A tall man in a Stetson & yellow cowboy boots sits next to you at the Peter Pan Bar. You interrupt his cartoon viewing: psychopathic pilots tank-killing over dangerous terrain. Splat! Bang! You ask him if he thinks the left brain is different from the right. He gets up, swallows his scotch & strides away, cracking his crop. Casting you forever into the female class.

People said he was a famous artist. He picked a drunken fight with his best friend: who will win the award? His best friend was a not-so-famous artist full of rancor. Famous artist threw his model out.

Here You Are! Grimm's Fun Park! Children Welcome!
No Speeding. Radar.

In a hotel lobby in Edmonton two dozen women, men & children sit mesmerized, staring at the TV set in right-hand corner. Left-brain-mad humanoids dispatch spaced-out enemies in star-wars cartoon choreograph. Splat! Bang! Boom! A father turns & slaps a small boy sitting next to him pedaling his feet.
  Speed Limit 55
  Swift's Take-Out — Snappy Snacks

In Calgary your bus crosses the Bow River at breakneck speed. You take in a movie to calm your spirit. Goldilocks & the Three Musketeers: three men get turned out of town, ride lunatic in the moonlight, curse the universe. At dawn rape a blonde in the next town, curse the universe.
  In the bus terminal, a young girl in black sings solo, her guitar full of flying silverfish & rainy weekends.
  Falling Rocks
  Slow —

❖

Someone jostles you as you enter the Vancouver bus depot. A tight squeeze. Your severed feelings begin to surface, your eyes brim over. You halt, at your wit's end. You visit the Museum of Anthropology wearing crocodile mirrored glasses. You open long shallow drawers. Stone arrowheads 25,000 years old. Where was your face before you were conceived?
  In the conservatory a distinguished grey-haired man with a cane sits opposite you on an apple-green painted bench under a ficus tree. He stares at you, his arm shoulder-high, his

hand on the canehead. You look away. Look back. He is still staring, wriggling in the oddest way. His dark blue suit wrinkling & unwrinkling over his body. Something pops out between his legs, startling bit of white against his dark suit.

Anon — a woman — once said:
I sometimes think we're best to weep
Than sing the praises of hu-man-ity.

You climb a hilly street with leafy trees in West Van. Your friend is not at home. You continue climbing. A marmalade cat crosses your path. It has a torn ear. Your memory grinds in its rusted crib.

Yourself as a child. You once tortured a small animal. Its eyes looking at you. A cat your family had. A cat with yellow eyes. Your mother would fondle its long body, its ears. You & your brother tortured it. Heat rises behind your ears. You have trouble swallowing. The path is steep & you are choking from the tightness of your exertions.

You reach the top of the rise. A leafy lone tree leans towards you as you lean against it. Emily once said: Far safer — meeting external Ghost — Than Unarmed — One's self encounter — In lonesome Place. You massage your throat. Slowly you begin to know your shame, your stabbing self-hate. Your banal story ends here.

You look up. You see the ocean,
the sea of Aphrodite.

You open wide your eyes. A gold moon gallops past ragged clouds, bursts into gales of laughter, dancing on the waves, on the sea's bosom; the threefold moon-Goddess shakes with laughter. You feel alive. You remember the artist you once were: your big canvasses, colour on colour, sheets of colour, walls of discourse, the dialectic so long denied. The canvasses warp & bulge, they begin to shout: passivity is a form of guilt. You awake into the silence around you: this precious Time, this Space of majesty, this your Life.

You regress, reprogress across the country. You love the white noise of the fat rubber wheels on the wet macadam. You hear singing. A voyage long & long.

In patience — in affectionate regard — you will speak — a force of phrasing — to establish the covenant — that was never acknowledged — between him & you.

You walk Montreal hilly streets. Greystone on cul-de-sac crescent. Late October leaves, yellow & sere, a fallen windblown vortex of leaves tickles your cheek. Air is fresh, bracing. Famous artist with hidden affliction has normal face. Paints colour-clashing cartoons of nude women gagged & bound & hanging from trees. Has nightmares. Periodic violent outbursts. His stifled right brain past recollection.

Irrevocably, your cross-country journey has changed you. Irrevocable decision: to feel yourself alive. Your unpainted images, your unborn art, your unlived life, you.

You throw yourself out. Of your own accord.

LEARNING WELSH

Gayla Reid

THERE ARE MOMENTS in August when the wind comes in from the west, bringing with it the cold dust off the plains. Today such a wind is blowing across the town and into the convent yard, where it seethes around the laundry block and catches at the pieces of nun's attire, starched and stretched out on low platforms by the tanks.

It nibbles at the little cuffs worn by postulants, then it takes on the gamps, the big bibs worn by the nuns.

For a moment, the wind dies down.

Now it's back.

This time, a willy-willy, a small dust storm, is making straight for the platforms. It scoops up the cuffs and the gamps. It carries them away, across the yard, over the fence, over the roof of the presbytery next door, right over to the park on the other side of the road.

Where it dumps them.

I see all this and so does Sister Winifred. So do Maria Dwyer and Rita O'Toole.

We are having our English honours class in the sun, behind the hedge.

We are all very senior girls, most responsible.

Sister Winifred looks around the yard, a small, hopeful

glance. Some other nun, surely, has seen the willy-willy lift up the intimate pieces of clothing and carry them off to the public world?

But there is no-one in sight.

Something will have to be done.

You can't leave nunly objects lying around in the town's central park, there to become objects of scorn and wonder to passing non-believers. This is a university town; non-believers are everywhere.

Her face, bright pink, is looking into mine.

I am unable to move, totally at a loss.

But Maria Dwyer and Rita O'Toole are on their feet.

"I'll go, Sister," they say, in turn. "I'll go." "I'll go."

Off they dash, not even stopping to fetch their hats and gloves, although nobody leaves the convent grounds without hats and gloves, not ever.

This is the first time I have been alone with her since I made my move.

I look at Sister Winifred. She looks at me. Dust blows into our faces.

Did it really happen like this or do I exaggerate?

This is the image: the willy-willy is whisking away the medieval clothes and Sister Winifred and I are face to face.

This is the emotion that accompanies the image: It is as if, in a dream, I am walking naked down the street. The same trapped humiliation.

Sister Winifred has a university degree — a most unusual thing, amongst our nuns. She is tremendously overworked. On Saturday nights, when we have films in the rec hall, she huddles by the projector, correcting papers by the dim light.

I think she is too earnest.

Yet here it is: I am craning my neck for a glimpse of Sister

Winifred's face as she comes back from communion (a voyeur of the holy, intimate moment). I am careful to arrive at Latin class early, so that I can sit at the top of the table. That way, when she has to move her arms to write on the blackboard, I can look up under her gamp.

If I'm lucky I get a glimpse of her neck, naked and interesting.

I can also see, tucked up under her gamp, a pocket where she keeps her fountain pen and pencils. And her act beads. Act beads are little beads, usually half a dozen, which you can push up and down. You push one up when you've committed an act. An act is something you don't like doing, but you do it and you offer it up.

Latin is at eight-thirty in the morning. By that time Sister Winifred has already notched up two beads.

What has she forced herself to do?

There are lots of things one can offer up, she tells us. You can put salt on your jam all through Lent.

She doesn't come from round here. If she did, I'd know what her real name had been before she entered. Lots of the nuns are Old Girls. Some have sisters at school. Rita O'Toole's sister is a nun. In real life she was Eileen O'Toole. Rita is going to enter, too.

To know the real name of a nun — we all want this.

I make inquires about her, but nobody knows. Some say she comes from Queensland, and went to the convent at Brisbane. Some say she comes from down the coast, dairy country. That her father is a grocer, a dairy farmer, a doctor.

At least I can look up Saint Winifred. Patron saint of the Welsh.

Saint Winifred was a seventh-century Welsh virgin. The son of a neighbouring prince wanted to marry her, but she had dedicated herself to the bridegroom of her soul. Enraged at being turned down, the prince pursued her as she fled for sanctuary. He caught her and chopped off her head. At the point where her head touched the ground, a fountain sprang up.

Sister Winifred would not have chosen this name. When she became a nun, the name was given to her. She herself would have heard it for the first time during the dedication ceremony.

In our English honours class, we are specializing in Gerard Manley Hopkins. Maria Dwyer and Rita O'Toole are keeping notes. Inscape, they write. Duns Scotus, they write. How do you spell that? Maria Dwyer wants to know. She really is a dunce, she'll be lucky to get a pass, much less honours.

I'm not taking notes. (All that stuff is in the introduction to the book.) I'm waiting for Sister Winifred to read out loud.

I'm waiting to see her face go open and serious as she reads "The Windhover." When she reads she is, I know, speaking only to me. Maria Dwyer and Rita O'Toole are just along as chaperones.

"He didn't write a word for seven years," Sister Winifred explains. "He was a poet before he joined the Jesuits. But when he was in the seminary he gave it all up. Then his rector said that he could write again and 'The Wreck of the Deutschland' came bursting out of him."

"It was," she said, "as if all that poetry had been building up inside of him, under such tremendous pressure."

"Like oil," I say.

"Yes, yes," she says, relieved. "Like oil."

And smiles.

At me.

Maria Dwyer can't stand Hopkins. "What's that wreck thing

supposed to be about? A bunch of nuns going down in the drink?"

Maria acts as if this were a great joke.

Maria says: "When Winnie gets going on that stuff it's like she's taking off all her clothes in front of us."

She makes me anxious, Maria Dwyer.

Sister Winifred's face has become daring and determined, like somebody about to dive off the high board (or at least this is how I imagine they'd look; you can't see their faces, way up there).

"Blue-bleak embers," she says. She has committed herself now, she looks a little desperate. "Fall, gall themselves, and gash gold-vermillion."

Ever so quietly, Maria Dwyer sniggers.

In Latin class, I get Maria Dwyer's basic exercises by mistake.

Maria Dwyer has taken the sentence, The boy who loves the master is good, and translated it as, *Puer, quem magister amat, bonus est.* Which means, The boy, whom the master loves, is good.

Trust Maria Dwyer to get it back to front.

Sister Winifred has corrected it. In the margin, she has written, for Maria Dwyer's instruction: *Quem* - Acc. as Obj. to *amat.*

She even fixes it for her: *qui magistrum.*

Not that that will do dim Dwyer any good.

"He was in a seminary in the Welsh hills," Sister Winifred says. "Studying theology. He wanted to learn Welsh, he was drawn to the music of it. But the rector said he could not approve unless it was for the purpose of labouring among the Welsh, to convert them."

As she is saying this, I am watching her hands. She doesn't

use any hand cream, of course. Her hands are cracked and dry and there are fine residues of chalk sitting in the lines.

"But it wasn't, you see. It was for the poetry."

Now she is looking right at me.

"Maybe Welsh could have made his poetry better," I say. "And if his poetry was for the greater glory of God... ." I trail off.

"Do you think it was the wrong decision?" Sister Winifred asks me. I can feel some need coming from her.

"The poetry is what survived," I argue.

I am into this now, I have to keep going. "It serves the greater glory of God even though Hopkins himself is long dead."

(Where did that come from? I am out of my depth.)

"But the rector said," she replies.

With this, I feel her going away from me. Literally, I see her shrink back into her habit.

I understand what she means: the vow of obedience, the chain of command. If the rector decrees that black is white, so be it.

I do not accept.

"He should have learned Welsh," I insist. "He should have."

I am horrified to hear my voice as it comes out. Shaking, near tears.

At benediction I cry into my mantilla. I keep my head bowed, and hope nobody can see. I believe I am weeping for Hopkins, the poet, denied his opportunity to learn the lovely language of Welsh.

I become more critical of her, more nervous.

He was sent to a parish in Liverpool, in an industrial area, a poor district.

I see him walking down the street in his soutane — timid, frail, with soft skin that never sees the sun. He comes to a smithy's. The fire burns and the big smithy raises those powerful arms and the horses stand in massive nakedness.

We have a grey shire horse at home on the property. He doesn't work any more. Now we use the Ferguson tractor. He lives in the house paddock, this big horse, gone at the knees.

"Somebody should send him on his way," my brother says, fooling around. "Off to the knackers. Glue, anyone? "

"Leave him be," my father says.

I watch my father go over to him, sink his head into the horse's neck. My father puts his arms around the old horse and caresses him.

"Stupid old sook," my brother says, embarrassed.

Something happens. Rita O'Toole's sister is moved to our convent. On visiting Sundays Rita is allowed to sit in the front parlour with her sister, Sister Ambrose, who tells her this: she was a postulant with Sister Winifred.

Postulants tell each other everything, Rita O'Toole says, happily. Rita has a vocation, she can't wait.

Sister Winifred entered the convent, Sister Ambrose says, because of the Kempsey floods.

She was at home from uni, and looking after a neighbour's family. The mother had just had another baby and wasn't well. So Sister Winifred, not yet a Sister, whose real name is Gertrude, goes to the farm to help out. Takes care of the baby, feeds the kids, so the mother can get better.

Down comes the flood, one of those huge floods of the early Fifties that took all before them.

The mother and the kids drive out in the Dodge. Sister Winifred is following in her father's Austin, with the crib in the back. (There are so many kids there's not enough room in the Dodge.)

The mum and kids get out okay, but when Sister Winifred is driving the Austin through the last creek, she is swept away. The car sinks.

Sister Winifred escapes. Ends up high in a gum tree, clutching the baby and watching the water swirl higher, higher. She makes a solemn vow.

God, if you let this baby live, I will enter the convent. I will become a bride of Christ.

I have lots to think about.

Gertrude, her real name is Gertrude.

Saint Gertrude was a Cistercian nun who entered the convent at the age of five. Cistercians take a vow of silence, they are an enclosed order. At the age of twenty-five, the spouse of her soul revealed Himself to her and favoured her with remarkable visions. She died consumed by love rather than by disease.

I decide I prefer Saint Winifred's story. On the lam from a love-starved suitor. Up and down the steep hills of Wales, she would have given him a run for his money. It would have been an adventure, before the capture, the beheading.

And that tale about being up a gum tree during the Kempsey floods. Surely she would have said, If you let *me* live, I will enter. She would have known that a baby, baptized and innocent, can shoot right into heaven, no questions asked. Why even bargain about a baby? If for some reason it hadn't already been baptized, she could have scooped up some flood water and done it herself, right there.

But Sister Winifred — Gertrude — how was it for her that day up a gum tree, watching the flood waters rise?

She is wearing a wide, polished cotton skirt and a white blouse. (What colour hair does she have?) Fighting her way out of the car, quickly quickly, get the baby out of the nice warm crib, and hang on, for Christ's sake hang on. The water is fast and cold even though it's February. It smells of mud and putrefaction.

The floodwaters have spread out across the paddocks so that everything is changed, completely changed.

It tells her that the unimaginable does happen. Only days ago, cows moved along their usual paths by the river, and it seemed as if things would stay like that forever, that that was the problem.

Too late to think about it now. Forget the tracks by the river, forget the slow movement of cows. All that exists today is water, and terrified stock, bellowing in fear, being carried along. Dead stock, dead chooks, miserable still-alive chooks, lounge chairs, sheets of corrugated iron, kero tins, tractor parts, nighties, meat-safes, mattresses, dead wallabies, baling wire. Towards evening, something dark and wet and solid goes by. It could be a pile of blankets; it could be a human corpse.

It could be a time for rash promises.

What kind of God would hold you to a deal made up a gum tree, *in extremis?*

Sister Winifred advises us to learn some of the poetry off by heart, so we will be able to quote it in the exam.

I learn the passages about the falcon: how he rebuffed the big wind. There are falcons at home; I have seen their swift flickering. I know how they soar on flat wings.

Rita O'Toole learns that poem about a nun taking the veil: I have asked to be where no storms come.

Maria Dwyer doesn't remember to learn anything.

Maybe Rita O'Toole just made up that bit about the baby. Maybe Rita O'Toole's sister, Sister Ambrose, made it up. Maybe Sister Winifred herself made the whole thing up. Maybe postulants pass their limited leisure time telling each other tall stories.

"Is the windhover a particular kind of falcon?" I demand.

Sister Winifred looks worried. "I'm not sure," she replies. "I think he might have invented it. Because of the way the falcon hovers in the wind. It is an image of Christ, he was referring to Christ," she adds, on firmer ground.

Is it the name of a bird or isn't it? She's supposed to be the teacher.

"He said it was the best thing he ever wrote," Sister Winifred says.

She is reaching out to me, in conciliation.

I do not manage to smile.

"They sent him to Ireland," Sister Winifred says. "To teach. He felt cut-off from his friends and the countryside that inspired his poetry. 'I am in Ireland now,' he wrote. 'I am at a third remove.'

"This was when he produced his terrible, desolate sonnets," she continues. "He talks about how he has had to 'hoard unheard.' "

Sister Winifred cannot leave this alone.

"In his whole life," Sister Winifred says, "only six people knew he even wrote poetry."

Maria Dwyer is picking her nose.

"He felt his poems were cries like dead letters to a loved one."

I don't know what to say.

"When he was in Ireland," Sister Winifred goes on, "he went to a gathering at a house in Dublin and Yeats was there. The two had nothing to say to one another."

She looks to me.

"Imagine," Sister Winifred says, "the two greatest poets in the same room together and they said nothing. They did not exchange a single word."

I wish this were for Maria Dwyer and Rita O'Toole as well as for me.

It is only two weeks until the end of second term and I get sick. I lie in my bed in the dormitory surrounded by books. I cannot stop now. Next term I sit for the exams that will take me to uni, where there will be people I can talk to.

Sister Winifred visits.

Our school has been doing better in the Leaving Certificate ever since Sister Winifred arrived. And I am their best bet this year; I am going to show them that convent girls can do just as well as those brainy kids from the state schools.

"Study, study," Sister Winifred says. "*Ora et labore.*"

"Don't study too hard," she adds.

She is jumpy, uneasy with me.

I lie back and shut my eyes. She goes away.

As soon as she's gone I open my eyes. I feel I've made a mess of something.

I am neither praying nor working, but thinking about Sister Winifred. Not as Sister Winifred, but as Gertrude. (I wish she had a decent real name.)

I should be coming down with her out of the hills, after we'd spent the morning watching the birds.

Her hair would be windblown. She would be leaping from boulder to boulder.

I would have shown her the small falcons.

She would have said, "Ah, bright wings."

One of the old nuns dies. This is the mother house for the order in Australia. The old nuns come back here at the end of their lives. You see them sitting on the balcony in the cloister.

Sister Winifred says, "The earthly circle is closing but the heavenly circle is widening."

There is a special requiem mass mid-morning. The bishop is coming. Everyone goes, except for the lay sisters, who are working in the dining-room, getting the midday meal.

They're all in the chapel, watching the heavenly circle widening.

I am in the dormitory and there is nobody around.

I get up, put on my slippers and dressing-gown, and go down the corridor. Past the pictures of the Old Girls. The most famous Old Girls of all — a novelist who writes about people who commit adultery; a Communist — aren't there.

Down the corridor and to the left and you come to the cloister. It is consecrated ground; only nuns are allowed to go there. Except for the priest. If a nun is sick, a priest carrying the host in the ciborium goes into the cloister. A nun hurries ahead of him, ringing a bell.

It is a mortal sin for anyone else to go into the cloister.

But nobody is around. I put one foot, two feet over the line, and then I am speeding down the corridor. Around the corner, I know, there's a row of three cells. Sister Winifred's is the one with the window facing the tennis court. (Rita O'Toole's intelligence.)

I pass one cell, then another, and here, with the door open, is hers. It must be. Yes, there's the window.

There is a bed. It's made, of course. There's an indentation where her body lies.

A table, not a real desk. She corrects papers late at night, prepares lessons. Here she opens my exercise book, sees my handwriting, reads what I have written.

A kneeler, with one prayerbook on it, open at the Litany of the Saints.

No drawers. Where does she keep her underwear? Perhaps they have some communal cupboard down the hall. Her Moddess. Because she must.

But on a peg behind the door, there's a long white flannel nightgown. I hold it in my hands. I bring it up to my cheek.

I lie down in the indentation on the bed and look up at the ceiling. The bed is harder than the ones in the dormitory. Which aren't anything to write home about.

I have to leave a message for her, a sign that I've been here. She has to know.

I get up and look around for a pen. Nothing. Her pen would be in the pocket of her habit, up under her gamp. I've seen the pen-holder when I've looked at her neck.

Back I go, down the hall, retracing my steps, down the stairs, to the right, out of the cloister. To the dormitory, for a pen.

Then I run back, along the corridor, into the cloister, all the way to her cell. Feeling a bit faint.

I look at the litany of saints. *Sancta Maria Magalena, Ora pro nobis. Sancta Agnes, Ora pro nobis. Sancta Caecilia, Ora pro nobis. Sancta Agatha, Ora pro nobis. Sancta Anastasia, Ora pro nobis.*

I write in the margins of the litany the one word of Welsh I have memorized from the introduction to the Hopkins poetry book: *cywydd*.

I believe that it means a poem. I don't know how this word might sound in someone's mouth. I do not attempt to pronounce it. I see the letters silently, in my mind.

After I have written this undeniable message in her prayer book, I lie down again.

I stare up at the ceiling, and cross my hands over my chest, as if preparing to die.

I think about the falcons at home, hovering, tail-feathers fanned.

I think about the wedgies, hunting wallabies, rabbits. Making do with a dead sheep instead, ripping it apart.

Wedge-tailed eagles, eight-foot wing span. Lounging in the thermals, then swooping in a long, lanky sideways dive after prey.

Has Sister Winifred ever seen them mating, in May? The male coming down upon the female, then pulling out at the last moment, his wings half closed.

The female turning on her back, in mid-air, showing him her talons.

The pair of them soaring high on upswept wings, sailing out across their countryside, looping and turning in the big wind as they shriek their intentions to the whole wide sky.

That is what I would show her, if she came home with me in the holidays.

I would lead her across the dry yellow grass and up into the hills, among the granite boulders. Get her to look up at the winter shafts of air, the birds. Show her — make her realize — that it was a matter of life and death.

But she will never go anywhere outside the convent. She has chosen. She has been chosen.

Beauty Incarnate and the Supreme Singer

(For Oscar Wilde)

Suniti Namjoshi

"Look," said the wren to the iris. "I'm not a nightingale. You're not a rose. But we too have a tale to tell, a song to sing, that sort of thing."

The iris was startled. She hadn't noticed the wren. She was engaged in letting the sun shine through her translucent skin, shaping and concentrating so that she glowed blue, with here and there a deep purple, modulating into darkness. "What do you mean?" she said.

The wren was taken aback. She had thought that her meaning was clear. "Well," she began, "you are not Beauty Incarnate like the rose —"

"I am beautiful!" The iris was irritated.

"Well, yes, that's just what I was getting at," replied the wren. She hadn't meant to annoy the iris, just the reverse. "What I was saying was that I am not a Supreme Singer, and you, of course, are not a rose —"

"Don't want to be a rose!" snapped the iris.

"No, of course not," soothed the wren. "You are not a rose, but you are very beautiful, and I would very much like to sing your praises."

"Oh. Go ahead then, but I'm busy at the moment."

"It's not that simple," the wren explained. "Don't you remember? The nightingale sang all night long —"

"*Not* all night," said the iris firmly.

The wren ignored the interruption. "— with her heart pressed against a thorn —"

"I haven't any thorns." The iris gazed down her long, green stalk, her smooth green leaves, with a certain smugness.

"— and bled to death," the wren finished triumphantly.

"Why?" asked the iris, jolted at last into proper awareness.

"Because she was suffering. In order to sing you have to suffer," the wren told her.

"But you're not suffering, are you?"

"I am a little," replied the wren modestly.

"Are you going to bleed?" By now the iris was thoroughly alarmed.

"Not if you're nice."

"I am nice. I'm very nice," the iris assured the wren earnestly. "And please, you don't have to sing my praises. I don't really care for poetry much."

"Now you're being cruel."

"No, no. I am not cruel. And I am not a rose!" the iris protested. But the wren wasn't listening. She had already begun her plaint.

BETTER HOMES AND GARDENS

Helen J. Rosta

HURRICANE HUGO HAS STRIPPED the trees of Spanish moss, exposing the azaleas to the sun and Steve, the tour guide, is worried. "The sun kills them," he tells the group.

Brenda nods. At home, she has potted azaleas so she's seen the withered leaves and shrivelled buds of plants scalded by the sun. She imagines that blight here at Magnolia Plantation.

"In the spring when the azaleas bloom, the garden's breathtaking. Now, I don't know what will happen —," Steve's voice breaks off.

The brochure from Brenda's hotel features Magnolia's spring garden, ancient moss-draped trees sheltering azalea bushes which, brilliant with colour, are massed along old brick-lined paths and around the edges of small lakes, their hues of rose and pink and pearly-white glimmering in the black waters of the lakes, lakes which were once plantation rice fields.

"Flowerdale, the formal garden," Steve says, slipping into his tour guide voice, "dates back to the seventeenth century. It was constructed at the same time as the first house."

"House/home." When she and Mike bought their house, their first and the one where they still live, the realtor didn't talk of houses; he talked of homes, showed them homes, sold them a home. He was selling a refuge — a place of warmth, comfort and affection, a family home. Family home. Words, Brenda thinks wryly, can be deceptive.

In any case, the great plantation houses, the Boone Halls and the Magnolia mansions, surely were meant to embody more than the realtor's concept of home. While they may have been, Brenda concedes, places of warmth, certainly of comfort (and perhaps of affection) she regards them as Family statements, the country seats of the Boones and Draytons transported to the New World.

"What happened to the first house?" she asks.

"I was coming to that." Brenda thinks she detects a note of irritation in Steve's voice.

"The house survived the Revolution. It burned accidentally thirty years later." Steve resumes his tour guide tempo. "The Drayton family was one of the richest in the colonies, so rich that in 1798, an Englishman by the name of John Davis mentioned its wealth in a book he wrote. 'These people,' he said, 'never move but in a carriage, and are always attended by their Negroes to fan them with a peacock feather.' "

"Way to go," the stout man with the red face guffaws.

There are a few chuckles. Steve smiles and continues. "Royal Judge John Drayton was born here in 1715. When he died, he was the wealthiest man in the colony. He left one hundred thousand pounds — a lot of money in those days — Magnolia plantation, several other great plantations, and over five hundred slaves."

The stout man sinks onto a bench beside the path and wipes the sweat from his face with a handkerchief. His wife sits down beside him and fans him with her hat. "Five hundred slaves," the man marvels. "Five hundred. I could use a load of peacock feathers and the whole bunch now."

There are no Blacks in this group. Brenda's hotel is teeming with Black women attending (according to the banner strung across the foyer) the Carolinas' Black Women's Baptist Convention but she's seen no Blacks among the tourists at any of the plantations.

Steve glances at his watch. "We can take a short rest. As long as we're back at the bus by five."

Brenda leans against the ribbed bark of a tree whose protruding roots reach into the dark water. On a tree across from her, a large black squirrel is spread-eagled, its mouth clenched around a huge nut. Food gathering ... . At home, Brenda can see squirrels, little brown squirrels, from the kitchen window. They run along the telephone wire to the bird feeder, back and forth along the telephone wire. Gathering food for the long winter.

Idle, for a moment at the kitchen window, just for a moment. Brenda! Mike's voice. Brenda! What are you doing? Where's my — ? When's my — ? Brenda!

The squirrel, dinner in mouth, continues its headfirst journey. The moment it reaches the ground, it flees.

Brushing away sweat with his forearm, the stout man bends into the breeze of the waving hat. Brenda folds her brochure and pushes a current of heavy air across her face. ... always attended by their Negroes ... . Always attended. What would always attended feel like?

"Politically, the Drayton family played a major role in the shaping of early America," Steve says. "Plantation ownership held the greatest prestige in the Colony because it insured both the time and means to pursue government service. To prepare them for public life, the sons were educated in England."

"What about the girls?" someone asks.

"The daughters were schooled at home. Their education was limited to art, literature, and, of course, etiquette."

A tall man at the back of the group laughs. "Small bodies, small heads."

Brenda remembers him from the Boone Hall tour, looking on as, one by one, the women in Steve's group stepped in front of the mirror that stood at the foot of the mansion's stairway. "Can you see your feet?" Steve had asked. No-one could. "Before they proceeded into the presence of the gentlemen in the parlour," Steve explained, "the ladies looked in that mirror to check whether or not their petticoats were showing. You can't see your feet because all of you are taller than ladies were in those days."

Does he mean small heads, small brains? Judging by the expression on his face, it's likely.

But, Brenda wonders, other than the shame of exposed petticoats, what did those tiny hoop-skirted women think about as they glided, agreeably pleasing, into the presence of the men; what occupied their minds as they sat, all smiles and fans and coquetry, with their beaus in the cooling breeze of Boone Hall's pillared balcony? The balconies of all the plantation houses, Brenda's noticed, somehow catch a breeze even when the work fields around the mansions are sweltering.

Boone Hall's balcony had looked down an avenue, a long avenue lined on each side with two-hundred-year-old oaks, oaks which, Steve said sadly, had been draped with festoons of Spanish moss — before the hurricane.

The stout man, leaning back, closes his eyes. Brenda, watching his red-faced, perspiring wife fanning him envisions his paunch in an easy chair and imagines a refrain, what're you doing what's for dinner when's dinner.

When's dinner? There would have been no such domestic duties for a Boone Hall mistress; behind the oaks, slave street sat within beck and call of the plantation house. But, Brenda reflects, the mistress would have had other duties — the obligation to please, to be charming and agreeable. And a duty to produce sons. Otherwise, the family name would be only a footnote in the annals of early America; that had been yesterday's history lesson. As the group crowded together on the pillared balcony of Boone Hall, Steve had briefly recounted the Boone family history, "Sarah Boone, a daughter of Major John Boone, the first owner of the plantation, became the wife of Andrew Rutledge and the grandmother of two of South Carolina's most noted sons: Edward Rutledge, a signer of the Declaration of Independence, and John Rutledge, the first governor of South Carolina."

A duty to produce sons, and not let her petticoats show. That last injunction, Brenda thinks ironically, surely involved more than petticoats. Didn't it all sometimes rankle?

"The second Magnolia house," Steve is saying, "also met a fiery end. In 1865, it was set ablaze by General Sherman's marauders." He motions to the seated couple. "We'll move on now, I'm going to show you a tree which played a part in the Drayton saga."

Brenda has read about the tree. In her brochure, on the same page as the picture of the famous tree, there's a photograph of a Black family. "Seated: Slave superintendent Adam Bennett and wife, Hannah. Standing: Sons John and Ezekiel." The three men, sepia-toned, clad in darker sepia-coloured suits, are ramrod stiff. Adam and Ezekiel hold books, Adam's between his palms, Ezekiel's in his left hand. John, too, may hold a book; his left hand is hidden behind his father's back. Hannah, a white shawl draped over her shoulders, sits slightly hunched. Her hands, curiously limp, lie palms down on her lap. The faces in the photograph are solemn, the men staring at the camera. Hannah's gaze — did her eyes shift as the shutter clicked? — is to the right, away from her husband. The caption reads: "MAGNOLIA'S ROYAL FAMILY."

The group walks slowly along the path and over a footbridge into a glade. Steve opens his arms to the encircling trees. "The day after the hurricane, I came here to help with the clean-up." He looks about gravely. "You can't imagine the devastation. Thankfully, our historical tree was still standing. But before you hear its story, you need to know something about the master-slave relationship of Magnolia's last antebellum owner, the Reverend John Drayton."

The Reverend John Drayton. His portrait, too, is in the brochure, a handsome but colourless face framed by sideburns and wings of black hair.

"Reverend Drayton," Steve says, "not only gave spiritual guidance to his three hundred slaves; he went so far as to build them a school house. There, under the guise of religious instruction, he taught the three R's."

Aha, John and Ezekiel hold books — bibles — to show that they can read. Did Hannah learn to read, or was her mind, her time, were her hands filled with duties — duties at the big house and at the little slave cabin? Perhaps the hands in the photograph are limp because they aren't holding anything or doing anything. Waiting for the shutter to click, they have been forced into unaccustomed idleness.

"In the school house which still stands on this plantation," Steve continues, "the reverend taught his slaves the basic skills of reading and 'riting and 'rithmetic — "

The tall man interrupts. "You told us yesterday that Boone Hall was the first plantation to educate its slaves."

"That's as far as historical records are concerned. Reverend Drayton provided education off the record; he taught his slaves when educating slaves was against the law."

"Brave of him."

"And good," a woman adds.

"Yes," Steve agrees, then says with a chuckle, "The reverend had a rather affectionate term for his slaves. He referred to them as his 'black roses.' "

A woman calls out "Three hundred black roses!" and

warbles in a light soprano, "I'm sending you a big bouquet of roses."

Steve acknowledges her with a strained smile. "In his youth, Reverend Drayton had been influenced by his aunts, the abolitionists, Angelena and Sarah Grimke. Eventually, because of their opposition to slavery, the notorious Grimke sisters were officially banished from South Carolina."

Notorious? Brenda wants to protest, notorious in ante-bellum parlance. But now? She bites back the words; Brenda has learned the wisdom of silence. She could say, however, that Angelena and Sarah Grimke let their petticoats show because they had more on their minds than their petticoats. And she might add, Angelena and Sarah Grimke aren't, and weren't, defined solely in relation to Reverend John Drayton. Those two 'notorious' women have names — written, spoken, living names. Unlike two other women in the reverend's life.

Flipping through her brochure, Brenda finds the picture of the church, the three portraits above it. Even the reverend's church, she notes, a substantial, uninspired-looking building, has a name, Saint Andrews. "Saint Andrews Church, the Episcopal Church of Saint Andrews Parish over which the Rev. John Drayton presided before, during, and after the Civil War."

The portraits and their captions imprint themselves on Brenda's mind:

Mother   Rev. John Drayton   Wife

"Over here," Steve calls. "We're waiting."

Brenda, startled, sees that the group has moved a short distance away and is now gathered around a large tree — the Tree. She hurries over.

"During the Civil War," Steve begins, "a scene which confirmed Reverend Drayton's close master-slave relationship was played out at this tree. Prior to the invasion of South Carolina, the reverend's wife and children had been sent to the safety of Philadelphia. When Union troops moved from Savannah to South Carolina, Reverend Drayton took refuge at his summer residence in Flat Rock, North Carolina. Magnolia plantation —" Steve pauses dramatically. "Magnolia plantation was left in the hands of the slaves. And that's where the story of this tree, Union troops, and Adam Bennett comes in."

Brenda knows this story, is puzzled by it. She has studied the solemn face in the photograph, searching for clues.

"Adam Bennett, Magnolia's slave foreman, former slave foreman," Steve corrects himself, "was seized by Sherman's men. As the plantation house was going up in flames, they strung him from this tree." Steve places a reverent hand on the grey trunk. "They threatened to kill him if he didn't tell them where the family's valuables were hidden. Adam Bennett, the former slave — " Brenda hears a swell of sentiment building in Steve's voice. "— in the face of death, Adam Bennett steadfastly refused to disclose the spot where he had buried the family treasure."

The blazing mansion, firelight dancing on the faces of the men, on the sweat-drenched face of the Black man.

Brave of him.

But the sentiment she heard in Steve's voice was not an affirmation of Adam Bennett's bravery; the sentiment had to do with loyalty. Good master/good slave. Good former slave, that is. The story, Brenda decides, is meant to validate the relationship and, by implication, to validate the Old South.

The Old South. "Nowhere does the mood and grace of the Old South live as here at Boone Hall."

"There's more on Adam Bennett," Steve tells the group. "While at Flat Rock, Reverend Drayton received a letter from his mother informing him that his former slaves had taken possession of Magnolia. Naturally, he remained in refuge. Months later, Adam Bennett appeared at his door. Adam had walked two hundred and fifty miles to bring the news that while the house was destroyed, the garden remained and— " Again Brenda hears the swelling of emotion. "— the reverend's former slaves were caring for the plantation. Together, Reverend Drayton and Adam Bennett returned to Magnolia and the unfinished work."

Steve thoughtfully strokes the trunk of the historic tree. "Devastation," he says quietly, and then, "The war had reduced Reverend Drayton to near poverty. He had to sacrifice his sea island plantation, his town house, and much of Magnolia in order to rebuild."

"Not my idea of poverty," the stout man comments.

Steve laughs. "You have to look at it from the Drayton point of view. For example, the plantation house you see today was originally a modest summer house the reverend owned at Summerville, fourteen miles up the Ashley River."

"Whew!" The man rolls his eyes. "Modest? Not by my standards."

Not by Brenda's either, and probably not by Steve's.

"The original house was smaller than the present house," Steve explains. "The dining-room, living-room, and water tower were added later."

"I'd call my home 'modest,' " the man persists. "Not as modest as those slave cabins we saw at Boone Hall, but modest."

Magnolia, too, has a slave street. It's featured on the same page as the Bennett family and the famous tree but it isn't on today's tour. Probably because slave cabins, unlike plantation houses, are basically the same: one room, a door, a window, a jutting fireplace chimney. Brenda wouldn't want to go anyway. "Some of the cabins are still occupied by descendants of those who occupied them prior to the Civil War." In the picture, smoke rises from one of the chimneys.

One-room shacks, but not different really from the shacks

perched on stilts in North Charleston. Steve, Brenda has noticed, always falls silent when the bus passes through Charleston's shanty town.

There's a better home awaiting —. Yesterday, at the hotel, she heard that song coming from the meeting room of the Black Women's Baptist Convention. There's a better home awaiting in the sky Lord in the sky.

"How'd he get it here? The house?" the tall man asks.

"The reverend disassembled it, loaded it on barges, and floated it down the Ashley River."

With a little help from his friends, but no-one mentions that. The aura around the gentlemen of the Old South makes them god-like. Let there be cotton fields, rice paddies, pecan groves, and crops of indigo and sugar cane. Let there be imposing plantation houses and beautiful gardens —. Let there be Magnolia. "On the south side of the Ashley River, Thomas Drayton settled and adorned a beautiful country seat. There he built a Mansion House of Brick."

In my Father's house are many mansions. In the sky Lord.

When Brenda enters the hotel lobby, it's electric with energy. The banquet for the Carolinas' Black Women's Baptist Convention is being held in the big reception room off the lobby. The women are waiting for the doors to open. No, they are not waiting; they are exuberantly milling about, chattering, laughing, humming snatches of gospel songs. Brilliant in satins and silks, vibrating in a kaleidoscope of colour. At their centre is a lone male, someone of consequence Brenda guesses, in formal black and white. She can't imagine any of them coming out of the shacks of North Charleston.

Brenda sets her suitcase on the bed and begins to pack. Tomorrow, she is going home. Going home. Like the Reverend John Drayton and Adam Bennett; the reverend to his beautiful garden and to, eventually, a "modest summer house" transformed; Adam Bennett, the former slave, to his cabin. Was it a place of warmth and affection?

In the photograph Hannah leans slightly to the right, an expression of resigned discontent on her face. Adam Bennett, hands cupping the bible, looks composed and almost stern, his expression that of an exacting superintendent. Did he ever, Brenda wonders, abuse his power? Or was he, like his master, good? But then, Brenda has heard of no bad masters, only good masters and loyal slaves. Loyal even in freedom.

Brenda understands, or thinks she does, why Adam Bennett, a free man, stayed on at Magnolia and why he walked two hundred and fifty miles and returned with Reverend Drayton to the plantation. Magnolia meant safety, security and, for Adam Bennett, status.

But why did he face death rather than tell where he'd hidden the treasure? Was his life of so little consequence? Or, having been elevated so far above his fellow slaves, had he lost himself? In his mind, was Adam Bennett a Drayton strung against the tree, a Drayton risking his life for the Family treasure?

That is the puzzle.

It's easy to understand why he returned, Brenda thinks. It was home. And where else could he go? Where else?

SUMMER COLD

Cynthia Holz

"SUMMER COLDS ARE the worst," Mother used to say. She would have gone on to scold me for spending too many chilly evenings at the pier, watching the Island Queen come in. "That's how you caught your cold," she would have summed up, and I would've admired her certainty, the way in which she overruled the world of germs in favour of a more personal wisdom. She'd feed me chicken soup and smear the red tracks under my nose with Vaseline. Then we would sit close around a hooded vaporizer, breathing the hot and blooming mentholated steam.

Now, with no-one nursing me, I stay in bed for two days, dozy and bored, and when I can't resist any more the sound of movement downstairs, switch to the living-room sofa. Sal walks by a couple of times before he sees me lying there propped on faded throw cushions, a child-sized blanket over my legs. "What're you doing here?" he asks, lifting his arms as if to fend off airborne viruses, then, glancing around, he adds, "Where's your friend?"

"Out shopping."

"So, did you ask how long she's staying?"

"Not yet."

"It's not like you invited her here."

"I didn't invite you either."

He sits down on an arm of the couch and squeezes my bare ankle under the blanket. "It's just that we're never alone any more." He is bare-chested, in swim trunks, a towel hooked around his neck like a horse collar, his skin flushed. When he lets go of my ankle a cold draft circles my leg.

He stands up. "Glad you're feeling better," he says, inching towards the patio doors. "I'm off for a swim."

All of a sudden I don't want him leaving me alone in the house. He's already opened the door when I wheeze, "At least you could ask if I need anything before you go."

He pauses. "Sorry. What do you need?"

"Something to drink. Hot soup."

He walks back to the kitchen and I hear him shutting cupboard doors. "There's only instant."

"That'll do."

He brings me a mug of yellow soup with dehydrated vegetables, splintery noodles and pebbly peas floating like sewage on the broth. I take this as a sign of our relationship. Then he's gone. I stare at his retreating back through the glass doors, his shoulder blades and the cleft of his spine, until I lose sight of him and the doors fill with afternoon light, uncommonly sharp, a light that makes the room seem indefinite, like a blurred photo.

After a while Helene comes in by the same door, in a stream of cooler evening air, and I'm glad to see her. She's carrying a string bag of groceries she hoists onto a kitchen counter and unpacks. "Oh!" she says when she sees me in the living-room, "you're downstairs. You look better."

"I feel lousy."

"We're having tofu casserole for dinner, that'll fix you up."

"I'm not much of a hostess either. You're doing all the work."

"Since when am I a guest? And the way I just turned up

like some abandoned baby at your door, I don't expect any privileges."

"Besides, I'm sick."

"Of course you are!" She sweeps across the room and sits on the edge of the couch, her skirt opening into blots of colour, like a peacock's tail. Her large eyes, rimmed in black and blue-shaded, seem extremely sorry. "Summer colds are the worst," she says, patting my blanket-covered knee. A knob of gratitude jumps in my throat.

"I think I have a fever too."

She leans forward and touches her palm to my forehead, "A little warm." And though she's only eight years older than me her motherliness is convincing. I might have crawled into her lap if she didn't suddenly shoot back and say, "You must be bored stiff. Why don't I get my Tarot cards, they're in my bag, and give you a little reading?" She vanishes into the guest room and reappears with a pack of cards and a thin book. Rearranging my legs on the couch she sits across from me, inches away, then shuffles the deck, counts out ten cards and lays them face-up between us, cross-like. As she bends low to study them I examine the gleaming crown of her head, the black polished hairs and the centre part along her scalp as milky as the white of an eye. She wears a silver-threaded blouse under a loosely-woven shawl, and her musky scent is strong enough to penetrate my stuffy nose.

"The King of Cups," she announces, and I look down at a picture of a crowned figure on a throne holding a cup in one hand and a scepter in the other.

"Is that good?"

"He symbolizes different men, good or bad." She opens the slim soft-covered book and reads aloud, "'The King also represents imagination, success and power, the power within each of us to do what we must in order to achieve our goals... .'" Her voice becomes stronger as she reads, lilting and clear. "My

God," she says, grabbing my wrist, "doesn't that give you so much hope?"

I stiffen at the stranglehold of her fingers, as if she would pull me out of my seat and into a world peopled by the Tarot creatures on the couch. And then I feel ashamed and try to relax my arm: Helene is still my father's glamorous girlfriend, someone I remember dressed in a blue sheath with tapered darts pointing to the astonishing fullness of her breasts. Someone I feel obliged to be familiar with. I make a joke: I say that when I think about men I don't feel very hopeful.

She draws her fingers back and cradles her hands in her lap. "I knew you'd understand," she says, "that's why I had to see you."

"How long has it been, three years? Before I met Sal, for sure."

"Too long."

"We keep in touch," I add quickly, "don't we? Only a few weeks ago I phoned Dad, I spoke to him — to both of you — remember?"

"Your father... ." Her voice drops. "I didn't leave for a week or two, you ought to know, this isn't a trial separation — I'm never going back to him. I mean it." Her gaze wanders then and she chews a thumbnail. "Oh Annie, I'd like to stay the rest of the summer if that's okay. Just to get my head together, maybe figure out what I should do next."

I start sneezing, once, twice, three times. Helene draws a balled-up tissue from her skirt and dabs my nose. "Unless I'm in the way," she says. "I don't want to ruin your holiday with Sal, of course."

"Holiday with Sal? I want him to go home."

She looks puzzled, then, "Oh, I'm sorry!" reaching out and hugging me as I squirm against her hot bosom. The breath goes out of me suddenly and I mold to the shape of her breasts. "Is it over?" she asks quietly.

I mutter acknowledgment into her neck.

"What a shame. He seems so nice."

"He *is* nice, it's just — I can't — "

Helene rubs a widening circle on my back. "Maybe we can help each other."

Yes, I nod. Oh yes!

When we break apart we're fidgety and stare at the crossing card again, the King of Cups. "He reminds me of your father," she says and I agree, a father-card. Fish and ocean, red ship, blue dolphin, blue moon; his baritone, his big hand, papery lips, scratchy kiss. His girlfriend.

Going to live with his girlfriend. Going away.

"The Empress is your centre card," Helene says, pointing at a seated woman in a gown. "She's a kind of heart card — follow your heart," but she doesn't tell me more than that, she seems to have lost interest.

The Empress: rings and pearls and party dresses, taffeta, chiffon and lace, a crown of stars; slender neck and long legs, a blue heron, lonely bird.

Blue river, blue, he left her, blue, blue, he let her go. Standing in the blue water, floating, going under, gone. Blue lips.

("Your mother, may she rest in peace, used to say..." is how people remember my mother, by her maxims. "Love is a woman's whole existence," she would say.)

The patio door rushes open on its rail and Helene calls out, "This one's Sal!" holding up a picture of a knight on horseback riding through the desert with his visor up, an orange plume streaming from his helmet.

Sal pauses across the room, peering over the rim of a tall bottle of beer. "Looks just like me. Where'd you get the mug shot?"

"It's Tarot." She scoops the cards off the cushion and shuffles them into a deck again. "Want a reading?"

"I don't go for that mumbo-jumbo." Sal looks uncomfortable.

He shifts his weight from leg to leg but doesn't leave.

"Come over here," Helene says, "we don't bite." She speaks to him in a mother-tone, although she's a few years younger. Passing in front of the couch on his way to an armchair, he casts an odour of hops and sweat.

Helene frowns, "I don't really go for that mystical stuff myself, but I thought Anna would be amused. She looked so unhappy lying there." She tips her head to one side and fluffs her hair, which rises and settles like a wave. "Isn't this cottage wonderful? And the island, such a beautiful place. You know, in all the years I lived with Anna's dad he never took me any- where as nice as this. In fact we almost never went out, period. Work, work, work, that's all he knew, that's the kind of man he was."

"Is," I correct.

"*Was* to me." She shifts her knees to face Sal directly. "Dead-meat."

He shoots me a look I don't care to interpret. Instead I begin sneezing again. They ignore me as I root through my pockets for a Kleenex.

"I left him yesterday morning — Anna tell you that? No going back either. When two people are bad together, drag each other down instead of lifting each other to new heights, there's no point staying together, don't you agree?"

I spread the Kleenex over my nose and mouth like a sur- geon's mask and think of my father working late, tired out, in his office that smells of lotion and alcohol, sweet and sharp. Will he sleep on a cot beside his desk instead of going into an empty bedroom? Will he try to get in touch with me?

When I look up again Sal is looking down at his beer, tilt- ing the bottle from side to side. He isn't saying anything.

Helene resumes, "So tell me about yourself, Sal. What do you do?"

"He's a journalist," I offer. "A very good one."

Sal upends the brown bottle and gulps beer. Then he says, "I'm taking a couple of months off to write a book."

"What sort of book?"

"Something political. Also I'm thinking of doing a thriller, I've already started one."

"Maybe a political thriller? Something with spies, that's an idea. John le Carré's a millionaire." She opens a black folder on the coffee table. "Is this it, the thriller book? Why don't you read us some of it."

"Nah, I don't think so." His eyes unfocus, sweeping across the cottage walls, the windows filled with hard light. "Anna's heard it anyway."

"I haven't." Helene hands him the folder. "Read me some, I'm interested."

"I don't know...."

"I'd like you to."

He blows across the rim of the bottle, making a hollow sound. Then he puts the bottle down and picks up the manuscript, pulling his eyes in line with a page. "'She had the ripe blond looks of Cybill Shepherd,'" he begins. When he gets to the bit about melon breasts and a pear-shaped ass I honk my nose in the Kleenex.

Helene purses her lips, "Go on," but Sal shuts the folder. "Well," he sighs, "we can't all be John le Carré."

"Of course not," Helene says, "but think about this: each of us has the power within to do what we must to meet our goals."

He blinks hard, then drops the folder back on the table. "Yeah, sure, but it helps to have someone believe in you."

"Please," I say.

Helene glances from him to me to him again, like she's figuring sums in her head — one plus zero, one plus one, one plus two.

Sal stands up abruptly and I gaze at his bare chest, how

smooth it looks, a sheen where the evening light from a window grazes his softening muscles. How cool it would feel to press my cheek against his chest. That would fix everything, wouldn't it, the sealing pressure of flesh on flesh.

"I'll start supper," he says and heads for the kitchen.

Helene jumps in front of him. "I'm cooking tonight," she says. "Tofu and brown rice casserole."

I wait for Sal to roll his eyes, wrinkle his nose and screw up his lips, but his face is still. "But come join me," she tells him, "there's lots to do." Arms at his sides, plastic sandals slapping the floor, he follows her into the U of the kitchen where the work is done. I twist on the sofa for a better view, but at such a distance, in smudged light, it's hard to discern small acts.

The rap of the knife on the cutting board, the hiss of running water and the opening and slamming of drawers remind me of family dinners long ago. Of sitting between Mother and Daddy, heads lowered over our plates as if in prayer.

"Here," Helene is saying, handing Sal a knife, "you can cut the onions, they make me cry." I hear the click of it, chop-chop-chop, and see the pumping of Sal's arm, then she commands, "Smaller — let me do it." He mumbles in reply and she counters with a laugh like the ring of two glasses touching in a toast. To love! to health! the future! As Sal steps aside he brushes his hand across the back of her waist and something crackles in the air. I hear it.

She tosses her head, hair glinting, and takes the knife, the blade tapping the wooden board. The only sound. Suddenly she cries out. Then, in a thin voice, "My thumb, it's bleeding."

Sal grabbing her by the wrist, her hand in the sink, in a stream of water from the tap. Sal yanking open a drawer, squeezing her thumb, taping the wound in a band-aid and guiding her to a kitchen stool. "There," he says. He's breathing hard. Helene sits down gingerly, her finger raised like she's thumbing a ride, the round pink tip of the digit peeking over its bandage. She is shivering. I see it — feel it — the slight wavering of her hips, the quick dance of her body, and I start shuddering too, jamming the blanket around my legs, but it doesn't help.

She slides off the stool, her skirt swishing against the wood with a liquid sound, holding her bandaged thumb in front of her like a torch. Her hair and shawl, her silvery blouse, flowing skirt: she crosses the room like someone walking in a dream, a Tarot queen, a creature risen from the sea.

She kneels beside the sofa, slips her arm around my back and draws me close. "You're cold," she says. Opening the shawl she hoods it over our heads. It radiates heat, as if there weren't round holes between its stitches but panes of glass catching the last of the sun's rays. In the silence I hear my heartbeat, I hear the surf, the murmur and crash of an old machine.

"Summer Cold" is excerpted from "ONLYVILLE", a current novel-in-progress.

MEETING JESUS AT THE RODEO COWBOY CHURCH

Gertrude Story

I DIDN'T GO THERE to meet Jesus, I went because Kim Bendicks, he told me if you went to Sunday morning service at the Swift Current arena the week Rodeo was on you could hide away in the washrooms when it was done, and then sneak out again when the after dinner stuff was on and Cal Rogers would be riding the bulls.

I wanted to ride bulls but I'd never even been on a horse. My dad was a rodeo cowboy, my mom said once to some guy when they were drinking beer in the kitchen the day the cheque came. Every month, the day the cheque came, my mom would be drinking beer in the kitchen with somebody and laughing a lot.

I was watching the Calgary Stampede. We were still living in Wainright then. The TV rolled like anything just about every time anything good was going on. When the soap and hair junk and McDonald's stuff was on, the TV was good, but as soon as something good came on it started to roll and heave. Like a good bull giving the cowboy a ride for his life.

I was going to be a bull rider back then. I was young. Four, five, maybe. But this one night, with the TV heaving and rolling I wasn't thinking about that, I was getting so mad at the TV I wanted to kick it, but that would just bring the old lady in flying if there was a new guy drinking beer in the kitchen. So I shut it off instead. And I heard her say then to this new guy, "The kid in there, his dad was a bull rider, did I ever tell you that?" And they both laughed. And the guy — he didn't stay around too long, that one — he said something about a lotta bull and they both laughed again and got up and went into the bedroom and shut the door.

And I got madder than ever at the stupid TV then, so I got up and went out and went over to Kim Bendicks' house across the street.

I thought maybe they'd be watching the rodeo at his house but his mom, she came to the door and she said, "Kimberley isn't allowed out at this time of day and you shouldn't be out, either; you go home like a good boy and tell your mother I said so." So that was that.

At least she didn't tell me to wipe my nose or wash my face. At least I think she wasn't doing that any more by then, but maybe I just don't remember.

Anyway, I'd started wanting to be a bull rider when I was pretty little. And I wanted cowboy boots and a cowboy hat and the whole bit and my mom used to tell me she'd get them for me for Christmas. Or my birthday. Or whatever wasn't coming up on the calendar for a while. But whenever the cheque came there was never any money left, so one day — I was going to school already by the time she did that — she took me down to the Sally Ann store and she got me a pair of cowboy heel rubber boots that were too big. They cost a dollar. They were blue. You never saw blue boots on a bull rider but anyway she stuffed old socks into the toes and I wore them for a while. But they leaked, so they were only good on dry days and then the kids at school had lots to say about that and so, to hell with it, I pitched them down the basement with all the other junk that got pitched down there and when we left that house it all stayed down there like the junk stuff always did whenever we moved to another place, and I never asked for cowboy boots again.

But at least with the new guy in Swift Current we got a good TV and I got a baseball glove his own kid didn't want any more. I tried taking it to school for a while but a baseball glove is no use when nobody lets you play baseball so I pitched it down the dark of the new basement and the guy, Erskine, he never asked about it the whole time he stayed.

I was twelve when he left. Erskine. It was my birthday. It was Erskine's birthday too. I don't know how old he was and I don't care.

So I wasn't wearing cowboy boots and I wasn't wearing a cowboy hat neither the day I went to the Rodeo Cowboy Church in the rain and the snow, to the exhibition arena in Swift Current. The cold was a bugger and I had to keep my hands in my pockets all the while I was running. And the steam of my breath in the cold got in the way so I couldn't see and this truck nearly got me and they honked so quick and so loud and so long I got warmed up all over with the scare.

There was two big cowboys in the truck. "Why the hell don'tcha watch where you're goin', Kid? You'll be crow bait if you keep that up," said the one who was driving.

"Better go git yer bow and arraz," the other one said. (I can't really remember what they said, but they said pretty close to what I'm saying they said.) "Better go git your bow and arraz, there's a posse after you, I hear."

And they laughed real loud with their mouths wide open and their heads laid back, and then they took off. I watched and seen where they parked. Lots of others were parked there too and going in by the side door of the arena so I went there too and did that.

For a while it was warm. Well, compared to outside. There

was that nice smell of horse shit but not strong, just enough to tell you the horses had been there yesterday with cowboys on them doing all the things that rodeo cowboys do. They weren't showing it on the TV. The TV we had now from Erskine was still working good but they weren't showing the rodeo on the TV.

There was singing. They had a band. For a while when I was younger Kim Bendicks' mom, she took me along with them to church, and there was no band there, that's for sure, just a piano somebody played with lots of rolls and finger swipes up and down the keyboard; it was okay but it sure wasn't any band. I couldn't hear the words much that the singers were singing when I got into the main hall of the Swift Current rodeo arena; I couldn't see the singers neither; but once in a while from way back in the bleachers part I made out *Jesus*, and then *rodeo*, and then *cowboy party time*. Maybe that's what they were singing about, I'm not sure. But I followed the sound up out of the main hall and up into the bleachers part and there was a whole bunch of people sitting up there, the men and the guys, even the little suckers hardly walking yet, they all had their cowboy hats on. But not the girls. The girls, lots of the ladies, too, had this real long curly piled-up hair like Dolly Parton's and it looked good, I liked it.

Everybody was all sitting up close together in one part of one side of the grandstand in the arena that was like the biggest horse barn you ever saw in your life. All closed in and closed over but so cold your jeans felt like ice bags hanging around your legs. And everybody was watching a line of people in front of the grandstand seats. Those were the singers. They weren't in the arena part with the clean sand and the horse dumps, they were just inside the railing part that stops the big bulls from jumping into people's hotdogs when the rodeo is on.

They were all in a row and they didn't have a band at all,

they had a piano box, like the bands on TV, so I don't know how it was you could hear the fiddle and the guitars and everything like that, because all there was was this one little old piano box and a nice lookin' lady with Dolly Parton hair giving it what for. Later I thought about it and I guessed they had a tape hidden somewheres, but it sounded alright. In fact, good.

Anyways, I climbed up right to the top of the next empty section and then I sneaked along until I got to the same row in the part where all the church people were. There was nobody in that row but a cat and when I sat down the cat left. I was cold and he would've felt good if you could've caught him and held him on your lap.

The whole row of singers was wearing yellow jackets. When they turned their backs on you there was something written there. I thought for a minute maybe I'd got into the wrong place and they had to do with bowling or something, but later I got close and saw it said I'M FOR JESUS HOW ABOUT YOU?

It was cold. The seats too. Then this one real big fat cowboy was sayin', "Let's pray, folks, and see can we warm up this big old cow palace with the love of Jesus and his holy name." And everybody wearing a cowboy hat took it off. I didn't think a Canada Tire cap would count so I kept it on, but this one old lady, she turned around and glared at me — the cat had come back and I hadn't meant to but I'd kicked it trying to get my legs underneath me enough to get them warmed up. It was quicker to squall than any cat I ever saw. She had pretty mean eyes. The lady. And she said in a big, man's voice, "Get that hat off your head, don't you know no better?" and so I did.

I waited till all the cowboy hats got put on again before I put on my cap, wishing to hell it had ear laps like Erskine's winter cap from the post office, or else that I had that cat to wear around my ears. But it didn't come back for a long time.

Then the fat cowboy said something into the microphone about giving testimony, and I thought, My luck! It's really a court place, not church, and I guess cowboys don't have to go to the same place downtown that Erskine had to go to when his real wife made him pay up money for something or other and my mom made him take me along even if I didn't want to go. When we got home she asked me what the wife looked like, was she pretty, and things like that, but the wife wasn't even there, only my mom said did Erskine tell me to lie about it so finally I said yeah. A while after that he left.

So now there was this big tall cowboy making his way down to the front where the singing had been going on. He had all the gear and everything, he even had the roper's gloves and he carried them in one hand, whipping his pants with them as he went. He had a big black book in the other hand, that'd be the Bible no doubt, but he didn't whip that any-wheres, he hung onto it tight.

So he gets to the front and takes the microphone — he has to put his gloves down to do it. At first he puts the black book down but that doesn't seem to suit him, so he picks it up again and puts the gloves down instead, and then he does all that all over again.

And in the meantime somebody sneaks up beside me say-ing, "Move over, Gimp!" It's Kim Bendicks. Everybody else calls me Leroy only mostly they say it *Lee*-roy. My mom says it's from some French greatgreatgrampa and it means "the king" and I should be proud of it, but she should try being proud of it sometime when half the kids in your grade are tail-ing you home hollering *Lee*-roy! at your hustling rear end.

Right away the mean-eyed woman turned around and said, "Shhh!" so loud the tall cowboy in front looked up from his book as if to see what was going on. And Kim shoved me with his rear to get me moving down along the long top empty row until we got right out on the aisle and there he let me stop.

The long lean cowboy was telling a story now. It was about himself. He said how he had been into the booze for years and it was awful, it crippled his head and it crippled his stomach and it crippled his life, he said. He said it just like Erskine used to say it, as if he really meant he was sorry about it, as if he was gonna cry if he told you any more of it. And he told how he used to play around with other women when he was doing the rodeo and his wife was at home with the kids, all five of them. And that was like Erskine too, in a way, and I felt kind of like crying myself and wished Kim Bendicks wasn't there; if he asked me something and made me answer I might blubber and then guess what I'd hear for the next forty years.

"And then along came Jesus," said the cowboy. And into the big rodeo barn galloped these seven brahma bulls, their heels clicking. They were tossing their heads this way and that at each other and they came to a fast stop, all in a row like sparrows on a high wire, as if to give the once-over to the long lean cowboy with his black book and sorrowful voice and to check out all of us sitting there in the stands freezing our butts and maybe only hanging in there to see the rodeo free when the church stuff was over and done.

And the biggest bull, he put his head down and scrubbed at the dirt and manure with one front foot and sent some of it flying over his own rump. And I whispered to Kim Bendicks, "I'm glad we're in the top back row if that sucker comes flying!"

And Kim Bendicks snorted and made pawing motions with his hands. The tall cowboy was thanking the lord now for the big bulls that had just been run in and for all the big bulls he had ridden down to the glory of Lord Jesus for the last seven years. Next he gave thanks for the handlers who had run the bulls in and said he hoped, in fact he knew, they knew what they were doing even though it was two hours before the afternoon show and then some. After that he gave thanks for the cowboy rodeo circuit and for Jesus and his rodeo cowboy church.

"Blessud be the day that I met Jesus!" swore the cowboy. "Blessud be the day that I met Jesus!" he hollered for all the world to hear.

"Jesus!" called out a little thin lady dressed all in red — red cowgirl suit with danglers and spangles, red furs over top, fox, I bet. "Jesus!" she called out again as she stood up and hurried as best she could past people's knees to the tall cowboy and there she put her arms around him. He had trouble, what with her and his roper gloves and the black book he was so careful of, handling them all; and then the lady turned around and smiled a big white smile and nodded her Dolly Parton head and five kids got up in the row she'd just left and filed their way or got lifted on their way by other people to the aisle, and from there they piddle-ran to the tall cowboy and the red lady and everybody had their arms around everybody and nobody.

It made me feel kind of all alone; it made me think of Erskine when he came back from seeing his own kid and had been gone for three days and how when he came in the door he'd yell out, "Come on down here, Leroy, ya little sucker, and show me if ya lost your arm muscle since I bin gone!"

And the music got upped so loud now you had to hold your ears. And "Jesus!" into the microphone bellered a big fat cowboy who seemed to be in charge of things. And "Jesus!" yelled the mean-eyed lady who had told us to hush up.

"Jee-*sus*!" said Kim Bendicks. Just *after* everything had got as quiet as it gets when the school principal walks into the room to find out who cut up three basketballs and tried to flush them down the toilets in the boys'.

The mean-eyed lady didn't turn around, she was down on her knees, squiggled down somehow in the narrow aisle, and crying into a big blue bandanna hanky. I was so glad she was busy enough not to notice Kim Bendicks snorting away that I said, "Thank Christ!" to myself. And I got this funny warm feeling spreading through my whole body and it lasted for quite a while, only not nearly long enough.

I wanted out. "I'm going," I whispered to Kim Bendicks. "My arse end is bloody well froze to the plank."

"And miss the bull riding? Are you crazy? You might as well not have bothered if you're gonna give up now, it's soon done!"

A lot he knew!

For now the music started up again, only this time soft and low. The bulls seemed to like it and they started to pick their way around the ring. "Blessud be the holy name of the lord!" calls out the big fat cowboy in charge of things, "and blessud be his holy word delivered to us this day." Two of the bulls upped their tails and shat, that real runny stuff, and Kim Bendicks said again, "Jesus!" And he snorted and took off his cowboy hat and hid his face in it for a while. The mean-eyed lady was back to sitting by now and she turned around and said "Shh!" again, real loud, but there was only the cat there now in our seats where we'd started out and it didn't seem to care what she did or said because it wiped its long tail along the lady's neck as it slid by, taking its time to do it.

That cowboy church music! It was so sad, it was so awful sad I could hardly stand it. It was all coming out of this same little piano, but there was fiddles coming out too, along with the piano sounds; and Hawaiian guitar — sad, sad, sad, I wanted to get up and go out and get away from it. Only thing, Kim Bendicks would have called me chicken and cluck-clucked all next day every time he saw me, his hands under his armpits and flapping his elbows up and down until everybody asked him what it was all for and then he'd tell, if I left.

"Once upon a time," the big fat cowboy was saying now, over top of the sad music, "there was a young boy, and he was alone and lonely and he was travelling in these parts, walking by hisself in the heat and the dust of the country roads.

"And he come to maybe ten miles the west side of Swift Current here, and he was mighty tuckered, mighty tired, mighty scairt and mighty lonely. Hungry and thirsty — oh, *so* hungry and thirsty — too.

"And this big Ford half-ton come up on him on the dusty hot road and the boy flags him down. And the truck stops. And this great big cowboy leans out and says, 'What kin I do for ya, Son?'

"And the boy says, the boy says, 'I'm hot and I'm dirty and I'm tired and sore and I'm as hungry and thirsty as a boy can be. So, Mister, do you know any place I could get me a bed for the night? Just a place to lay down my tired little head for the night? Can ya, Mister? Can ya, Mister, please!' "

Right then, to tell you the truth, I had this idea I wouldn't mind being out on some hot dusty road somewheres, it would beat freezing your butt off in the Swift Current rodeo arena when you're not even sure you're gonna get to hide away in the men's and get to see the afternoon events free. But this big fat cowboy was kind of crying while he talked, like that old Hank Snow did sometimes on my mom's old cowboy records, so I figured I'd hang in for a while yet and see if this was one of those Old-Shep-was-a-dog kind of stories that you didn't have to believe in unless you wanted to.

"A bed for the night, Son?" the big cowboy said (the Swift Current big cowboy was saying). "Why, shore. I'll tell ya what. You just go down that west road a few miles and you'll come to a big white house." (Sure, don't drive the poor little sucker there, I says to myself, what's another few miles to somebody who's dead beat and buggered? Erskine would have said, "Pile in the back, Kid, and if we don't hit a McDonald's in the next town we'll put on the feedbag when we get home. Meanwhiles, here's a chew a gum, let's see if you can fool your stomach with that until we can find it something better.")

"A nice old lady will come to the door there," the cowboy was crying, "and you just say to her, John three-sixteen. Can you remember that?"

So, according to the fat cowboy's story, the kid says to himself, John three-sixteen, John three-sixteen, over and over again, his tongue sticking to the roof of his mouth with the heat and the dust, but he keeps saying it so's he won't forget. And he gets to the house. And the old lady takes him in and first thing she does is wash him up in a big bathtub. (I'da drunk some of that bath water, was it me, if the first thing anybody did on a day you could fry eggs on the back step was *stick* me into water instead of giving me a big pitcher of it to drink after an all day hike. But I suppose these crying church cowboys know how the story happened so they have to tell it that way, it wouldn't be right to make something up, it likely wouldn't be right to do that.)

And so it seems the kid gets out of the tub feeling good and he says to himself, he says, "Hmm, John three-sixteen. I don't know who is this John three-sixteen. All I know is I was a dirty boy and now I'm a clean one, so I wish I knew what this John was all about, I do."

And I kind of wished I did, myself. Kim Bendicks didn't seem to care. He'd snagged the cat and was trying to make it sit on his knee, I suppose he wasn't wearing long gotchies, either, so anything to get warm. But the idea wasn't too popular with the cat, like Erskine would have said, and he squiggled so bad I guess Kim squoze him a little too hard to keep him in place. And the cat yelled and scratched and Kim yelled and scratched the scratch. And the old lady with the hard eyes she stood right up at her seat and turned around and sent us a *Shhhhh!* they could have heard in Moose Jaw.

The crying cowboy didn't seem to be too happy about it, neither, but he kept on talking and the fiddles from the music box kept on crying too. And the long and the short of it is that this old lady, the one in the story, then finally did give the kid a drink of water — "all the water a young boy could possibly want to drink." And she fed him a spread. The cowboy named it off: pizza and pie and turkey and a ham sandwich — I got stitches inside just to hear about all that good stuff on a empty stomach. "All the good food that ever a young boy could possibly want to eat," he cried, and Kim Bendicks' stomach started rumbling, I could hear it plain as anything and I figured, This is gonna get us another big Shhh! from Old Hard Eyes! But she never even turned around, she was crying again into the big blue bandanna hanky and then blowing her nose in one corner of it and then turning it around to another part of it to wipe her eyes.

And every time something new and good happened to him the kid says, "Hmm, John three-sixteen. I don't know this John but I know I was a hungry boy and now I am fed." And, "I was a thirsty boy and I got give something to drink." And so on down the line of good things that happened; every time he told himself in that way that he was having pretty good luck out of this John three-sixteen, whoever that was.

He never asked the old lady. I guess, was it me, I wouldn't have asked anybody about it, either, in case the John three-sixteen luck dried up all of a sudden with the curiosity. Curiosity killed the cat, like Erskine used to say, when you asked too many questions and he was six into the beer.

And then the big fat cowboy was really crying. Great big tears were running down his fat cheeks and I felt kind of embarrassed for him. Erskine said a guy never cries; crying is for women and girls; a man never cries. So I just kind of wished this cowboy would quit it and I guess the brahmas did too.

They'd just been farting and rustling around the ring, the bulls had, and once in a while one of them would take on another and horn butt him halfway down the arena through the sand and crap. But after this cowboy got into the crying story about old John three-sixteen they'd somehow lined themselves up at the opposite end of the arena, all in a row, and they just sort of stood there as if they were trying to figure out what was gonna happen out of it all. Once in a while the big ugly grey one would look over the shoulder of the runty little blue one beside him as if to say to the next in line, "Can *you* figure it, Big Louie?" That's just the way it looked.

Erskine used to say that animals talked to him. Especially cats. Especially his wife's big ugly tomcat. When he was really into the beer Erskine would tell how that cat never liked him. And every time he came home drunk and made his wife do him up eats at one o'clock in the morning he would set himself down before the plate that had been waiting for him on the table since supper time. And every damn time that cat would parachute down from the high buffet hutch onto Erskine's plate and sit there and wipe his rear arse end around on it and look him in the eye and say, "Get the hell out of here if you don't want your eyeballs made into cat food some dark night!"

The last time his wife's cat told him that he left for good, Erskine always said. And my mom said, "Do we have to hear about *her* every time you have one too many beers?" And Erskine would say, "I was talkin' about the cat, fer chrisake!" And he would get up and go around the other side of the table and put his arms around her and say to me, "Don't she look cute when she's mad, eh, Lee-roy?" I somehow could never get mad when Erskine called me Lee-roy.

The big fat cowboy wasn't crying any more. But he took up the microphone again and hoped the spirit of Jesus had entered each and every one there, every cowboy and his lady, every heart and every mind, and had warmed them up good, real good, because the Swift Current weatherman sure didn't seem about to do that this weekend.

And then he said they weren't going to pass the hat for collection because they already had a big old cowboy hat on a table in the main hall of the arena where there was books and papers and tapes of the Rodeo Cowboy Church Singers you could buy. And then he said, "And, folks, please, we ask that not a one of us has come to church today with a view to staying behind to see a free show. Everybody's eyes are on us," he said. "The Lord's eyes and the eyes of the community. And the Rodeo Committee has to make money to pay its cowboys, so, please, folks, play it square today for the sake of Jesus Lord, I know you will. For when you meet him again in that Great Beyond and he asks you if you ever cheated on a cowboy, you will want to be able to say, Never, dear Lord Jesus, I always paid my way."

And when he said that, he looked right at me. I don't care that he was way down there at the railing and me and Kim Bendicks was way up top. His look went right through my heart. It was like Erskine's real wife's tomcat, only maybe a little bit kinder, I don't know about that. And Kim Bendicks and me, we cut it outta there and as we was flyin' past the washrooms he shoved me through a door and there was no wall buckets so Kim Bendicks says, "Shit! The women's."

And he hustles us out and into the john next door.

"Get your feet up offa the floor and shut your yap and when everything's quiet stay put and when everything's noisy again just wander out and into the crowd and if I see you I see you and if I don't I don't." Kim Bendicks pushed me into the first stall and I heard his feet go slipper, slipper, slipper and a door creak once, twice, and then I heard nothing.

I sat with my back up against the toilet tank and for a while it felt good, I was sweating bullets. It's no lead pipe cinch, like Erskine would say, to hunker on top of an open toilet with your feet up off the floor, trying not to breathe and trying to tell yourself you really don't have to pee yet. After only a while it was awful. I closed my eyes and hung on. Then all at once it was nothing. No feeling. Nothing. Like I was floating above the toilet seat, maybe.

And there inside my eyes I saw a white light. It wasn't made up of light, it was made up of words. But the words made a light. A light so bright I didn't really want to look at it. I looked at it, though. It didn't hurt, it just was there.

The words of the light said: Jesus! Jesus! Jesus! Over and over and over again. And then the words were being said into my head: Jesus! Jesus! Jesus!

And I felt awful because I'd swore and I said to the words in my head, "I'm sorry, Jesus, I wish I hadn't swore."

The words said back, "What the hell is all this? Swore? I thought you were *calling* me!"

"Well, in a way, I was," I said.

"Shut up!" Kim Bendicks hissed from the far stall.

So from then on I just worked my tongue and my mouth and I said the words inside me. I *was* calling you, I guess, I said. I never expected to find you inside my own head. I went once out on the prairie with Erskine and I thought I saw you in a willow bluff but it turned out to be Erskine's brother's white Charollais cow, the one that was lost for a week.

"It was me," he said.

Careful, I said, Kim Bendicks will hear you.

"Na," he said, "I have clouded his mind for a while. Like they do sometimes on the Good Ship Enterprise. Don't worry, he'll be alright. You're a good boy, Le-roy, king of kings, to worry about your friends."

He'll kick the ... supper out of me if I don't do this right, I said.

"We'll do it right, not to worry. In fact, it's done. Let's go. Keep your eye on that little blue bull, he's gonna turf the best rider they got out there this afternoon."

Hey, I'm not gonna go into that rodeo, I said. The big

cowboy said the eyes of the Lord are upon us. I know what that means: they've got the Mounties out in civvies here today.

"The eyes of the Lord will be upon them too then," he said. "Trust me," he said. "Let's go."

I didn't mean to. But all at once my body just sort of curled itself off the toilet and we went through that stall door as if it wasn't there and out into the hall that was churning like Speedy Creek in spring, only with people.

And before I knew it I was in the stands, way up high, feeling warm, feeling fed, feeling washed clean (that was likely the sweat I'd worked up in the john) and feeling happy. And if I felt a little thirsty I only had to remember I hadn't got to pee down in the john and that scared the thirst away in a hurry.

Finally it got so bad I thought I'd better tell him. "Jesus, I gotta go pee," I said.

"Watch your mouth, young man," said somebody. It was the mean-eyed lady from church. "Wash your hands when you're done and, here, on your way back get yourself some eats and bring me a hot dog too. With lots of mustard, mind." She handed me a five.

"Beat it," she said. "Do you think I want to smell wet pants all afternoon here?"

I went.

It was a great time.

When I was going home it was nearly dark. It came to me that I'd never come across Kim Bendicks and I hadn't even said another word to Jesus after I got back with the pop and the grub, I'd talked to the old mean-eyed lady all the rest of the time.

I stood still in the cool clear of evening and listened to my head. Nothing. "I'm sorry, Jesus," I said, out loud. "I didn't mean to be like that. I just forgot. I didn't mean to be like that."

Nothing. For a long time. Then it was like the broken TV

all of a sudden, I just got so mad all at once. "Jesus Christ!" I said, "I *said* I was sorry."

Into my right ear crept a warmness. Like a little breeze. Only it had words. "He's busy just now," the words said. "Can I help you? I'm John."

It was good enough for me. When I got home I told my mom I had lied about Erskine and it was all her fault. She went to clip me one but John said "Duck!" so loud she heard it. It put her swing off.

Besides that, she went to her knees — kind of heavy and slow but sure and certain, like the young cow Erskine's brother whapped with the sledge hammer the day we went to the farm to help butcher. And before she even hit the floor my mom she was startin' to pray and cry. John and I went to bed.

Next week, when I know better how to do it, I'm gonna ask for Erskine back.

WANDERING

Maureen Hynes

SEND ONE PHOTO, says the form, one photo taken within the last three months, three by five inches, head and shoulders of the patient. Black-and-white or colour. The photo to accompany the application form my sister and I have already filled out.

The form that asks about her middle name (oh, she hates Gertrude so much). Date of Birth: 13/11/13. Height: 5'2". But she used to be 5'5". Weight: about 140, my sister and I guess. (And what does *your* mother weigh? I want to write). Colour of Eyes: grey-hazel. Colour of Hair: brown-grey. Even at 77, still so little grey. Thin Eyebrows or Thick: very thin. Any Scars: many scars; a very old thyroid operation scar at base of throat, recent lumpectomy scar on left breast, recent scar on left hip from surgery for broken hip, scars on left arm from pins for a broken wrist, toenails removed on both big toes. Amputations: no, we shudder. Prostheses: no. False Teeth: yes. Hearing Aid: no. Glasses: yes, on a string round her neck. Tattoos: no, we chuckle. How about a snake entwined around her right forearm? 'Mother' surrounded by hearts and flowers? Mother. No, no tattoos. And so many other details: build, precise skin colour and complexion (ruddy, freckled, pockmarked?); hair style (bald, receding, curly, wavy, sideburns, wig or toupee?), eye defects, moustache, disabilities, birth-marks, any special medications.

And where is the patient likely to wander, the form asks. We print three locations: to the Dominion Store at the Yonge-Eglinton Centre; Saint Michael's Cathedral, for the 12:15 Mass; 26 St. Hilda's Avenue, her mother's old home.

Send one photo. Today, alone, I look at the eight shiny black-and-white photos I picked up from the camera store. Six of my mother, two of me taken on a warm and brilliant sunny Saturday, a surprise in early March. But the weather scares us now, because the deep cold has kept her in all winter. Now, we think, in the warm weather, she's more likely to go out.

I'll take the pictures on Saturday, I'd told my sister. I trick my mother a bit, to take the photos. I hide in the living-room winding a new spool of TMAX 400 black-and-white film into my camera, walk into the kitchen. What a gorgeous day, I say. It's spring, I say. Look, it's so mild. I open the back door, the one off the kitchen. Feel that, I say. Oooh, we both exclaim, our pleasure immediate, welcoming the warmth. Look, I say, I want to finish this roll of film, can I take some pictures. Let's go out on the porch. Just step out on the porch. Just there. She looks nervously at me, at the camera. Okay, she says, just out on the porch. She steps out into the sunshine and looks around the yard. We both take deep breaths and smile at the new warmth. It's lovely, isn't it, I say. I just want to finish this roll, I tell her, lifting the camera to my eyes. *Head and shoulders*, I remind myself, focussing quickly through the viewfinder. Isn't it gorgeous out? I snap a photo. Hey, I laugh, can you manage to look a little bit *friendly*? She breaks into a great smile. I snap another. Oh, the roll's not finished, I say, pretending annoyance. I snap another. That's enough, she tells me.

Just one more, I snap another. Here, you take some of me, I say, handing her the camera. Just press *here*, I show her. She snaps one. Take another, I tell her, and quickly advance the film for her, not caring if she focuses or not. Oh, *still* not finished, I say, taking the camera from her. I pretend annoyance again. Let's trade places, I say, you stand over here. The late afternoon light is casting long sharp shadows. I want to bracket the shots; don't want to repeat all this. I take two more. Let's go inside, she says. Okay, Mom, just one more. But she won't allow one more. That's enough, she says. No more, she says. She goes inside with relief, having indulged me. Her anxiety to get back into the kitchen is like a taste I can hold in my mouth. I wonder if we can count on it, her wanting to stay inside the house. Or does she sense my dishonesty, the purpose I am pretending not to have? Oh, it's finished now anyway, I tell her, eight shots into my roll of twenty-four. I rewind the film, open the camera, fish out the roll and put it in my purse. You want a cup of Nescafé? she asks, the tenth time in an hour.

Send one photo. Almost every day she talks about her mother, about going to see her. She packs a plastic bag with a few things, a towel, some underwear, a sweater, a new pair of pantyhose, a nightgown, and something that looks like it might be a gift, a pair of shiny turquoise plastic earrings in an old blue Birks box, an expensive little bar of soap or a cheap china figurine. Little things I never knew she had. She ties up the plastic bag tight by its two plastic handles and puts it in a corner of her room. The next day she stashes the bag in the back of her closet, and packs a new bag. On her really bad days she comes downstairs with her plastic bag and looks at it in confusion. I was going to take this down to Mom's... she starts to say, but doesn't finish. Oh, that's okay, we say. We'll do that later. Okay, she says, and lets us take the bag from her hands. When she isn't looking we take it back upstairs and unpack it.

If I haven't been there for a few days, I have to go up to her room and unpack three or four of these bags and put their contents away. We don't like to do this, go through her things, but we have to because fairly often she's packed away all her underwear. Sometimes she comes downstairs for dinner, looks in the dining-room and then looks at me puzzled. Where's Mom? she asks. My mind scrambles. Ahh, I say soothingly, remembering the information sheets from the Alzheimer Society about how to handle these behaviours.

Ahh, you're missing Nan a lot, I say. You're thinking about Nan again, I say. Address the emotion, not the facts, the information sheet says, the sense of loss, the nostalgia for a safer, surer time. Don't tell the patient her mother is dead. You run the risk of tripping off the grieving process again. Don't say, she's in Heaven, which she might understand, or she died in 1964, which she won't. You're missing Nan again? Yeah, she says, shaking her head, I haven't seen her in *so long*. I give her a small hug. It's Sunday, I say, remember how she used to come here almost every Sunday night after Devotions at church? And she always brought Maple Walnut ice cream. And I never liked Maple Walnut ice cream? Sometimes Neapolitan, and I didn't like that much either. It was always so soft and melted and, I pause, ersatz. Ersatz? she says blankly, and I remember the precise moment she taught me that word, in the basement of Eaton's Annex, cheap merchandise, she said, ersatz.

I keep going, what I liked was Butterscotch Ripple, but Nan never brought that. But *you* used to buy Butterscotch Ripple for me at Hall's Dairy, I end brightly. We both laugh. I have edged her past the bad moment again. Or is that what she thinks? What does she think? Oh, but I am not always this kind. Sometimes if it's the fourth or fifth time in an hour that

she's asked about going down to her mom's, I get exasperated.
Mom! I say sharply. Nan's not there. She's not there and we're
not going. She turns and leaves the room and I feel awful.

Send one photo. I am looking at the six shiny black-and-white
photos on the desk, lined up in front of the keyboard. There
are two really good shots.

I like the one with the great smile the best. But it's a little dark,
too. I decide on the one that has the best light. She looks just
about to speak. Her forehead is furrowed a bit, and fine wrinkles cushion her skin. Laugh-lines emanate from the corners of
her eyes, across her cheeks. Deep folds run from her nose to
the corners of her mouth and down her chin; the folds are
familiar — I recognize the beginnings of them in my own face.
Her throat looks corded but soft, too. Her hair is lifted up in
small wisps in the mild afternoon breeze. She's wearing her
white cardigan over a green and blue blouse. Of course her
glasses are hanging around her neck, as they have for years.
Her new glasses that I bought her in a pharmacy, because now
she refuses to go to an eye doctor for a check-up.

I'll keep the one with the great smile for myself. It's a little
dark, and besides, she won't be wandering around smiling like
that.

Yesterday on the way to the doctor's in a taxi, she turns to me
in the back seat. She leans over and whispers, so the cabby
can't hear, in a voice so urgent and panic-filled that chills ripple across my shoulders, *I don't know where my kids are.* Panicked
like she's lost sight of us at a beach. I take her hand, Your kids
are fine, I say. We're all grown up now. We're all fine, we're all
okay. I'm Maureen, I'm one of your kids, and I very slowly
detail where we all are, where we all live. Oh yeah, she says,

oh yeah, that's right, and she comes back slowly to the present. For the moment.

Send one photo to the Wandering Patients' Registry at the Alzheimer Society. The Alzheimer Society sent us the form, but they'll forward it to the police. The police will keep it on file. Sometimes inside the subway you see a photo of an older person taped inside the glass ticket taker's booth. Missing, it says above the photo of the old man in his long winter coat, staring flatly out at you. If the patient goes missing, you call the police immediately and tell them she's registered. One day last fall, about five o'clock in the afternoon, my father had a big scare. My mother hadn't come home yet from the noon Mass at St. Michael's Cathedral. He saw a police car on the street and went out to talk to the policemen in it. I'm worried about my wife, he said. He explained that she was in the early stages of Alzheimer's, but still pretty independent and reliable. Is she registered, they asked. When he said no, they said, there's not much we can do about it. When she got back about a half an hour later, she was upset. She didn't want to talk much about it, but my father pressed her. I got turned around on the subway, she said. I got on at a new entrance. A man gave me the wrong directions. I went down to Union Station instead. I had to come all the way back. Then she changed the subject. She said that at the cathedral she met a woman who had twins; the woman's husband was away in the Air Force, and she was taking in roomers to pay the mortgage. My father noticed the woman had the same life story as my mother. She hasn't wanted to go out on her own since that September day. But every day she wants to see her mother. Now that the cold weather is ending, we get scared, we ask each other, do you think she'd go out? It would only take a few moments. She's so much worse now, we tell each other.

Send one photo. Grieving in pieces, that's what the social workers are telling us to do. You have to mourn the loss of what your mother was and accept what she still is. You have to grieve the part of her that has wandered away and will never come back.

DOREEN'S KITCHEN

Marina Endicott

WE ALL TALK about Doreen as a monster, a giant, a little bit crazy. She lives with our father, Patrick. I don't have to have anything to do with her any more if I don't want to, but Irene has to go to the island every Christmas and Easter, because she's only eight and Patrick still has visiting rights for her. I think he may have a right to me too, but it's fallen into the dusty corners, with one thing and another. So I wouldn't have gone with Irene except she said she couldn't bear to go unless I went.

Christmas is not the best time to travel if you don't want to get where you're going, because everybody else does, and at all the airports and bus stations everybody's being greeted by people who are ecstatic to see them, crying and hugging, touching reunions — there was none of that when Irene and I got off the ferry. Just Doreen standing huge-legged, as big as a house, a mansion, an army barracks, six feet tall and about four feet around. Patrick was not there.

"Two hours late!" was the first thing she said, as if the snow was our fault. Neither of us said anything. She didn't meet our eyes. I was pretty sure she would have phoned to find out how late the boat was going to be. She should have, anyway.

"You'll have to carry your own bags, girls," she told us, as if we wouldn't have realized that for ourselves, and then she stomped away.

"She's started it already," Irene whispered to me, and pulled at my arm as if we could still get back on the ferry and go home. She knew we couldn't, she knew the return tickets weren't until January 2nd, and what would we do until then in Vancouver?

"We could live in the museum like those guys in the book," she said, as close as she will come to begging, but I had to march her forwards anyway. I picked up our bags, only knapsacks because we weren't going to need good clothes for all the magnificent Boxing Day parties that Doreen wouldn't give. Beside us a man was finding his mother or some older lady — enough older that there was no question even in our sensitive minds that she was his girlfriend or anything, she had to be a mother or an aunt. "In Nova Scotia," I told Irene as we watched, "they say *awnt*; but here they say *ant*."

He put his arm around her and kissed her on the nose, and her face which had been anxious and quiet till then went into a million wrinkles of pleasure and trying not to cry. "I miss you so much," he said, and she said, "Oh, I miss you so much!" I think she must have been his mother.

I took Irene's hand and we walked after Doreen out into the evening wind, the street covered with a sifting of snow. "It's terribly sentimental," I said, "Meeting people like this, Christmas. It makes people say loving things that aren't even true — at least Doreen is honest."

"Sometimes when you don't mean something but you say it, then you do mean it after all," she said.

Doreen was half a block ahead of us by the time we got outside, and the distance didn't narrow even though we almost ran to catch up with her. She had on a red coat that wouldn't button up in the front, because of her belly, so it flapped in the wind. We could follow her like a ship with red sails. She has stumpy legs that don't wind down at all at the ankles, straight sausage from knee to foot. She also has red hair: hennaed, Isabel says. She's got a big messy mouth that goes up on one side and down on the other and little pebble eyes you can't tell the colour of. The big mystery is why Patrick likes her at all. She's an editor, maybe he thinks she will advance his career. They are not married; apparently he told her he'd had enough of getting married. Katherine and Isabel, our mothers, who were each married to Patrick for a while, could probably have said the same thing. We didn't know Doreen's position on married or not married, or whether it had changed when she found out about having the twins.

"She must be ready to pop," I said to Irene as we jogged along. "Maybe it makes you bad-tempered."

"She's always bad-tempered," she said, out of breath. I slowed down a little. "Or else stupid and telling lies."

The light poles stretched out in front of us, puddles of light on the skimpy snow and mud. We ran out of one and into the dark, and then into light again, and in the light I could see that Irene was probably going to have to cry.

I stopped. "She doesn't hate us, she's just worried. Personally I would rather be married to Jimmy Bakker or Donald Trump or somebody than Patrick. Even when he was younger he was no picnic, and now he's old and cranky. Plus she's going to have a baby any minute."

"Two," Irene said, putting her hand on the pole. "Two huge babies as big as cars."

"Anyway, we can't expect her to like us a lot, we remind her of Katherine and Isabel."

"Mommy likes you, and I like Isabel," she said, staring at me.

"Yes, but it's a long time ago."

"When I was born did my mother hate you?"

I took a minute, I thought she'd like me to consider it

seriously. "Well, when you were born she didn't know me yet, it was only afterwards that they started living together, when you were six months old. Then she liked me. I was surprised, I didn't think she would." I was not doing a very good job. "Look, she's way ahead, we'll never catch her."

"I don't want to catch her. I want Daddy to come and take us to a hotel instead and have pancakes."

"He doesn't have any money."

"I know."

She was crying to herself, not sobbing, a couple of tears running out of her eyes.

"I have fifty bucks," I said. "We could get back on the ferry and get a hotel in Vancouver and call home, and they could send us some money, and we'd be home tomorrow." It was a kind of plan. If she wanted to do it I thought we should.

A dog came running along the pavement and swerved to come over to us. Irene put out her hand and he sniffed at it and then licked it. She knelt down and scratched his back. He lifted up his head and sang, his mouth in a tiny little o to let the sound out.

"If Doreen was a dog she would like me," Irene said.

"If Doreen was a dog she would be the biggest pit-bull in the world and someone would shoot her."

She almost laughed. "This dog has no collar."

"He doesn't look hungry though, maybe he lost it."

"Maybe he'll follow us home and Doreen will have to let him in."

That made me laugh. The idea of Doreen coming to the door with a lamp and maybe a couple of cups of cocoa on a tray, seeing the dog, saying Oh poor doggie, let him come in and warm himself at the fire and sleep on my bed.

"We could give it a try," I said, and took her hand again. But the dog ran off, had somewhere else to go — we could have followed him home. We went on through the snowy night, all the way down the mile and a half to the turn-off to Patrick's house.

Patrick's house is not actually his house. It belongs to Doreen, but Doreen didn't live in it when she was alone, she was too chicken. When Patrick met her she was living in a room in Kitsilano in the same house where he was staying for a week. When I try to think of how they hit it off and decided to move to the house on the island my mind veers away. It has to have sex in it, but the thought that Patrick could possibly have sex with Doreen or want to after my mother and Irene's mother who are both beautiful although in completely different ways and interesting and intelligent — it wouldn't matter if Doreen was only ugly, but she's grotesque.

But she has a nice house. And she works for a publisher.

The porch light was on but the door was shut when we got there — it would have to be, of course, the wind was blowing and it was still snowing a little. Irene was walking blind wherever I took her by then, and she stood numbly while I got the door open and then steered her inside.

Doreen got up from the table. She had a hot drink in her hand, coffee or tea, steam coming up from it.

"You'll be tired," she said. She couldn't look us in the face. "I put the TV in your bedroom."

She has a face that can go dark, it can look almost black, you can't stand to look at it when she's angry. Her eyes, which she could not swing up to look at us, were all brown shadowed. She stood there beside the table, stubbing her cigarette out and holding her cup. She hadn't even taken her coat off, it was gaping open over the stomach.

I put the knapsacks down, took off my coat and boots, took off Irene's coat and knelt to undo her boots. Irene stood still, her face was bent down too. In the whole room I was the only one who could look around the walls and see all the paintings Doreen's father had done, heavily under the influence of Emily Carr if you ask me. It was easier to look at the paintings than at Doreen.

She didn't say anything, she didn't move.

I stood up and picked up the bags and got Irene's hand in mine again. Nobody said anything. After a minute, when nobody, not even me, could look straight ahead, I took Irene into our usual bedroom, the small one at the back of the house.

It was only nine o'clock, but I opened up one of the beds and helped Irene undress — she was crying so hard she couldn't get her buttons undone. Her little body was shaking and shaking, it made me so angry that I started to shake too, and I couldn't talk about it even though I should have found some way to make Irene think it wasn't her fault. "Never mind, never mind," was all I could say, which was stupid, because why shouldn't she mind?

After she was lying down and not shaking so badly I went to the bathroom down the hall and got a washcloth. I put it under the hot tap. While it was getting warmed up I looked up at myself in the mirror and in that sudden glance it seemed to me that I had the same brown mask over my own face, like Doreen's. I wrung the washcloth out and took it back to our room.

Irene was calmer, she was turned towards the door waiting for me, with her hand under her ear. "Roll your head a little," I told her, "So I can wash your face."

"It's warm," she said.

"We can fix it, we can go home tomorrow," I said.

"It's okay."

The bed was covered with a white Hudson's Bay blanket, with beautiful coloured stripes. "Do you always get this blanket even when I'm not here?"

"I like it."

"We're not prisoners or anything, we'll call our mothers and they'll send us a new ticket. We don't have to stay." I was worried that maybe I was making it worse, because she wasn't really listening to me.

"The first little bit is always hard," she said, and that filled me up with anger to the roof of my head.

"Where's Patrick, that's what I'd like to know?"

"That's probably why she's mad," Irene said, closing her eyes to let me put the washcloth on them.

I was afraid she would be cold, so I lay down with her for a while. The one lucky thing was that Katherine had enough money to buy tickets for us. So far I've found that the thing I want most often is enough money to leave places. If Isabel had had more money a long time ago I wouldn't have had to stay with my grandparents in Mahone Bay. She wouldn't have had to share a house with Katherine, and Katherine wouldn't have had to either if she'd had a job then. But then I wouldn't have ever met Irene except maybe by accident here at Patrick's — and if he'd had money I bet he wouldn't have taken up with Doreen. If he'd had enough money to take off I bet none of us would have ever seen him again. Maybe he had some money, maybe that was why he wasn't home.

When I woke up I didn't know where I was for a second — I knew I was with Irene, but it wasn't my own bed or hers. Then I saw the wooden slat blinds shining and I remembered I was at Patrick's. My watch was hard to see, I had to hold it right under the window without waking Irene up. The moon was out of the clouds, it must have stopped snowing. It was eleven-thirty.

I got up carefully and put the blankets back around her and I left her my watch in case she got worried. I put it on the pillow beside her.

Then I went out into the hall, even though I was afraid to do it — I thought I'd better talk to Doreen. I was amazed at how scared I was.

The hall seemed long before I could turn into the living-room. My socks weren't making any noise on the carpet, so she didn't turn around when I came in. She was still sitting at the table. She still had her coat on.

I couldn't speak for a minute, because I was afraid I'd start yelling. Not only would this be a stupid thing to do and take away my dignity, I would also lose, because Doreen can really holler.

"I need to use the phone," I said, finally.

"It's on the kitchen counter." She didn't jump or turn her head, it sounded as if we'd been having a conversation all night.

I had to walk past her. She didn't move anything, not even a finger or a muscle in her face, she stared down at the table like she had been doing, like a stone woman. I was double afraid now, because she was being so weird, but it came out of me like diarrhea or something, by mistake.

"Where's Patrick?"

She looked at me then; it took her head a while to get back in gear for turning. "Patrick?" she asked me. "I don't know where Patrick is. He went for coffee."

"When did he go?"

"On Tuesday."

"This is Friday."

"Yes. It's Friday."

I had this really vivid memory of when Irene was about five, Katherine saying "he went for coffee" when I asked her how Patrick left her. It might have been a joke; he left Katherine long before Irene was born, a couple of months at least, and here was Doreen obviously nearly ready to reproduce. In the same moment I also remembered Doreen taking me to shop one day in Vancouver and buying me a good leather skirt and a Walkman; she must have spent about six hundred dollars in one day, but the thing was it was a nice day, we went to Stanley Park and I got a peacock feather, and we had fried chicken in the park.

"Did he phone?"

She looked up then, I thought she might laugh. It was a stupid thing to ask. I felt even worse.

"You could have called and told us not to come," I said.

"I thought he'd come back." She tapped her finger on the table. "I wanted company."

What would you want us for? Call your friends! I wanted to say, but I had a feeling she didn't have any friends. Even her parents were both dead: that's why she had the house.

She got up, she took off her coat and went to hang it up. As she walked, all lumbering, she said, "If you want to go home tomorrow I'll arrange for it."

That was exactly what I'd come out here for anyway, but as soon as she said it I thought maybe we should stay for a couple of days anyway and see what happened when Patrick came back. And if he didn't, then I didn't know what we would do.

I couldn't like her, she was impossible to like, but it looked to me as if she was taking her coat off because she knew Patrick wasn't coming back tonight; she wouldn't need her armour. She was so huge with the babies that I didn't see how we could leave her alone right away. I would have to find some way to talk Irene into it.

She stopped over by the wall with her hands on it, leaning into it. "Oh God," she said, in that extreme way she has; it made me afraid that she was going into labour right there. "I didn't give you anything to eat. Do you want a cup of tea?"

This seemed to me to be the most selfish and disgusting thing she'd said or done yet, to offer me a cup of tea at midnight when Irene had gone to sleep with nothing. I almost decided to phone Katherine right away, even though it was two in the morning in Saskatoon. But Doreen stayed bowed over by the wall, resting her head on it, looking like a child sent to the corner; also I'd been thinking it might be more mature to wait until the morning to call them instead of waking them up in the middle of the night all panicky. I wouldn't have the tea, though.

"No thank you," I said. "I'll just go back to bed."

You get these notions of what is loyal and what isn't, I don't know where they come from. Irene wouldn't ever know that I'd had a cup of tea. But if Orpheus or somebody hadn't had a piece of pomegranate — no, it was Persephone, even better. If she hadn't eaten a little seed of pomegranate on the way out of hell, just to get the taste of the juice on her tongue, it would be summer all the time, never winter, never Christmas. I must have been tired: all the way to bed and into bed and into sleep, I was thinking about Persephone climbing that long dark hallway out of hell.

Irene woke me up by staring at me — she does that all the time at home, you get a feeling in your dream that someone's watching you, and you open your eyes, and there are her clean white and green eyes looking into yours. She isn't really awake herself, she's just thinking and looking. I say good morning and she says good morning, and I put my arm around her, and then we close our eyes again and go back to sleep. So far we could have been at home. The next thing is about ten minutes later she starts to draw on my face. She's painting my face on for the day.

She did that too, so I got to lie there with my eyes closed and her delicate fingers touching me like soft brushes, like the fronds of a juniper bush. Irene is like a smell of juniper in the room.

"What are you drawing me," I asked her in my unused early voice. It was almost dark in the room.

"You have big black eyebrows," she told me, tracing them. "And your cheeks are full like the wind on the map, and your mouth has a sharp edge to it." She used her fingernail.

"I am the war queen."

"But you have a huge double chin — " Two tickling loops under my chin made me crouch my head down to my chest. "And your ears can hear everything in the world." Her finger fiddled inside the curls of my ear, first one and then the other — my head went side to side on the pillow. "And your whole face is bright bright green," she said, laughing so no-one would hear us.

I pulled myself up on my side to do her. I started at her forehead and washed my hand all down her face. "Your skin is purple like blueberries with sugar on them. You have a spear for a nose ... ." I pinched it gently all the way down like clay. "Your eyes see things hidden under rocks or water." I pressed lightly on the inside of her eyeballs, by her nose. "Each of your teeth — open your mouth — each tooth is three feet long and has a bell on the end." She was laughing again, making almost no sound to match my whispering, trying not to open her eyes. "And you have a beard as long as a carpet, a red carpet rolling off you for fancy people to walk on."

"Then Doreen can't walk on it," she said, which gave me those two hard heartbeats — I'd almost thought she was okay.

She opened her eyes. She caught me watching her carefully and she screwed up her face and burst out laughing, too loud for however early it was. "Okay, okay," I said, "She can't, you get to pick — with teeth like that, no-one will dare to walk on it if you don't invite them to."

"*You* can walk on it," she said, still laughing when the door opened.

Doreen nearly filled up the whole door. She either hadn't

taken her dress off or she'd put it on again.

We both shut up.

"I'll make you some breakfast," she said. Then she left.

We stayed shut up. After a minute I scrabbled under the pillow for my watch.

"It's six-thirty."

She looked scared and giddy both. "It can't be, it's getting light out."

"Well, it's *dawn*, yes. They have daylight saving here. And it's farther south."

We were both about to get hysterical, like being tickled until you can't stand it. It was either laugh or bawl.

We put our same sweaters back on so we wouldn't take too long in case she was waiting for us, and we put our shoes on too, to feel more stable.

"We are the warrior queens," I told her. "Your teeth like spears can vanquish any terrible spider-witch; my windy cheeks will blow her into next week."

I hadn't told her yet that I didn't phone home, or that I thought we might have to stay. Feed her up first and then get her aside, I thought, feeling guilty for being so manipulative but also grateful that she was so young she could wake up happy even in this house, even without Patrick, even having breakfast with Doreen.

The whole house was grey-blue, twilight in that early early morning. I nearly turned on a light switch, I had my hand out, but then I thought Doreen might want it dim.

Irene held my hand when we got to the living-room. The table was set with place mats and everything — jars of jam and butter already there. Doreen came in from the kitchen carrying a big glass jug of orange juice, Patrick's jug that he used for making sangria in the summer.

"Hey there," I said, being polite. "I'm sorry we woke you up."

"I wasn't sleeping," she said. "Sit down."

"Can I help you?" Why does it always have to be so awkward? Even when Patrick's there making dumb jokes the first couple of mornings are this stiff. Sometimes it's been worse, really. She said no and went back to the kitchen, so Irene and I sat down like good girls. Irene's foot kept kicking me under the table. I pinched her knee where it really makes her laugh and grinned at her as if Doreen was a nothing, a tiny mosquito.

"Did you call home?" she whispered, just as Doreen came back with a plate of eggs.

"I just fried them," Doreen announced with her usual too-loud voice, plunking it down in front of us. Then she stopped. "If you want scrambled, Bess, you can make some more."

"Fried is great," I said. What else could I possibly say anyway, since she was trying not to be the ogress this morning. She went back to the kitchen again.

Irene turned one over with her fork. They were hard as rocks and black on the bottom. I put one on my plate anyway.

Doreen came back with some toast, that special thin-slice kind of bread, as if she could possibly lose weight at the moment. I thought she might sit down with us, there was a place set for her, but she went back again, her bunchy yellow feet slap-slapping in red slippers without backs. Irene took a piece of toast and put it on her plate. It was like being in some horrible movie that would last for three hours, Doreen would just keep bringing things in all morning, all day, the food would gradually turn into lunch and then dinner and we'd still have to sit there eating. The egg on my plate had two yolks — I suddenly almost had to puke. Two hard yellow ping-pong balls in a greasy white bed.

I looked at Irene instead of puking. She looked back at me. "I didn't call," I said. I was afraid Doreen would hear me, or come back. "I couldn't call last night, it was too late." That was no good, my mother would have been out taking the paper to the paper-boys, but Katherine would not have been asleep, and she never minds being woken up anyway. Irene looked at me (ashamed of me?).

Doreen came in with a pot of coffee. She poured me a cup. "Irene?" Irene looked at her instead of me; then looked away again quickly. "Do you drink coffee yet?"

"She doesn't like it," I said in case Irene didn't talk. "She'll just drink juice."

"There's your breakfast then," Doreen said.

Out she went.

Five eggs on the plate, four pieces of toast.

"Can you eat?"

Irene shook her head. Shit, I thought, I am so bad at this — it's a good thing I don't have some poor child to look after all by myself. But then I thought that Doreen would have two soon, and they would be a lot worse off than Irene with Katherine and Isabel and me around her.

"Eat an egg," I told her. "It won't kill you and you'll need your strength." I leaned over. "We may not live till lunch," I said faintly in her ear. Nothing for a minute, but then she looked up at me sideways.

"Can I have some ketchup?" she asked me in a small voice — not like last night in bed, but the good bad small voice she uses when she wants something evil. Katherine doesn't buy ketchup, we have to get it at McDonald's. She grinned at me a little, just showed me the top row of her teeth. "Three feet long," she said. Then she laughed her head off without making a single bit of noise. I hit her on the head with my knuckles and went to the kitchen. It was darker in there, the north side of the house. So it took me a minute to see her.

Their kitchen is weird, for colour, because everything in it is plum, even a big plum-coloured fridge and stove, and also for shape. It's a tunnel, sort of, cupboards on both sides of the narrow narrow room, and then at the end a nook or something that used to be a greenhouse when Doreen's father was around. They'd taken out the greenhouse shelves and put in a daybed instead like a window seat, an armless thing with cushions at one end. The glass goes right up to the roof, bending into the house at the top, so it's a good place to lie down at night. You can look down the path to the shore from there.

Doreen was crouched on the daybed like an animal, going hoo, hoo, with her mouth, her breath. She had one foot on the floor and one knee on the bed, both arms bracing her, her huge belly touching down on it. She couldn't see me; even if she could have I don't think she would have noticed me. Her heel was bare, the slipper was falling off. I wanted to leave, but if I did Irene would think something was wrong. Something was wrong, she'd be right.

Everything in that dark plum kitchen looked like blood — all I could do was stand there. I didn't like it, I wanted to go home.

Her neck stretched out, she seemed to be looking out the window, but she was still making that noise. I couldn't even put my hand on the counter.

"Hi," she said — the most ridiculous thing to say. I don't know how she knew I was there. Everything smelled like fried eggs.

She stopped. She was quiet for a minute, then she pushed herself back off the bed.

"Did you need something?" she asked, not looking at me, standing with her back to the kitchen.

"Um, ketchup," I said.

"Ketchup. In the fridge."

I got the fridge door open. The light from inside it shone out into the gloomy room, made all that dark red glow instead of smoulder. It lit her back up too, in her red dress. It was only the colour of bricks, not blood.

"Do you need the doctor?" I was getting the ketchup out,

not looking at her in case she didn't want me to.

"No," she said; I was only a child, she was saying.

I took the ketchup bottle out to Irene.

"It's no-name," she said, yanking her mouth down — I could have slapped her face, which really surprised me, I don't think I ever wanted to slap Irene before. It was the surprise that fixed me up, made my mind start again.

"I'm going to be a minute," I told her.

"Has she started?" she asked, face lighting up, shoving her chair out. All excited for somebody she couldn't stand, and there was me being such a baby, I couldn't even stay in the same room.

I hurt in my stomach. "I think maybe she has. She's — not really friendly."

"She's probably just busy," she said. She pulled her chair in again and poured herself some ketchup. Then I could think, look, that looks like blood too, and see how stupid I was being.

"Okay, stay out here until I say, okay?"

"Okay," she said. She cut up her egg.

I was going back, the whole six steps from the table to the kitchen, which that morning was like walking over the Alps or something, when Doreen started to yell.

Oh God, I thought, dead babies pouring out of her, oh God, but when I got to the doorway, Irene right behind me, it was the pan on fire, the pan she'd fried the eggs in — a bright little fire on the stove. Doreen was yelping, waving her hands in the air, she looked like a scarecrow, if you could get one that large. There was an acid, metallish stink.

"Water, get water!" she was shrieking.

I grabbed the frying pan off the burner, found the lid of a pot hanging under the counter and jammed it down.

"If you put water in it just burns more," Irene shouted at her to stop her yelling. She got around me and went to Doreen. "It's okay now, Bessie got it," she said.

The handle was hot, but it was plastic, not hot enough to burn me. I put the frying pan down in the sink.

"My grandmother does this every year at Thanksgiving," I said. I was in an amazingly good mood all of a sudden. It's being useful, being good in emergencies, I really like to do that. If I went crazy I'd probably go around setting fires and putting them out.

Doreen sat down on the edge of the daybed, she used Irene's shoulder to get down with.

"She puts brown paper over the turkey, that's what her mother used to do. But it catches fire every year."

"So Bessie puts it out," Irene said. She was watching Doreen calm down. "With baking soda."

"Do you want a cup of coffee?" I asked her. "I mean, do you want anything?"

Doreen started to laugh haw-haw-haw through her nose. "You didn't use baking soda, Bess," she said, between brays.

"The lid works too," Irene said, perfectly serious. That made me laugh, a bit. I went and got the coffee and poured her a cup. I put some sugar in it, because if people are in shock they need it. I thought if Doreen kept laughing like that she might get hysterical and then we'd have to pour water on her. Or jam a lid on her head.

"Isn't this idiotic. It's simple reaction," she said. "I'm fine."

"Are you having the babies?" I asked her — Irene was going to ask her if I didn't.

She gulped some coffee, she coughed.

"Should we phone the doctor?"

"I've got a midwife, I called her at five." She paused, she put her hands down on her knees. "The doctor will come later on, but Janice is coming at eight."

"Is that soon enough?" I was surprised — the way she was panting before, I thought they were being pretty casual.

"It takes a while, Bessie," she said. She took a big breath, and then she put her hand on Irene's shoulder. "It'll be a Christmas present," she said. That's what people say to their own children when they're having a baby, that it'll be a Christmas present for them, or a birthday present. It sounded crazy coming out of Doreen's mouth, but she meant it to be kind, in her ungainly way.

"You should lie down," I said, trying to be kinder myself.

"Yes, I should get out of this firetrap, too." She hoisted herself up again, and we all went into the living-room in a line, playing follow-the-leader. I had this urge to duck down and crawl under the table to see if she'd do it, but I got over it immediately.

There wasn't anything to say in the living-room. We stood around. Neither Irene nor I wanted to sit down before she did, and she didn't seem to feel like it. It was getting lighter, even through the fir trees outside the living-room windows. Doreen wandered around touching things, flicking her big finger on picture frames and the edge of the mantel. Irene and I stood awkwardly, trying to think what to say.

"Do you want to play cards?" Irene asked — then she looked at me in agony in case she'd said the wrong thing.

Doreen looked around. "I can't think of anything else to do," she said. She seemed to be pretty helpless for a big woman. It didn't take away her size, it made it more obvious. She pouted out her lips. "Nope, I can't think of one thing I'd rather do."

Irene got the cards out of the wooden box on the mantelpiece. It was seven in the morning and we were going to sit around playing cards with a pregnant woman we couldn't stand.

"If I go get some wood, can we have a fire?" Then it would be like evening, I thought. Doreen said sure, and I left Irene to set up the cards. She loves playing cards. I think maybe it's the only thing she and Doreen could possibly do together — Irene doesn't like to shop that much yet. But she would like Stanley Park, and the peacocks.

"Doreen's Kitchen" is excerpted from a longer story, titled "Doreen."

CITY: ROMANCE

Rachel Wyatt

A CLOUD OF inefficiency had settled over the city. Some said it was the hole in the ozone layer that was causing it. Others blamed it on the fumes of diesel and oil we were inhaling all the time and said that cars must be banned from downtown. Marie's mother said that it was to be expected, young people did not care and the fact that the chiropodist was two hours late was a perfect example. He knew she would wait for him. Her time, to him, had no value whatever. But her feet needed his care. She sat. She waited. And later she called the office to tell Marie all about it.

All the same there was music to be heard. People driving by in their cars left their windows down and a patchwork of sounds zipped out into the air. The birds in the trees round Osgoode Hall chirped out their little notes. And Marie knew that her own briefcase was an emblem of things done right, achievements, appointments met, promises kept. And Sam accepted that.

"So good of Sam," Sheila said. But Sheila always saw the downside.

In the office maze, corridors, bypasses, sunlight shining in some windows, Marie crossed Sam's path, he crossed hers. Papers were exchanged, books from the highest shelves, and words and looks. The phone brought in the tragic people. Marie and Sam listened and occasionally spoke. A good day's work. The praise came from above.

Marie skipped along the sidewalk and then marched in a more orderly fashion hearing glad songs sung in a pure soprano voice. Words floated up from beneath the street. There was an argument going on about responsibility. The last man out leaves all tidy, they said. Nothing though was written and not all of them agreed. The foreman, paid more, should stay late and make sure the street was safe. The foreman said he was paid to delegate. The others told him what he could do with "delegate."

She walked down the steps, paid her token and took off her dark glasses and stood on the subway platform with all those others, all of them standing there, staring ahead of them, trying to decipher the writing on the wall until the train came.

Kids had taken over the deli in the Mall. Its garbage cans were dripping over with used plates and forks and empty sauce containers. There was a sour smell of decaying meat. Three boys were sharing a milkshake behind the counter, three straws in one half-litre of strawberry special. And when Marie asked them for her medium-sized sandwich plate, ordered at 2:00 to be ready at 6:30, they told her it was already on its way in a cab across the city. Had she not said "the Beaches"?

They made several phone calls and tried to get the cab to return but it and the sandwiches, ham, egg, cheese, tastefully arranged with cut up raw veggies, had disappeared into the cool evening. So they insisted she go into the kitchen with them and help make up a new platter regardless of time and her new outfit.

Jurgen arrived at the subway depot to find his office door locked. Hanno had left early. He had not waited as he was supposed to do, as the written rules said. Jurgen kicked at the door. Hanno might be in there, despairing, dead. "Hanno!" he yelled. "What the fuck! What the fuck! What the fuck!" And then he sent out the signal that stopped all trains in their tracks. If Hanno was on an Eastbound train going home, he had to be made aware of his error.

Everyone in the great hall could see that two of the second violinists were missing and that no-one had bothered to remove their chairs. Oboes, double basses, percussion, all tried to draw the audience into the music. But the audience, and the conductor must be aware of it, was watching, waiting for those two renegades to come creeping in, sidle to their places, fastening their ties, rustling pages, and trying to catch up. The music's tempo quickened. Lyricism fell by the wayside. Romance died.

Sam whispered to Marie that he had paid $67.50 for his ticket and was entitled to a full orchestra. Mortifyingly he got up in the middle of the last stanza of the first movement and stomped out. There was slight applause from those nearby. Others hissed. She sat tight. If he read that as betrayal, that was his problem.

"He was fucking supposed to wait!" Jurgen yelled down the phone to his boss. Hanno was supposed to wait and hand over his sheet and to wait so that they could have coffee together and talk about last night's game, about women, Hanno's kids, or the weather maybe.

A stranger put his head round the office door and screamed, "Are you bastards on strike again!"

Marie had spent evenings checking out the wine, the cloth, the recipe for the fish. Sheila, copying it from her book, had missed out only two of the vital ingredients. The whole apartment smelt of the cabbage which she had substituted for broccoli. Sam was late. What excuse this time? He couldn't get a taxi? Something wrong on the subway? Stuck in an elevator? And the fish lay drying up amid onions on the brightly coloured plate she had bought two years ago in Quimper.

It was simple. It was the rule. The day man was supposed to wait until the evening man arrived, to hand over his sheet showing any irregularities, and then they shared coffee and their views on the state of the world, kids, women, the Jays' lousy batting average. Then Hanno went off home to dinner and Jurgen began his evening of watching and waiting and writing his report, dated clearly, written neatly. What was he supposed to do if he couldn't get into the office?

"Are you bastards on strike?" the passenger shouted again.

"I tried to cancel your appointment," the woman in the beauty salon said over the phone. "But you were not there and so you will have to come in. Henri won't tolerate missed appointments. You either come in or you pay. Which is it to be?"

Marie said, "I tried to let you know. I'm due in court in ten minutes. I can't come now."

"Don't expect Henri to do your hair again."

The teacher said plaintively that she had only received fifteen notices about the school concert. She had put them into those hands which reached out and when the bell rang she had, as usual, run out into the street whispering "Hallelujah." Another day finished.

Sheila said every teacher she had in high school had been unfair to her.

Hanno's home life had gone to pieces on the day when the plumber put the wrong piece of pipe in the joint. Rina said, Rina shrieked, that it was not her fault that the water had run down the stairs and ruined a thousand dollars' worth of broadloom. The phone had rung. She had to rush out to the hairdressers because there was a gap in Henri's schedule. Someone had let him down.

"I'm being charged with racism," the teacher said, the following week. "All the kids who got notices for the concert were the grabby ones who pushed forward to take them."

Marie looked at the teacher's dossier and saw that several pages were missing. She sent for the clerk and discovered that there had been a spill in that office, papers had been chewed up by the machine which had not been serviced now for over a year. The teacher obviously did not fit into the system. She had to go.

Jurgen tried to defend himself. Could they not see that Hanno might have killed himself and been lying in there, shot?

Marie loved Sam. But ever since the affair of the sandwiches when she had turned up at the office party three hours late, covered in chopped egg salad, crying and carrying an empty tray, he been cool towards her. As distant as a cold planet. He was not leaving love messages on her answering machine. He had also said something about her hair looking different these days.

Her next case concerned the security services of the subway. Employees had made a citizen's arrest of their supervisor who appeared to have gone berserk one afternoon when he came to the office and found it locked.

Marie was trying hard to hear music. The habit had helped her always in school. There were, in most places, sounds that could be forced into a symphony if you listened hard enough. Her own voice, she liked to think, added something to the melody of the world around her.

"I can't believe you've cut off my phone," she roared to Claudine the operator who was trying to put her through to the business office. "I did not pay my bill because I never received it."

"It was mailed from here."

Marie bought a CD player. She set the little silver disk into the slot and let Shostakovich show her what he had done with the sounds of his life.

The news on TV showed groups of people beating other people with sticks mainly in foreign countries. And while she felt sad for them, disturbed even, wishing to help, there was nothing she could do. Had she made her way to one of those countries, paying her own fare, carrying meat and bandages, she would not have known whose side to be on.

The symphony was soothing, it planed the edges from

her mind and let her accept notes, easily, randomly, like following a stream.

Sheila said that was her whole trouble.

"Your mother called me," Sam said harshly at the office. "She's fond of you."

"She wants to know when we'll be married."

It crossed Marie's mind to apologize but she held back.

Her mother's question was reasonable. For a long time she had wanted to know the answer to it herself.

"I went home to save my wall-to-wall," Hanno pleaded.

"My neighbour phoned me at the office because he heard the sound of rushing water, he saw water coming out under my front door. I saved for that rug. It was blue with a classical pattern. All my life I wanted a rug like that and now the insurance company won't pay."

You could not, in law, indict the hairdresser.

For a week a new mailman had delivered Marie's mail to number thirty-five and the woman inside lying helpless from a stroke had been unable to redirect it. Only the woman's daughter had finally, angrily brought Marie a little bag of letters and told her to put her proper return address on the envelope. Did she and her mother not have enough problems?

"I tried to call you, last night," said Sam.

Marie burst into tears.

He backed away.

"The repairman," she shouted after him, "Has promised to come on three separate occasions. And has not turned up."

He marched away from her voice, down the steps and

onto the street. She interpreted his scream as one of joy, she pictured him leaping into the air, free at last. Now he need not pretend affection where he felt none. Now, as he, probably, went hopping down the street, he was telling passersby of his blessed release. And she let herself into her office and turned to her files for comfort.

"Good riddance," Sheila said.

Marie went to the hospital to visit Sam. It was a time for discretion. She silently reproached herself for not following him out onto the street. He was bitter about those passersby who had seen him there, half in and half out of the hole in the road, and had not come to help him. He was suing the workman who had failed to replace the manhole cover at the end of the day. He did not offer the case to her.

At the wedding, the bride was late because, as she told the guests later, she had second thoughts about marriage and more specifically about going on honeymoon with a man whose leg was encased in plaster hip to heel.

After she had caught the bouquet of freesias and baby's breath, Marie wished Sam and his nurse well. They were driven away in an ambulance, the nurse looking trapped as she peered from the little round window at the back.

Her mother, home at last from the chiropodist's said, "See. This city is falling apart."

Sheila said, "There are other fish in the sea, Marie."

Marie still heard music. The Wedding March faded into the sterner brassy notes of a school band practising inside the building next door. Birds, knowing that they would soon be on their way South, were singing a more cheerful song. She waved to the workman who stuck his head up out of the manhole. He whistled. She didn't know the tune but it had a good lilt to it. She walked lightly to his rhythm and, further along the road, dropped the bouquet into a trashcan and decided to make up a song of her own.

A CHINESE WEDDING

Margaret Hollingsworth

I KNEW SHE'D be all right. She was a friendly, outgoing girl and she was the star of my class; they were all fresh out of the Chinese equivalent of high school, and it was as much as I could do to draw a couple of words out of them. Not her though. She'd been tuning in to Voice of America since she was twelve.

I gave every one of them an English name — the boys I named after Canadian prime-ministers, John A, Pierre, Brian, Lester B.

I named the girls for their wives, but I ran dry after Mila and Maggie and Maureen, so I moved over to characters in books of fiction. I'd've liked to have used biblical names but my colleagues got in first, the school was swarming with Mary's and Martha's.

She was the only Wendy.

I don't pretend to be an intellectual, but I liked teaching them. I've never been listened to by so many people — I guess it made me feel important. All I had to do was follow the textbook, they never gave me any flack, though sometimes they fell asleep as soon as they hit the bench. That threw me off till I found out one Sunday halfway through my second year that it wasn't because I was boring.

I always got together with the other three Christian teachers and a few students on Sunday morning for prayers and bible study, then we'd go out for lunch at a little hole-in-the-wall restaurant we all liked. It was a special treat; we didn't get much of an allowance, nothing like some of the salaried teachers with their MA's and PHD's. What we made we tithed back to the church. Anyway, on this day it was just the four of us, no students, and one of the guys happened to mention that someone had been snoring in his American poetry class. It was a revelation. It turned out that it happened to all of us and we all thought it was our fault. Nobody gets much sleep in China, they're jammed into their sleeping quarters like matches and the street noises start up at about 4:30 am.

Wendy never fell asleep. She was always the first on her feet with a question and she'd stay behind after class to help clean the board or discuss some point she hadn't understood. About a third of the way into the session she started coming to our Sunday morning gatherings. Uninvited. I'd never taken much notice of her. She was heavier than the other students and it had occurred to me that she must be better fed. When I looked at her closely I saw that her eyes bulged a little and her glasses gave her pupils a kind of furry, splayed-out look, like she was dreaming. I liked that. She wore very red lipstick which didn't do anything for me. The first time I kissed her I mentioned this, and she never wore it again. I guess she was pretty. The Chinese said she was, but they have different standards. She was definitely lively.

She took to bible study like a pup to the nipple. Everyone remarked on it. She was real intense about it, and she managed to come up with questions that none of us four white guys could answer. She learned whole books of the Old Testament — she'd ask us one week what the next week's text would be, and she'd show up with the whole chapter memorized. She wasn't one bit superstitious like most of the students. She was open and ready to let Jesus enter her heart.

I can only say that it was the Lord's will. She proposed to me the second time we were alone together. Naturally I laughed. I never usually had students in my room, and never women. The residence was filled with *foreign experts*, all nationalities, all teaching at the university. Mrs. Wong downstairs kept a sharp eye on us. She came into our rooms every morning at 6:30, with the excuse of leaving thermos flasks of hot water. There are people at every corner watching your activities in China, but it only bothers you if you have something to hide. Wendy always arrived on my mat at a respectable hour with a watertight excuse for her presence. She was one of the few people Mrs. Wong ever smiled at. She had a million questions about North America — well, all the students dreamed of getting there, (they didn't differentiate between the States and Canada) but none of them were as single-minded as her. Oh, I knew she was more interested in my passport than she was in my nonexistent muscles. I didn't encourage her, but I didn't discourage her either.

We got engaged just before Christmas. We kept it quiet, but I found out when I left in June that everyone'd known we were an item for six months. Everyone, that is, except my bible study group. When they heard, they prophesied doom — though as it turned out, two of them married Chinese women themselves.

I decided not to renew my contract for a third year. I talked it over with Wendy and she was all in favour of me going back home as soon as possible, as long as we got married first. I tried to sidetrack her by saying I had to get the ring first, and I wanted a Canadian one, not a piece of glass. She produced a Sears mail-order catalogue; it was five years out of date but it featured diamond rings. I promised her one when we got back to Canada.

We were married the day before I left; it happened in a

borrowed third floor apartment. It was just one room, hung with red banners, and cutouts of the Mandarin symbol for happiness stuck all over the walls. A city official in a tight gray suit did the honours, and I had one of my bible-study colleagues bless us. Wendy rented a fancy veil and a white dress and she had a bouquet of silk flowers. Her whole family was there, cousins and second cousins, her brother and nieces and her little old grandmother, who she was specially fond of. It made me think of my grandma; I was glad the old lady didn't have to witness me taking my wedding vows in Chinese. She'd've had a heart attack when there wasn't one mention of Our Heavenly Father. Deep down she thinks the whole world should speak Ukrainian.

Everyone made speeches and I made one too. I was nervous but it turned out pretty good. Her old grandma cried at the top of her lungs, and no-one tried to shut her up. They'd hired a band to serenade us as we left the apartment block to go back to the Foreign Teacher's residence. I thought they looked a bit pathetic standing there among the heaps of coal and garbage, playing *Oh how we danced on the night we were wed*, an accordion, a violin and a saxophone. It was raining. I didn't dare let on that I can't dance.

I got back to Saskatchewan with the wedding certificate and a couple of suitcases full of presents, jade, and hand-painted scrolls and stuff. The woman at customs let me through right away; she just touched my shoulder and wished me luck, and there I'd been rehearsing my spiel all through the flight, not wanting to pay hundreds of dollars in duty.

It was great to meet up with all my old circle, but I hadn't been home for more than a few days before I realized it wasn't the place to bring Wendy. They're good people, but they're not exactly unbiased. It's not their fault; most of them have never travelled further than Winnipeg. We needed to be where there wouldn't be any prejudgements made, where we'd both be starting fresh. For a time I considered going down to the States. I knew I could probably swing something, through the church, and the States is fertile ground for Christian teaching; but I figured I had enough challenges ahead getting myself set up as a married man. I had to try to plot out some kind of path for myself, no more low-paying jobs; before this I'd never minded what I did as long as there was a chance to spread the Word, but I was a family man now, and my first duty was to support my wife and help her become a Canadian. I realized I hadn't thought things through, it had been enough to try to imagine myself waking up next to a woman for the rest of my life. I put my fate in the Lord's hands and went down on my knees.

It took nearly a year for the paperwork to get sorted out between Canada and China. She wrote me just about every day, and I wrote back and corrected her letters. A guy from the Plymouth Brethren over in Moosemin landed a job out west in British Columbia. He said there was housing and work, so I drove out there to take a look. I knew it was a long ways away, but until you actually drive it, far doesn't mean a thing. I kept comparing the miles of empty landscape to China, where every inch of soil is swarming with reapers and sowers.

I called up the guy from Moosemin as soon as I got over the Rockies. He was in a place called Kelowna. He said he liked it out there. I was thinking of pushing on the extra few hundred miles to the coast, but he said people were more open to the Word in the interior of the province. So I wound up in a place called Castlegar. It was a small town in the middle of great scenery, a big river and mountains and stuff, and there was industry, so I was pretty sure I'd find work. I knew it was the place we were meant to be the minute I hit town.

I rented a trailer on a site a few miles outside town, bought some sheets and towels and dishes, then drove back home to wait for my wife and swallow my butterflies.

I picked her up in Regina at 3:45 pm on July 11th. We couldn't think of much to say to each other at first, but it got easier. She made a good impression on my family. The fact that she was a Christian helped — not to mention the bolts of silk her parents sent over. That stuff must've cost a fortune, and I knew they'd probably mortgaged the next ten years of their life for it.

My Grandpa joked that my wife fitted into life in our town like a well potted snooker ball. We only stayed a month, but in that time the choir master had her in the choir, she was playing bingo with my mom, and my sister JoAnne got the biggest kick out of taking her late shopping on Fridays. She wasn't a bit shy; in fact she had opinions on everything from the day after she arrived and nobody thought any the worse of her for holding forth. She'd read up on Canada and knew more about the history and geography than half my high school teachers. And it turned out she could play the piano by ear — hymns, country music, the Beatles and the Sound of Music, stuff like that. She was a big attraction, the house was always full of neighbours wanting to hear her talk. Before we left town my Grandma gave me a diamond ring. I knew it was her engagement ring and I didn't want to take it, but it fit my wife's hand like it was made for her. My grandma kissed her and told her not to be lonesome. I guess she was remembering when she first came here as a young girl, but Wendy wasn't the type to be lonely.

We loaded a few things into my truck and set off for BC. If the Lord hadn't been calling us to Castlegar I'd have cancelled the trip and toughed it out at home. As it was the family followed us along Highway 1 for about fifty miles, then honked three times and turned around. I had tears in my eyes. I asked her if she'd felt okay leaving China, and she said sure, no problem, and sat on the edge of the seat looking out, like a kid on a birthday treat. I told her I'd teach her how to drive, then I regretted it. I didn't want her taking off on me — we were in this together now. All the way across I squeezed her hand. I had a red indent on my palm where the diamond bit into me.

She liked Castlegar right off. My Grandpa hit it on the head when he said she was born to Canadian life. I couldn't've made a better choice. I had to beg her to cook her home recipes — she liked the Chinese take-out downtown, and she wouldn't have chopsticks in the house. She fell in love with the trailer. Over there it would've housed two families. I had difficulty folding myself into the shower, and I kept hitting my head on the bedroom light fixture, but I kept my complaints to myself. She had her hair cut off and never got out of her blue jeans and sweatshirts, except on Sunday. I told her I preferred her in her old frills and lacy blouses, but I guess she thought I was kidding.

The first week we were there I found a janitorial job. It was pretty humble, but I knew it could lead to something else and I gave it everything I had. She never complained when I was out of the house nine hours at a stretch. It didn't take long to organize a few of the guys in the shop for prayer meetings in the lunch hour, and even the odd time after the night shift. She busied herself with the church and with bible study. Sometimes I'd come home at night and there'd be one light on, and she'd be sitting on the couch with the bible spread on her knees, her finger following the words, mouthing them like a deaf mute. Other than that I think she slept in, wrote letters home, and watched TV; she liked the cartoons, though the mountain out back made the picture all snowy.

I taught her to skate that first winter. She was used to ice — they get plenty of it back in China — but she'd never owned skates. I got her a pair of the latest style for Christmas and she burst into tears. She had a tendency to cry when she was real happy. I joined the over-thirties hockey team and she came down to all the practices with a thermos of tea to cheer me on. It was a bit embarrassing at first, the other guys' wives didn't do that, but they accepted her and kind of adopted her as the team mascot. She even talked a couple of them into coming to church, guys I'd had no success with at all!

She didn't spend much of our money, but she could never pass by a shop that sold wool — she said she'd never seen so many colours. Pretty soon I had a hand-knit sweater for every month she'd been in Canada — all the same style since she couldn't follow our patterns. Twelve sweaters. Twelve different colours. She counted dates from the time she got here as if that was when time began. Chinese are funny about time, they count your age from the time you're conceived. Every month I'd start counting, but time passed and nothing happened in that area.

The second summer we were in Castlegar she asked for a bicycle. I told her it was madness — we lived at the top of a one-in-five hill — but I finally gave way and got her a three speed, nothing fancy. The ten mile ride to town didn't faze her, she liked the machine, and it made her more cheerful. I'd noticed that she wasn't talking as much as she used to, but I figured we were getting used to each other and didn't have as much to say, but now she was chattering away like she did when we were back in Saskatchewan. Her English was much better, though the words she chose were sometimes weird, influenced as they were by Goofy and Babar and her reading of the New Testament. There were a few other Chinese in town, mostly Cantonese tradespeople. She wasn't inclined to get to know them and I was just as happy. It needed a big effort from her to fit in, and she was making it.

That summer she was back to asking questions about everything, and she took my advice and joined the library. She read all the local history books from cover to cover. I knew what she was looking for, and I told her I'd never heard of them writing a history of the Chinese in Canada. She was too shy to ask the librarian. I told her they just weren't part of the overall picture, not yet. I guess I could've been more sensitive, but I felt she was comparing Canada to China, and we were losing out in the history stakes.

She joined the local historical society. It was no big deal. They met once a month. They brought in a speaker, and socialized after with coffee and cookies. She came home all happy and flustered after one meeting — they'd asked her to give them a talk about China. She worked on it for weeks, and when the time came I went with her, and she stood up and spoke about the Christian missions in Manchuria for an hour without notes. Word perfect. I was proud of her. The ones who stayed awake asked some real dumb questions; had she ever been a communist, did they still bind their feet, and what happened to all the girl babies? She was kinda upset. We didn't stay for coffee, and she hid inside herself a bit after that, but we knew there was nothing to worry about as long as Jesus was on our side.

I came home one night and found her on tenterhooks. She leapt on me the moment I got in the door and said someone'd told her a joke in the supermarket. It was about the steamers that used to go up and down Kootenay Lake. The old steamboats, way back when. She couldn't get her words straight, but as far as I could gather one of them was clipping along and suddenly a shout goes up, "man overboard." They cut down the speed and start to turn back when the shout goes up "no problem, he's Chinese" — so they carry on, full steam ahead. Well, I can see why she's mad. That kinda racist talk's right off the shop floor, you hear it all the time, but it won't wash in the supermarket where there are women and kids who might actually be influenced by it. I grabbed her and hugged her to me, but she pulled back.

"That's not the end of story," she said. "They turn round and pick him out."

"What for?"

"What you mean, what for?"

"I mean, why — I mean, what made them change their minds?"

"Because he was *cook*!"

She started to laugh. I laughed with her, I mean, it was meant to be a joke wasn't it? And then she locked herself in the bathroom.

All in all we were pretty happy. I'd taken a big chance bringing her over here, and I knew I was responsible for her. When it came my turn to testify in church the next Sunday I used the Chinese cook story as a text. I felt real stupid when she got up and walked out.

She kept telling me she was finding comfort in her faith and we prayed together that the Lord would help her, but bit by bit she began to drop out of most of the church activities. I got her an electric piano so she could learn the hymn tunes, and she played till the trailer rocked — sometimes she'd be up at three in the morning playing. Our pastor told me he often came across her, sitting in the empty church staring straight ahead like she was hearing voices.

I knew it would take time.

I began to put money aside to bring her mom and dad over for a visit but she said she didn't think they'd be allowed to leave. I suggested she should go to a retraining course they were organizing for women with English as a second language. Computers and office routines, stuff like that. I figured she could use a skill. I got the forms, but she never signed up. She said she wanted to sell real estate. I don't know where she got that idea, it seemed crazy to me, but I put her onto a guy in the church who was in construction. He told me he didn't think she was ready.

One night I came home and she was building a wall. It was the end of August, and just beginning to get dark. The door of the trailer was open and she was on her hands and knees on the steps. She had a bunch of bricks and a little pile of cement and she was building a wall along the top step, she had it jutting up maybe a foot over the threshold.

I said "Okay Wendy, you want me to fly in through the window like Peter Pan?"

She didn't see the joke. "Is done," she said, and she got up and stood back and admired it as if she'd just painted the Mona Lisa.

I'd steered clear of humour since the episode over the Chinese cook joke, but I couldn't hold back from laughing.

"What's it for?" I asked.

"To keep away bad spirits."

"Oh, they been nosing around, huh?"

"Yes."

"So how come they haven't bothered me?"

I followed her over the wall and into the trailer. There was no food ready that night. I showered, grabbed a sandwich, stepped back over the wall and went down to the church for a meeting with a visiting evangelist from Iowa. I didn't ask if she wanted to join me.

The wall stayed put, and, to tell the truth, I got kinda used to it. They have these raised sills in the doorways to Chinese temples. They figure that ghosts and bad spirits can only move in straight lines so they have to stay outside. The trailer did feel better after it went up. Calmer somehow. No-one was hurt by it.

She brought in the altar in September. It wasn't very big but it certainly wasn't small. She put it in our bedroom — there wasn't room anywhere else. She brought in fruit and flowers and incense and stuff. I tried to tell her it wouldn't do, but she sat down at the piano and played extra loud. I decided to let it go — I guess that wasn't too bright, looking back, but I figured she was homesick, and back in China lots of people have altars in their homes and they don't have any religious significance. I started talking to her in Mandarin at breakfast, when my brain was fresh. She usually answered in English, but I kept it up.

I thought it would do her good to make some more friends, so I asked a few of the guys from work over to the house with their wives, but she never made a move to see anyone on her own, and I had to put up with a lot of leg-pulling on account of the wall. She didn't ride her bike any more, didn't hardly leave the house except to stock up on instant dinners and soft drinks, and to come to hockey practice: I don't know why she kept that up. The fellows never commented on how fat she was getting; they probably thought we were expecting.

She was standing by the boards when we were all coming off the ice one night and one of the guys turned to her and asked if she was rehearsing for Halloween. It turned out he'd seen her hanging out at the graveyard. She didn't deny it, but she didn't try to explain it either.

I wondered if I should take her to a doctor, but I thought I'd try one last thing to cheer her up. We'd never got around to a Canadian wedding even though we'd promised it to ourselves when we were in China. I proposed we should tie the knot soon, and really do it properly. We knew enough people in town now. We could rent the church hall and have a big feast. Really do it up. One of the guys at church asked if we were figuring on buying ourselves a burial plot as a wedding gift — he'd seen Wendy at the graveyard too. I filed the information away. She was free to go where she liked.

I called my parents and they really went for the wedding idea. They proposed coming out to Castlegar with my grandma if we'd have it on Thanksgiving. My sister could stay home to look after my grandpa — he hadn't been the same since his knee replacement last winter. It didn't leave much time, but I figured we could get it organized, and it would give Wendy something to think about, even if there wasn't time to get her folks over. They came to the first wedding, so it wasn't as though we were leaving them out.

Two days before the wedding I asked her what she thought we should do about rings. That was when I looked at her hand and saw she wasn't wearing my grandma's diamond. I couldn't remember when I'd last seen it.

I didn't want to make a fuss, we had enough on our plate, but if it was missing, my grandma would notice for sure, so I enquired after it as casually as I could.

"I entombed it."

"What?"

"In his tomb."

"Who?"

"It's with him."

"What kind of craziness...?"

I had to remove myself. Half blind, I marched out and grabbed a spade and jumped in the truck. She followed.

"He's a wandering spirit alone, without a wife. Without company. For ever and ever." She was running alongside the truck, holding onto the door handle. Yelling. The doors of the other trailers all flew open.

I slammed on the brakes and she clambered up beside me. I put my elbows on the steering wheel to prop up my head, and let her have her say.

It seems this young Manchurian guy died in a house fire in 1981. He was buried in our local boneyard. She'd somehow found where he was from, some town close to where she was born and she'd started writing to his family. This was the first I'd heard. It seems he was twenty-one years of age, the same as her. He was on his own here. She'd been writing to his mother and father and his distant relatives, and I didn't even know. She'd been writing letters to his family. It suddenly hit me that she'd given my ring to a Chinese corpse. She'd wedded herself to a dead man! And all she could say was that he was a wandering spirit who couldn't rest if he had no wife.

I saw hellfire. I pushed her out the truck. I screeched up and down outside the trailer park a couple of times then I took off on the Nelson road and up Kootenay Lake as far as the hot springs. I only stopped because I was low on gas. The tank had been full. I didn't have a swimsuit or nothing, but I rented one, along with a towel, and I waded into those caves up to my thighs in hot water and stood under the falls letting the hot water pound me. There was steam everywhere. I hate the place, but I wanted it to cleanse me. I wanted to open my eyes and see ... and see what? God or something. Yes. I wanted to see Jesus coming out from behind those goddamn spears of rock. Stalactites or whatever. I wanted him to walk on the water. I wanted him to put his arms round me and tell me I'd done the right thing. Yes. I wanted affirmation. I felt like I was going nuts. I stood there under the falls and waited and watched the curls of steam, and not a goddamn thing happened.

One thing I knew for sure. The wedding was off. We weren't really married anyway. We'd never been married in the eyes of the church.

I could feel the hot water puckering up my skin, and that felt good. I wanted to pucker up all to hell. I wanted to stay in that cave all night, and never come out. But the place was closing down and they called to me over the sound system.

There were no lights on in the trailer when I got back. I kicked her wall and let myself in. It was neat and clean as usual, the TV was on, but there was no sign of her, and when I checked I saw that her things were gone. Her clothes, her bicycle, and the $40.00 we kept in the cutlery drawer for emergencies. She'd left her wall and her altar, and she'd left her wedding band in a saucer next to the sink. I ran round to the neighbours' and they all swore they hadn't seen her, though I could see from their eyes they were lying.

I got on the phone and headed off the wedding guests. My mom and dad and my sister insisted on coming anyway, and they helped me put my stuff together, so I could come back home as soon as I'd worked out my notice. I stayed cheerful — I didn't want them to worry. After they'd gone, the whole thing hit me, and I hung round the trailer biting my fingernails, waiting for her to come back. No-one mentioned her. It was like she'd gone up in smoke. The people at church invited me home to meals, but I wouldn't have any of their pity. I stayed clear of the church building, to set foot inside would've been to see her, or her ghost — sitting in our seats, raising her eyes, her voice, her palms. Praising.

I stayed on in the trailer even after I finished at the plant. I couldn't believe it was over. I hung round, dreaming up tasks, filling in time. In the end I had to admit that my folks were right, and I really had been taken for a sucker. Used. All she'd wanted was to get over here. They said it was obvious from the start, nobody tries that hard. I unravelled a couple of her sweaters, looping the spare wool round the back of a chair the way my grandma does. The wool was all crinkly like her black Chinese hair after she gave herself a perm. I made believe I was running my fingers through her hair. I could still smell it on the pillow. She wasn't much of a knitter, those sweaters were full of dropped stitches. I gave the other ten to the Sally Ann.

I didn't have any plans, but I didn't want to go back to Saskatchewan, I knew I'd never find her there. So I headed out to the Coast.

I took the first job that came up, in a pizza shop. I worked like a dog and pretty soon they made me manager, and I began to think about buying a franchise. I was too busy to get involved in the church again. I see now that you can't just order up a religious experience like it was a pizza with extra toppings.

At night I detoured home via the pawn shop on Hastings. I

always let my eye fall on the diamond rings, and I looked at the names of real estate sales persons on the For Sale signs on fences and lawns. One night I ducked into a store in China Town and bought one of those knee-high household gods. I kept it hidden behind a pile of empty boxes under the counter. One of my student helpers found it, and I made out someone'd left it in the shop. It was true in a way.

If a Chinese woman came in the shop I felt myself start to shake. They didn't come in often — the Chinese don't like cheese. She liked cheese though. Or at least she said she did. She ate it, what better proof is there than that?

CONTRIBUTORS

GAIL ANDERSON-DARGATZ's first collection of short fiction has been accepted for publication by Douglas & McIntrye. "The Girl With the Bell Necklace" won first for fiction in the CBC Radio Literary Competition in 1993. Anderson-Dargatz is now working on a novel from which "Bell Necklace" was taken. Her short stories and poetry have been published in a number of literary journals over the last couple of years. She is a graduating student of the University of Victoria's creative writing program. Before returning to university, she worked for a number of years as a journalist, photographer and cartoonist. She now writes and farms with her husband in Errington, on Vancouver Island.

CLARE BRAUX has sixteen short fictions published in literary magazines in Canada and the US. Four have been anthologized. Her novel, *Medusa & Her Sisters* will be published by Moonstone Press in Spring, 1994. Her collection of short stories is looking for a publisher.

ANNE CAMPBELL's previous books are poetry collections: *No Memory of a Move, Death Is An Anxious Mother,* and *Red Earth, Yellow Stone.* Campbell's stories have appeared in magazines and the anthologies: *Sundogs: Stories from Saskatchewan, The Old Dance: Love stories of one kind or another,* and *Lodestone.* Her award winning story, "Lily and the Light", appeared in *Room of One's Own.* Her day job is with the Regina Public Library where, among other things, she has administered Canada's longest running Writer-in-Residence program in a library.

BEVERLEY DAURIO is the author of three books, most recently *HELL & Other Novels.* Her short fiction has been published in journals in England and Australia, and across Canada in *Best Canadian Stories, Rampike, This Magazine, West Coast Line, Canadian Fiction Magazine,* and many others. A publisher, editor, and anthologist, Daurio was born and raised in Toronto and now lives in Stratford, Ontario.

MARINA ENDICOTT works as a dramaturge and director in the theatre. Her stories have appeared in several magazines and anthologies, including *Frictions, Coming Attractions 1992,* and the *Journey Prize Anthology 1993.* She now lives outside Mayerthorpe, Alberta, where she has almost finished a collection of long stories. "Doreen's Kitchen" is excerpted from one of these stories.

CLAIRE HARRIS came to Canada from Trinidad in 1966. She settled in Calgary where she teaches English in the Separate Schools. In 1975, during a leave of absence in Nigeria, she began to write for publication. She was poetry editor at *Dandelion* from 1981 to 1989. Her first book, *Fables from the Women's Quarters,* won a Commonwealth Regional Award. For *Travelling to Find a Remedy* she won the Writer's Guild of Alberta Award for Poetry and the first Alberta Culture Poetry

Prize. *The Conception of Winter* won an Alberta Culture Special Award for poetry. *Drawing Down a Daughter*, her sixth collection of poetry, was published in 1992. She is working on her eighth manuscript, "Return of the Native" and on a collection of prose and poetry, "Angelworks."

ELISABETH HARVOR's fiction and poetry have appeared in *Arc*, *The American Voice*, *Event*, *PRISM international*, *The Hudson Review*, *The Malahat Review*, *The New Yorker*, *Poetry Canada Review*, *Prairie Fire*, and *Saturday Night* as well as in several other periodicals and journals. Her first book of stories, *Women and Children*, has been reissued under the title *Our Lady of All the Distances*. *If Only We Could Drive Like This Forever* is her second collection of stories. She has recently published her first book of poetry, *Fortress of Chairs*. She has also won a number of awards for her stories and poems, most recently the Malahat Long Poem Prize, the League of Canadian Poets' National Poetry Prize and a National Magazine Award.

MARGARET HOLLINGSWORTH was born in England and has been a Canadian citizen for half her life. She has written widely for screen, radio and stage, and published two collections of stage plays: "Willful Acts" and "Endangered Species." Her collection of stories *Smiling under water* was published by Lazara Press in 1989. She teaches in the Creative Writing Department of the University of Victoria.

CYNTHIA HOLZ is the author of *Home Again*, a collection of short stories. Her work has appeared in numerous literary journals, including *The Malahat Review*, *Descant*, *Quarry*, *The Antigonish Review and Queen's Quarterly*. As well, her stories have been anthologized in *The New Press Anthology #2, Coming Attractions 5* and *Ounce of Cure*. She lives in Toronto, where she teaches creative writing. "Summer Cold" is an excerpt from her novel *ONLYVILLE* to be published in Spring, 1994.

MAUREEN HYNES has published *Letters from China*, featured in 1991 in "Nomads," a display of Canadian travel writing at the National Library in Ottawa. Her poetry has been published in *Quarry, The Fiddlehead, Geist* and *Contemporary Verse II*. She was selected for the May 1993 Writing Studio B at the Banff Centre for Fine Arts for her poetry.

ELISE LEVINE is a writer and editor living in Toronto. Her work has appeared, or is forthcoming, in *The Malahat Review, PRISM International, The Fiddlehead* and *CV2*. In addition, she is a runner-up winner in the 1993 *PRISM international* Short Fiction Contest.

SERENA LEE MIS.TA-NASH is Métis. She was born and raised in small town Saskatchewan, Canada. Although separated at birth from her Métis family, she spent many happy childhood hours listening to stories. In 1980, she moved to the Yukon, where she began to write and then to perform her stories. She has had a number of poems and short stories published and has written for television. As a storyteller, she has produced a one woman show that has travelled throughout North America. and toured her show on Sakahlin Island in the Russian Far East. Currently she is working on a collection of stories for children and new material for her storytelling show.

SUNITI NAMJOSHI was born in India in 1941. She has worked as an Officer in the Indian Administrative Service and in academic posts in India and Canada. Since 1972 she has taught in the Department of English of the University of Toronto and now lives and writes in Devon, England. She has published five books of poetry including *The Authentic Lie, From the Bedside Book of Nightmares* and *Because of India: Selected Poems*. Fiction publications include *Feminist Fables, The Conversations of Cow,* and *Aditi and the one-eyed monkey*, written for children. *The Blue Donkey Fables* was among the top twenty titles selected for Feminist Book Fortnight in 1988. *St. Suniti and the Dragon* and a new edition of *Feminist Fables* are forthcoming.

SUSAN PERLY was born in Toronto where she now lives. Perly lived for many years in Nova Scotia. She has also lived and worked in Latin America where she still continues to travel. Her story "Guatemala" appeared in the original *Frictions*. She is also a contributor to the anthology *Hard Times*.

PAULINE PETERS is a writer and storyteller living in Toronto. She is engaged in the challenge of using the English language to express an African-Canadian woman's soul. Most recently she performed a segment of her work "Dryland: In My Village" for Nightwood Theatre. At the moment she is looking forward to more writing and performing. Peters is also an occasional graphic artist and finds drawing and printmaking a sometime welcome relief from language.

FAUZIA RAFIQ is a Toronto writer and a member of the editorial collective of *Diva*, a quarterly journal of South Asian women. Her stories have been published in *Diva* and *Fireweed* as well as in *This Magazine*, and she is currently working on a collection of short fiction. She has edited and developed numerous handbooks and resource guides on anti-racism, wife assault and immigrant women for various groups in Toronto.

GAYLA REID was born and grew up in Australia. She came to Canada in 1967 and lives in Vancouver, where she writes and edits public legal information materials. She was a founder and for thirteen years an editor of *Room of One's Own*. Her stories have appeared in *The Malahat Review*, PRISM *international*, and *Island* (Australia). She was featured in the 1993 *Journey Prize Anthology*, and in this year's *Coming Attractions*, edited by Douglas Glover and Maggie Helwig, from Oberon Press. She won the 1993 Silver Medal National Magazine Award for fiction.

HELEN J. ROSTA lives in Edmonton. Her short stories have appeared in various magazines and anthologies, most recently in *Great Canadian Murder and Mystery Stories* and in *Kitchen Talk*. A collection of her stories, *In the Blood*, has been published by NeWest Press.

HOLLEY RUBINSKY, the author of *Rapid Transit and Other Stories* is the inaugural winner of the McClelland & Stewart Journey Prize and has won a National Magazine Gold Medal for fiction. She is presently working on her second collection of stories.

JENNIFER RUDDER was born and raised in Toronto. She studied Italian language and literature at Carleton University in Ottawa and the University of Bologna and works in the visual arts in Toronto. "Summer of Love" was written with the encouragement of the Aristazabal Women's writing group and is her first published short story.

GERTRUDE STORY was born in 1929 near the town of Sutherland, Saskatchewan, which is now a suburb of Saskatoon. Since her first book of poems, *The Book of Thirteen*, was published in 1981, she has become one of Saskatchewan's best known storytellers and most acclaimed writers. Her four collections of short stories and a recent memoir have earned her much critical praise.

RACHEL WYATT has been living and writing in Canada for thirty-five years. She is married and has four children. She has had four novels published by The House of Anansi Press, two stage plays produced at The Tarragon Theatre, Toronto, and has written countless radio dramas for the CBC and the BBC. Lately she has taken to writing short stories again. She is currently Director of the Writings Program at The Banff Centre for the Arts. She also directs the Radio Writing Workshop which takes place there in December.

❖

OTHER BOOKS FROM SECOND STORY PRESS